# Blue Murder

## ALSO BY WALTER WAGER

# Blue Murder

A NOVEL BY

## Walter Wager

ARBOR HOUSE NEW YORK

Library of Congress Catalog Card Number: 80–67622

ISBN: 0-87795-286-8

Manufactured in the United States of America

10 9 8 7 6 5 4 3 2 1

This book is dedicated to Dublin author and educator Jack McIvor, and his three splendid daughters.

# Author's Note

Everything in the pages that follow is fiction. If by any chance the names of people, companies or organizations in this novel should resemble or match those of ones that actually exist anywhere, that coincidence is wholly accidental. All the names and events in this book are the products of the author's imagination.

The author acknowledges with gratitude the cooperation of the public information units of the U. S. Army and Air Force in New York City, the public affairs office of the Treasury Department's Bureau of Alcohol, Tobacco and Firearms in Washington and the Special Agent in Charge of the A.T.F. team in Los Angeles. The public affairs division of the Central Intelligence Agency has also been helpful. Special thanks to weapons expert Sean Collinsworth of the Los Angeles County Sheriff's Department.

W.W.

# 1

THERE WERE three men in a dark green Volvo, three more in a blue Cadillac—one of the stubby Sevilles. Both cars were stolen. There was no apparent connection between them as they moved south from Los Angeles on the Santa Ana Freeway. The midmorning sun was bright, and the traffic heavy.

Following orders, the husky driver of the Cadillac kept three other cars between his own and the Volvo that was leading the way to the *objective*. Out of the army nineteen months, he still thought in military terminology. In today's *operation*, the timing would be critical.

When he saw the roadside billboard announcing that it was seven miles to Disneyland, he looked at the digital calendar clock in the center of the dashboard. 10:08 . . . April 1.

He checked the speedometer to make sure that the Cadillac was not exceeding the 55 m.p.h. limit. Most traffic on the busy freeway was doing 60 or 65, but they could risk attracting the Highway Patrol's attention; the men in the "hot" cars could not. Their *mission* had to be executed perfectly, and completed within the next thirty-seven minutes. Tomorrow it would be in all the papers, on all the radio and television news broadcasts. Major crimes always were.

Another billboard heralded the exit for the Japanese Deer Park. The Cadillac driver adjusted his silver-lensed aviator glasses as a Gray Line tourist bus slid by. When smiling children gestured from the windows he waved back benignly. He liked kids, had never intentionally killed any. That incident on the *recon patrol* north of Danang didn't really count.

He followed the Volvo off the main artery into the area of small factories that some politician had named City of Industry. Three quarters of a mile later, he watched the car stop as a man in its back seat spoke into a powerful walkie-talkie.

"Hello, High Guy. High Guy, this is Ground Hog. How's the weather?"

"All clear, Ground Hog," replied the helicopter pilot 3,000 feet overhead. "Repeat, all clear."

It was a good plan. With the chopper up there to warn them of approaching police cars, the raid ought to go off without interruption. Again the Volvo led the way, first four blocks further west, then three blocks north. There it was, Century Electronics, a one-story building of white cinderblock about forty feet wide, perhaps twice as long. For a moment, the man behind the wheel of the Cadillac wondered what they made in this windowless plant. He studied the dashboard clock again.

10:20. Almost time.

Maintaining their thirty-yard separation, the stolen cars circled the block to check out escape routes before taking their positions for the assault. The Volvo moved down a service road to the parking area behind the factory and came to a halt near the freight entrance. At almost the same moment the Cadillac stopped a dozen yards from the front door. It was 10:24.

"One minute," the Cadillac driver announced. His two passengers stepped out, walked back to the trunk and unlocked it. They took out a pair of long cardboard boxes, closed the lid and strode forward to speak to the man behind the wheel.

"All of them?"

"All of them. *Go,*" he said.

The clock showed 10:25 as they walked toward the building. The driver reached under his seat for a large brown paper bag, and watched the crew-cut one enter the plant while the other waited outside near the door. The reception area was small, but the woman at the desk was fat—at least a hundred and fifty pounds and only five and a half feet tall.

"Speak to you later, Gladys," she said, and hung up the telephone.

"Flowers," said the man with the box.

"I think you've got the wrong place."

"This is Century, isn't it?"

"Yeah. Who're they for?"

He looked at the package, shrugged.

"Name's probably on the card inside," he said and took the top off. Inside was a submachine gun with a silencer screwed to the end of the barrel.

"*What*—" she began to ask, but five bullets cut off the question, and her life.

The man with the automatic weapon looked down to make certain that she was dead, and paused to listen. He nodded as he heard machines pounding beyond the wall. Then he opened —just a few inches—the door he had come through.

"Ted," he called out softly. The man waiting outside came in and took out of his box another rapid-fire gun fitted with a silencer. At the same time, one of the men from the Volvo was using an identical weapon to blast the lock on the plant's rear door.

9

"The phone, Ted," the first man reminded him. His partner fired a short burst that sent bits of the telephone casing and short pieces of wire flying. That done, he swung his gun to the door that led into the production area. He smiled as he studied the sign mounted eighteen inches above the knob.

"No admittance," he read aloud.

"Ignore that."

Turning the knob with his palm to avoid leaving fingerprints, Ted opened the door. They stepped into a large chamber full of noise and machines and took positions on either side of it. They began to count the shirt-sleeved men working there. There were five . . . six . . . seven . . . all so busy that none had noticed the door open.

Ventilation was poor, and it was hot in the factory. One of the employees—a thin young Chicano wearing a T shirt that said "Latin Power"—walked to a vending machine against the wall and fed it coins to buy a soft drink. The can dropped with a thump, and as he reached for it the team from the Volvo came through the rear door with their automatic weapons ready— exactly on schedule. It was 10:28.

The Chicano lifted the can of root beer to his lips, took a gulp and froze as he saw them. Choking on raw fear, he struggled to decide whether to shout a warning. One of the gunners solved his problem with a burst that sent him crashing into the vending machine. It was a signal for the others to open fire.

The execution squad killed coolly and expertly. Screaming workers ran in blind panic toward the exits, and were gunned down. Others, terrified, tried to take cover behind their still running machines. The murder team moved methodically through the plant, hunting down the workers as if they were rabbits. They shot everyone several times, and kicked the bodies to be sure. The orders had been specific. No survivors.

Out front, the Cadillac driver saw a Honda pull up and watched its rider enter the building. It was a brief visit. The leather-jacketed stranger took one look at the dead receptionist and turned to run, but not far. He was halfway out the door when the man in the Cadillac drew a silenced .32-caliber pistol from the brown paper bag and shot him twice in the head. The cyclist fell back into the reception room, where one of the killers put three more rounds into his chest before returning the gun to the flower box.

A moment later, the crew-cut man joined him and reported that the Volvo team had already left via the rear freight exit. "They're rolling now," he said. "I checked the stiffs inside. Eight up and eight down. Clean sweep. Hey, who was the biker?"

"Beats the crap out of me."

They closed the front door behind them, walked to the Cadillac and put the flower boxes back in the trunk. As they were climbing back into the car the driver started the motor.

"All of them?" he asked in a taut voice.

"All of them. What's the matter, Carl? You sound nervous as hell."

"The goddamn matter," he replied as he guided the Seville out onto the road, "is that I don't like slicing things this fine. The Feds will be all over this place in about fourteen minutes."

"Maybe they'll be late."

"They'll be on time," he predicted grimly, and he was right.

# 2

SINCE BEVERLY Hills probably has the highest per-capita income in the United States, it is hardly surprising that this famed community is adorned with a great number of large houses. The one that private detective Alison Gordon drove up to at 11:30 A.M. was a *very* large house even by Beverly Hills standards—a $3,000,000 estate. It was surrounded by a high wall that was covered with some sort of thick green vine that made it look less forbidding, but the elegant-looking woman at the wheel of the Porsche recognized it as a nine-foot-high fortification—a stone security blanket for the living legend who owned it.

There was a big metal gate with a pane of bullet-proof glass set flush in the wall beside it. A guard in the tan uniform of one of Southern California's most prosperous protection services stared out for several seconds before his voice grated from the louvers of the intercom above the window.

"Help you, miss?"

"Please tell her that A. B. Gordon is here."

He spoke to somebody on the phone and pressed the button that opened the gates. She guided the sports car up an impressive driveway flanked by tall trees that had been there for a long time. The perfectly trimmed lawns and shrubs also reflected sustained care and expense. Alison Gordon recalled that it had been built by one of the top film stars of the 1930's—a dashing bisexual Adonis who thrilled audiences and earned millions. Out back were a tennis court, swimming pool and bath house. Alison Gordon had attended a barbecue on the flagstone rear terrace when Zanuck owned the place five years ago.

She parked the Porsche in front of the columned entrance and nodded in satisfaction as she caught a glimpse of herself in the side mirror. She was the best looking thirty-five-year-old woman she knew, and she knew half of the major actresses and sex symbols in Hollywood.

"Miss Gordon?" asked the middle-aged maid in the doorway.

"Yes."

"This way, please."

She entered the house and flinched at the decor. She recoiled several times more as she trailed the maid through room after room—each featuring the worst of Italian modern. The garish hues of the fabrics, the unnatural tints of the leather and the inhuman shapes of every piece assailed her sensibilities. Each room must have had $80,000 worth of furniture, and twice that much in contemporary art.

"Miss Gordon," the maid announced.

The room she now entered was equipped as a gymnasium. It had a wooden floor with basketball hoops at either end, a free-standing mini-sauna and a variety of exercise machines. Pumping away doggedly on a stationary bicycle was the lady of the house: short, curly-haired, topless. With her teeth gritted and sweaty breasts bobbing, the determined superstar panted and pedaled. Crouched over the handlebars, she radiated ferocity. Like almost everything else in the life of Lauri Adams, being

13

physically fit was a war. Pounds and weakness were the enemy, and she would destroy them as she had destroyed her other foes.

She grunted, strained and cursed. She neither spoke to nor otherwise acknowledged A. B. Gordon, who was not at all surprised. In the no-holds-barred entertainment world where cannibals were honored speakers at author luncheons and glib degenerates were prized guests on radio and TV talk shows, this talented woman was known as The Bitch. The competition for that hateful/admiring title had been fierce; but even her worst enemies—and there were scores of them—recognized her supremacy.

"Agnes!" she shouted in a voice that could crack a water glass. The maid walked to the machine, and studied the dial.

"Ten miles. You can get off now, honey," she said. Lauri Adams pumped on for another half minute out of bravado, establishing that she had not been defeated by the machine, then slapped the bicycle and dismounted, adjusting her green mini-panties in victory. She accepted a thick terry towel from the maid, and pointed her finger at the door in silent command.

"Take a look at that wall, Gordon," she said as the maid left. *That's* a Tony Award, and those two are Oscars. The thing on the left is the Emmy for my '78 TV special. That bunch on the far right—the ones that look like little phonographs—are the Grammies I got from the Recording Academy. I've copped *three* more than Streisand; that burns her ass. You get my message?"

"No, but I'm sure you'll explain it."

"I'm a winner, Gordon," she said as she toweled her face and breasts, "and I win because I'm the best. Number one." She jabbed a finger into the air. Alison decided that Lauri Adams was both serious and a bit insane—like most of the twenty other clients A. B. Gordon Investigations had served in the past year.

"They say you're Number one in your field, Gordon—the best

this side of Chicago. I heard what you did with the terrorist bombers in Vegas last winter. I've got all kinds of connections, if you know what I mean."

It didn't surprise Alison Gordon that the superstar had contacts in either the underworld or FBI, or was it both? She opened her purse to reach for the black and gold cardboard box that held her Sobranies.

"That was some number in Vegas—a real wipeout," the performer continued. "This job won't be anything like that. No violence, no danger."

"Mind if I smoke?"

The gold-tipped cigarette was in her hand, and she found the Dunhill lighter.

"Those things can kill you, Gordon. I was at a White House dinner last month, sat next to that fat guy who just won the Nobel Prize. Crackerjack scientist. He said cigarettes are suicide. If you gotta smoke, how about a joint?"

Alison Gordon shook her head.

"A little coke?" the gracious hostess offered.

"I'm not thirsty."

Adams started to smile. "That was a joke, right?" she asked.

"I hope so. What is the problem, Miss Adams?" The detective lit her gold-tipped cigarette.

"Like you to locate my kid brother, Sid. No big deal. You were in the CIA, right?"

Alison Gordon nodded, and exhaled a column of smoke.

"Then your outfit ought to find him in about three days."

"I should tell you our fee is five hundred dollars a day."

Adams shook her head, and threw the towel on the floor.

"No, you shouldn't. Tell my business manager. I'll give you Sid's address and a picture of him. Come on."

Alison Gordon followed her through the house and listened

15

to a running audit of what each piece of furniture and work of art had cost.

"Decorated the whole place myself," Adams boasted as they entered a room dominated by four huge speakers and the latest home electronic gear. There was a large stereo rig, a pair of twenty-five-inch TV sets, two videotape recorders, hundreds of audio and video tapes, a Moog synthesizer, Advent TV projector to throw magnified broadcast images on a six-foot screen, and a black leather wall decorated with a dozen round discs of yellow metal.

"Gold records, Gordon. Each one a million-seller. And my mom wanted me to marry a dentist and breed in some suburb."

There was a wedge-shaped desk of stainless steel and Lucite by the French windows, and a swivel chair of orange Naugahyde behind it. The singer-actress-director-producer dropped into its womblike cup and pushed aside a mound of cassettes and a miniature tape recorder to shuffle through a heap of papers. After a few moments, she found an envelope and thrust it at the detective.

"That's where he was till nine or ten weeks ago. Letter came back marked address unknown. The crazy kid just split, I guess."

"How old is he?" Alison Gordon asked as she found an onyx ashtray.

"Let's see. I'm twenty-nine. That would make him . . . twenty-six."

So she lied about her age, like a lot of other women—and men—in and out of show business. Even accountants and optometrists were doing it these days.

"Now where the hell did I put that picture?" Lauri Adams pressed one of the buttons on a red plastic intercom on the desk beside a mound of scripts.

"Philip!" she said, then began rooting among the piles of

16

letters, invitations and telegrams. Alison Gordon sat down on an uncomfortable aluminum chair, and realized that tomorrow would be the eleventh anniversary of her wedding. It was nearly eight years since the Agency told her that she was a widow—probably. They'd never found Mark's body, and to this moment it was strange being a widow. The fact that he was *legally* dead didn't make it any more real, she reflected as she puffed on the Sobranie.

"Where the hell are you, Philip?"

"Right here."

The black man in the doorway was tall and trim in a racing driver's jumpsuit. He wore horn-rimmed glasses and flashed a knowing smile as he walked to the desk and handed his employer a terrycloth robe.

"That's not what I need, Philip."

"A cold or sore throat is what you don't need—not with that recording session tomorrow," he told her. She put on the robe and pointed at the clutter of paper and gadgets.

"Sid's picture. Where is it?"

He reached into one of the mounds on the desk, pulled out a square envelope and gave it to her.

"I looked there," she grumbled.

"The reporter from *Time* will be here in forty minutes, and Kaplan phoned that it's time to sell the pork belly futures. Lunch today is—"

"Lamb chops," she said. "I know that damn Scarsdale thing by heart. Bye, Philip."

He left, and she handed the envelope to Alison Gordon, who took out the photo and scanned it. Sidney Adams had his sister's curly hair and wide eyes, but not the strength. He had an intelligent, wary look, and appeared even younger than twenty-six.

"What does he do, Miss Adams?"

"Do? He's a bright kid . . . Could do most anything. Wrote some songs that were damn promising. Played guitar in a rock group at high school. Worked for me, sort of an all-around helper . . . till three months ago. Went out on his own and hooked up with some new recording studio."

"Which one?"

"He wouldn't tell me. Didn't want Big Sister to butt in, I guess. Probably didn't want them to know he was my brother. Lot of pride, that kid."

The private detective sensed that there were things unsaid, perhaps things she wasn't supposed to find out—ever.

"Anything else?" she asked without much hope of a straight answer. Lauri Adams considered the question carefully. Alison Gordon had seen that tense mask and stance before. Another damn lie or half-truth was coming. Why did so many clients play these idiotic games?

"He drives a red Fiat I gave him for his birthday in September."

"Friends? Hobbies? Favorite restaurants?"

Lauri Adams pursed her lips again and frowned. "Mexican food. Ate two or three times a month at La Cantina, that restaurant near Century City. Friends? He talked about a woman named Clarice who lived across the hall. Wish I could remember her name."

"So do I," Alison Gordon said as she rose to leave. She ground out her cigarette, wondering why she had taken this case.

"Fleming—Clarice Fleming."

"That's fine, Miss Adams," she forced herself to say, and speculated that the problem might be medical. They'd check the area's hospitals routinely, of course. "Drugs? Alcohol? Fainting spells?" God, she sounded like the elevator operator an-

18

nouncing floors at a mental institution.

"A little grass . . . a little tequila . . . a nice, normal kid. This should be the easiest four hundred dollars a day you ever collected."

So The Bitch was a chiseler too. It figured.

"Five hundred." The detective corrected her coolly and got an answering look that wonderfully simulated confusion and innocence.

"Five hundred?"

The voice was very good too—about nine years old.

"My staff will bill your business manager—as you requested." Alison Gordon glanced at her wristwatch. "We'll be in touch, Miss Adams," she promised.

"How soon? When will you start working?"

"In about two hours. I've got a lunch date over in Hollywood —less than a mile from the address you gave me. I'll call you when I have something."

Lauri Adams guided her through the labyrinth to the front door, chatting about her new album—which she'd *have* to produce herself because nobody at the record company understood her *concept*—and the movie she was *forced* to direct next month in *simple self-defense*. The script that she had just rewritten was too good to let any of those thugs *butcher* it . . .

"After what they did to ruin the Midler picture—*pooor* Bette."

"I'll call you," Alison Gordon said. She'd had more than enough, and was in a hurry to get away. She started toward her car.

"Gordon, I dig that linen suit you're wearing. How much did it cost?"

"I'm the detective. *I* ask the questions."

Lauri Adams glared in undisguised astonishment. *Nobody*

19

talked that way to her. She *wanted* that suit. "Gordon!"

The elegantly dressed investigator got into her car and put the key into the ignition.

"*Where* did you buy it?"

Alison Gordon just waved in a parody of a warm farewell and drove off. The guard couldn't help smiling. It was difficult to resist a beautiful woman, he thought as he watched the Porsche roll down the hill.

When she reached the bottom, she turned on the radio to blow away the bad taste of her recent experience. The superb voice of Lauri Adams leaped at her in a marvelous rendition of Billy Joel's latest hit. Who Sidney Adams was and why he had disappeared might be uncertain, but one thing was definite. The Bitch could *really* sing.

As the Lauri Adams record ended, the driver of the blue Cadillac pulled the car to the curb and turned off the radio. His two passengers got out immediately and separated at once in accord with instructions. The submachine guns had been trans-ferred to a panel truck, and the Volvo had left them a mile earlier so that no one would see the two cars returning to the lot together or connect the six men.

It was going well, the man behind the wheel thought. He waited until they were out of sight before he swung the Cadillac back into the traffic. There was always a lot of it in this part of Hollywood near midday. It was 11:42. He still had eighteen minutes and five blocks left. No sweat. Hell, it was the FBI agents who were perspiring now, with a half-ton of corpses and not one damn clue worth anything. It would be interesting to see what bullshit story the Feds would put out on the one o'clock news.

He saw the lot, and nodded in satisfaction. His shift didn't start until noon, which left plenty of time to change his clothes. The guard at the entrance gestured in recognition and pointed —there was the Volvo, empty. He parked the Cadillac a dozen yards away from it before he entered the rear of the adjacent building at 11:49.

The well-lit but drab corridors were filled with a steady stream of muscular men, several of whom greeted him as he made his way to the locker room. He took off the sports jacket, polyester shirt and gray work pants and put them and the paper bag in the back of his locker. Then he put on a uniform shirt, tie, trousers and holstered .38 before making his way to the office on the second floor. The telephone rang as he sat down behind the desk. It was 11:59, a minute before the noon shift was to take charge. The man he was relieving was at the water cooler, so he answered it.

"Narcotics Division," he said in a firm voice. "No, sir, Sergeant Melendez isn't here right now. Can I help you?"

# 3

EVERY YEAR, Hollywood comes up with a busty new sex symbol, some remarkable innovations in accounting that dazzle the Internal Revenue Service and a wonderful new second-rate restaurant. This delights the locals and is fodder for the media, but it does not make for good dining. That was one of the reasons that A. B. Gordon felt sulky as she walked out of this year's "in" establishment at a quarter after two.

"Great, wasn't it?" Brad Manoff said. He was another reason for her sense of discomfort. One of the boy-wonder vice presidents at Warner's, he had the cunning of an Apache war chief. He was a doer, a problem solver, a go-getter—an intelligent pain in the ass.

"Thanks for lunch," she answered evasively.

"Now about those video cassettes—"

"Sorry, I can't help you."

"You agree that ninety-two hundred cassettes didn't just boogie out of the warehouse?"

"I already did that over the curried eggplant," she reminded him, "and I told you to let the insurance company investigators find them."

"I'm appealing to *you*," he said as he adjusted his gold neck chain.

"You're doing your job. You asked me eight times *nicely*, and I said no *nicely*. Let's leave it at that."

It was about time for him to invoke the deities, perhaps the head of the conglomerate itself. He didn't disappoint her.

"Steve said that you were the only person—"

"Wish him a happy birthday for me, will you?"

He looked stunned. "Jeezus, did I forget his birthday?"

The lie took away his momentum, but only for a moment. If charm and flattery wouldn't work, he'd try something else.

"Steve isn't going to like this," Manoff warned. "The whole company isn't going to like this, and you do a lot of business with us."

She lit a cigarette, and eyed him coldly.

"You threatening me?"

"Come on, Al," he said.

"Don't threaten me, and don't call me *Al*. You don't know me well enough for that. I've always been treated courteously by your people, so don't push your luck. You don't want me to call the big boys at Seventy-five Rock."

He winced at the mention of corporate headquarters in New York, but masked it with another large smile.

"Now *you're* threatening *me*."

"Damn right. I don't like your attitude. You need somebody to look into your missing cassettes tomorrow. We can't because we've got a lot of other cases. It's that simple, so don't play games with me. Go find somebody else to manipulate," she said as she opened the door of her car.

"Listen, I apologize. I was only following orders."

"Cheer up. I know people who are a lot worse than you," she confided and started the Porsche.

"Is it *really* his birthday?"

She winked. Eight minutes later, she parked the sports car across the street from a squat apartment house on one of the less elegant streets in a no-longer fashionable section of Hollywood. Constructed in 1931, the Casa Isabella had a vaguely Moorish exterior that hadn't been cleaned for a while. Like the much more famous Chateau Marmont and others, it had been the home of many aspiring actresses, actors, writers and directors on their way up the ladder in the 1930's, 40's and 50's. Now it seemed a bit shabby, although it was still favored by some sentimentalists, over-the-hill performers and writers who had come from New York or London to work on their first screenplays. The Casa Isabella had a certain frayed and tacky class. Alison Gordon wondered whether Sidney Adams had lived there because he had a romantic streak.

She rang the doorbell.

There was something familiar about the building superintendent in the cheap hairpiece and peppy yellow shirt who answered. She had seen him somewhere before—but could not dredge up a name to go with that rotund face. The man was at least sixty, with beer breath and the sad eyes of a clown. *That* was it.

"Uncle Howie?" she guessed.

"You remembered. You're a *goood* girl," he said in a voice right out of her childhood. For a few seconds she was seven or eight again, sitting in front of a television set, watching a show starring Mr. Marvel. Uncle Howie had been the frenetic "second banana," cavorting and mugging and mixing handsprings and clown falls with reminders about kindness to your plants and your mommy. A long time ago, she told herself as she regained control of her feelings.

"My name is Gordon, and I'm a private investigator."

"Did you drink your milk today?"

She felt a surge of guilt, then wanted to hit him.

"Are you the super here?"

He smiled broadly as he patted her cheek.

"Marvin Howard. Marvin T. Howard, actor . . . clown . . . and concierge of the Casa Isabella. Sounds better than 'super,' doesn't it?"

"A lot better. I'd like to talk to you about a former tenant named Sidney Adams."

"I still do an occasional commercial, you know, and I'm available for children's parties."

She felt depressed.

"Mr. Howard, I'm trying to find Sidney Adams. Do you remember him?"

"Sid? Sure, I'm not senile, damn it. Nice fellow. *Short*, that was his problem. Lived here about three years. Clean, honest, very polite—but *short*. That gets to them, you know."

"To whom?"

"*Short* people. Feel they're being looked down on. Some of them handle it pretty well . . . become rich doctors and lawyers to prove they're just as good or better than tall people. Sid wasn't one of those."

"Did Adams leave any forwarding address, Mr. Howard?"

He reflected only briefly, then shrugged.

"No. They don't look back. Maybe they don't look ahead either. Could be it's just *now* that counts . . . You a bill collector, miss?"

"Just the opposite," she said. "He won a third prize in our lottery—one of those magazine subscription promotions—and by state law we've *got* to get the check to him. Do you have any idea where we might find him?"

Howard reached into his breast pocket and took out a cheap

cigar. He stripped off the cellophane and lit up.

"He said something about a beach when he left. End of January. Nice boy, Sid. Left the apartment clean as a whistle. Some of them just *go*—without a word. Change wives, jobs, homes, like they were dirty socks . . . hope this cigar isn't bothering you."

"Not at all," she lied. "Maybe his neighbor, Miss Fleming, might have an address or phone number. I'll try her."

"Three-J," Howard said.

"Thanks. It was wonderful to meet you. I loved the shows for years."

"Remember the song?" he asked brightly.

She tried, and failed. "Sorry. Three-J?"

He nodded. Then he pointed across the dimly lit lobby to the aged elevator. It moved so slowly that she wondered whether it would ever reach the third floor. When it did she hurried out in unconscious flight for her safety. The carpets were worn, but there were large potted rubber plants in the corridors—along with smells of cooking. She found the door marked 3-J, heard no sounds from within and hoped that Clarice Fleming was (a) at home, (b) sane, (c) sober. She was in no mood to cope with "none of the above." She knocked. Someone looked out through a one-way peephole, then unlocked the door.

"Miss Fleming?"

The woman in 3-J smiled, exposing what Alison Gordon recognized as at least $4,000' worth of dental work. Big. Everything about her was big. At least five feet nine inches tall, over a hundred and sixty pounds and wearing a purple caftan dotted with crazy daisies.

"Clarice Fleming?"

"Of course. And who are you, darling?"

The blonde curls were reminiscent of the late Jayne Mansfield. The scent of Tabu was overwhelming.

"A. B. Gordon. I'm a private investigator, looking for Sidney Adams."

"Has the dear boy done something *naughty?*" the massive woman cooed in a husky voice.

"Won a prize in a lottery, and they want him to pick up his check. He didn't file a change of address when he moved."

"What a thoughtless boy!" Clarice Fleming laughed.

The woman needed a shave. Under all that eye shadow, powder, rouge, lipstick and other makeup was a chubby man in his early thirties. Alison Gordon recalled an incident with a male assassin in women's clothes in Bangkok, but that had been long ago and far away. Southern California's transvestites had never caused her any trouble, and she had learned how to handle them.

"That's a lovely outfit, Miss Fleming. *Stunning.*"

The transvestite glowed and preened, and dimples bloomed on the painted face.

"It's just something *silly* to wear around the house, but it's comfortable."

"Not *silly,*" Alison assured her. "Fun."

The makeup must have taken an hour to apply. It was . . . perfect.

"I *do* try to make life amusing," Fleming admitted. "Lord knows, it isn't easy. Most people barely exist. They're so sad, so lonely, so full of secret yearnings. I do what I can."

"You've got the gift."

"Miss Gordon, you're one of the few who notices," Fleming said with a flounce that stopped just short of being comic. "Most of them don't."

The detective wasn't sure whom Fleming meant by *"them,"*

but she certainly wasn't going to ask. She looked past the transvestite, then, saw the cat. She grinned, and blinked her eyes at it. The cat blinked back.

"Persian, isn't she?"

"You're a cat person! *Knew* it. Just sensed it the moment I laid eyes on you, dear. . . . Well, her name is Princess Joan—after the late Miss Crawford. Her brother is Prince Albert. Would you like to see him?"

"Who wouldn't?" Alison Gordon replied as she walked into the apartment. The theme was flowers—everywhere. Violets on the cushion fabric, roses woven into the rug, carnations in pink and white all over the wallpaper and a tablecloth exploding with orchids. All were complemented by ceramic table lamps that resembled spring bouquets.

"How lovely," the detective said as she sat down on a Victorian couch. It took her about four minutes to make friends with the amiable long-haired cats, and three more to get Clarice Fleming talking about Sidney Adams. Never made noise. Very few friends. There was that big fellow in the black leather jacket who rode the motorcycle, of course.

"Do you recall his name?" Alison asked.

"Never knew it. I called him Seventy-Seven." Fleming giggled. "Those were the last two numbers of his license plate. Peeping out the window's not very ladylike, but I can't resist it."

"Nobody's perfect. Did Sidney ever mention where his friend worked?"

"No. Did I tell you he had a mustache? Dark hair with a wonderful tan. Very handsome. Would you like some tea?"

"Wish I had the time," the detective replied as she got to her feet.

The Persians blinked regally as Fleming walked his/her guest to the door and accepted Alison's card, promising to phone if there was any news of Sidney Adams.

"You might run across him—or at least leave word—at The Steel Cellar," Fleming suggested. "He had some friends there too. Out on Melrose near the Paramount lot. Everybody knows it."

When Alison Gordon arrived at her Beverly Hills offices she found Andrew Agajanian waiting impatiently. A lean and worldly man who had served with her in the Central Intelligence Agency for six years, he was now her firm's accountant and special-projects man. He was a good-looking bachelor and familiar with many more bars and night clubs than she was.

"Some twitchy type from Warner's called twice," he reported, "and the CBS boys called to say they deeply and genuinely appreciate that number we did for them last week."

She dropped into her swivel chair and turned to look down at Wilshire Boulevard for a few moments. Then she rotated the chair to face him.

"I want to ask you about a bar," she said.

"Sure. By the way, the name of the Warner's guy was Brad Manoff—"

"Screw him. Tell me about a bar called The Steel Cellar. I gather everyone in town except me knows it."

"Don't feel bad, Al," Agajanian advised. "It's not your kind of place. It's not a bar either. It's a club."

"Indian, political or social?"

"Try kinky. Boots and saddles. Whips and chains. The whole beat-me-daddy routine. Leather, slaves—the works."

"Not my kind of place," she said. "So little Sidney is into s and m, and who knows what else?"

"I don't even know who little Sidney is."

Lighting a Sobranie and puffing, she explained that Sidney

29

Adams was Lauri's younger brother.

" 'The Bitch'?"

"All we're supposed to do is find him and send her business manager the bill. It's no big deal, Andy."

"No blackmail? No kidnapping?"

She shook her head as she took the photo from her purse and handed it across her large desk for him to study.

"Last address was the old Casa Isabella—couple of months ago. I stopped by there today after lunch. The transvestite who lived next door remembered that Sidney had a friend—large, male, mustachioed and fond of black leather jackets—who rides a cycle. Last two plate numbers are seventy-seven."

"Does Sidney have his *own* wheels?"

"Red Fiat Spider. Gift from his loving sister. Why don't you try your friend who plays the computer down at Motor Vehicles? Maybe he's picked up a speeding citation recently or filed a change of address. See what you can dig up in the next day or two."

It didn't take that long. He was back in her office a few minutes later with a cold look on his face, an expression she recognized immediately.

"Somebody's dead?"

"A lot of people are dead," Agajanian replied. My contact at Motor Vehicles gave me the plate number in ten seconds flat."

"God bless computers," she said wearily.

"He didn't even have to go to the computer, Al. He *knew* it. The FBI had just called in to ask about the car. Seems that some people with automatic weapons drove up to a small factory near Anaheim about four hours ago and blew everybody away. Chopped nine people into dog meat. A massacre."

"Oh, my God. Why?"

"Nobody knows why or who, or if they do they're not telling.

All he knew was that the Feds found six cars parked behind the plant, and one of them is our red Fiat."

She stood up and removed her jacket. She took a shoulder holster from the middle desk drawer, slipped the harness on and then unlocked another drawer to reach a .357-magnum pistol. After checking the clip, she slid it into the holster and put on the jacket again.

"You know where the factory is?" she asked.

"No, but I'm told it's all over the radio and the whole story should be in the afternoon papers."

"Take the picture," she instructed. He obeyed, and trailed her silently to the elevator and down to the garage. Three minutes later they were in the Porsche, fighting to slip through the heavy Beverly Hills traffic toward Anaheim and the Spider that Lauri Adams had given her brother for his birthday.

# 4

THERE ARE many graceful boulevards and tree-lined avenues in the capital of the Republic of Panama. This shabby back street, however, was full of sleazy bars, soon to be crowded with women and lustful American soldiers. It was only one day after payday, and the prostitutes knew that the bored young men still had plenty of money left to spend. Some whores were drifting in now to get good seats at the bar, testing their smiles and licking their carmine lips at the few males already present. Two or three flicked their tongues in mechanical promise, even though they realized the customers at the bar were more interested in rum and pisco than in oral sex.

The clientele was as seedy as the establishment. The clothes, the haircuts, the hands and faces of the men at this bar spoke of a lot of wear and little success. Hispanics, Indians, blacks, Anglo-Saxons and multiple mixtures had come from everywhere and were going nowhere.

At five after four, Private José Garcia of the U. S. Army Medical Corps entered the bar, shivered under the impact of the excessive air conditioning and gallantly declined a tart's offer to "go 'round the world" for $20. Even though he knew the price would drop to half in another ten days, he had other, more important matters on his mind. As the soldier paid for a rum and Coke at the bar, a black man dressed in a rumpled cotton-and-polyester suit rose with a sigh and made his way to the toilet. Private Garcia sipped at his drink for a minute, then slid from the plastic-covered stool. He finished the drink in a long gulp and gestured to the bartender for another.

"Gotta take a leak," he said as he started for the lavatory. Inside, he found the black man washing his hands at the sink.

"Speak, Joe. The booths are empty," the man said in tones that sounded British Caribbean.

"I think I'm onto something, but I don't know what it means."

"Go on," the black man said impatiently.

"They figure I'm just another dumb Puerto Rican, so they've put me on garbage duty."

"You didn't call me to this cesspool to discuss Yankee imperialism, did you?"

"Shit, no. Listen, something weird's going on in the nuthouse. Very hush-hush. They've got the whole psycho section rigged real strange in terms of security. You wouldn't believe it. It's ass-end-backwards."

"What is, Joe?" The black man saw that the towel dispenser was empty and began to dry his hands on his trousers.

"They've got it set up to keep people *out,* not *in.* And that's not the half of it. All the psychos in there are loose. Every door was open. People walking around free and easy without a single security guard."

"So there's something crazy in the crazy house, comrade?"

"What do you think it means?"

The black man shrugged, looked in the cracked mirror and thought.

"No idea. I never could understand the American Army—*never*. Fortunately, I'm just a messenger. I pick up information from you and a few other people, and I pass it on to my control twice a week. I think that he codes and radios it to his boss, who is presumably very clever and puts all the pieces together. It's *his* job to understand everything."

The door swung in. A man who smelled as if he had not bathed in two weeks walked through. He eyed them suspiciously, belched and made his way to the urinal as Private Garcia stepped into one of the booths. The lack of towels did not bother the intruder, for he left without any thought of washing his hands.

"You can come out, Joe."

Garcia emerged, looked around and shook his head.

"That fellow thinks we're faggots," he grumbled.

"Is that worse than being spies? Look, Joe, can you get inside that mental ward?"

"Don't know. They got it sealed up like a steel drum, with MPs at every entrance. Who ever heard of MPs guarding a nuthouse—even one for the violent types?"

"Joe—inside?"

"I'll try, but no promises. There's something *mean* about those MPs, something that bothers me."

"MPs are *supposed* to be mean, man. See you next week."

The black man left and, half a minute later, stepped from the chilly bar into the choking heat and humidity—93 degrees Fahrenheit, with 81 percent humidity. For a few moments he wondered about the significance of the information he had just received. Then, with sweat pouring from his body, he walked the patterns and tested the procedures that would warn him if he was under surveillance. If he was being followed, it had to involve something a lot more important than what was going on in the nuthouse.

No, he was not being watched. Garcia was probably confused or exaggerating, he told himself as he unlocked the five-year-old Ford they had provided him when he'd arrived in Panama. The rattling two-door fit his role of an alchoholic freelance photographer, Major Orloff had insisted. "Suits you just right, Bob," the facile bastard had assured him, but it was more likely a cheap way to save money. The major and minor powers had been skimping on budgets for field agents since the end of the Vietnam War and the start of the latest push for détente and disarmament.

He was back at his studio darkroom before five. The porno dealer would have to wait for the prints of the three nude Filipino girls and the burly Norwegian sailor. The report from Garcia had to be typed up and photographed for delivery to the "blind drop" this evening. All this skulking about because of a U. S. Army hospital seemed ridiculous, he thought as he set up his lights. Panama was little more than a steamy backwater. Nothing important had happened here in years, and there was no reason to think anything would now. The business at the psycho ward was probably some new form of experimental treatment and nothing more.

# 5

WHEN SHE saw the entrance to the Santa Ana Freeway ahead, A. B. Gordon pulled the Porsche off to the side and used her car phone to call an unlisted number in Sacramento. She explained that she was en route to Century, and was concerned that local or state police might bar her from the scene.

"Sorry to bother you about such a small thing, Jerry," she concluded, "but there may be something and someone a lot larger involved."

"You want to say who?"

"You know I can't," she answered. "Listen, if you're not in a position to do me this favor—I'll understand."

"*What* favor?" the governor countered. "Of course, I'll help you."

She turned on the all-news station and listened while she and Agajanian drove south. There were three separate reports— none very informative, all seething with sensationalism. As they turned off the freeway Agajanian pointed up to the helicopters circling nearby. One bore the emblem of CBS-TV News, the other of ABC-TV News.

"It's going to be a circus," she predicted. Using the rotorcraft as a beacon, she drove on almost half a mile before she was stopped by a roadblock. A California Highway Patrol car parked at right angles was obstructing both lanes. A young policeman pointed right to an intersecting street, ordering them to detour.

"Street's closed," he said briskly.

"My name is Gordon. Alison Gordon."

"Yes, ma'am," he answered in instant recognition. "Just got the word from Captain Champly on the radio. Go right ahead, ma'am."

"Thank you, officer," she said. Agajanian said nothing until they reached the Century Electronics plant. Then he took one look at the crowd and confusion and nodded.

"It's a circus," he agreed.

There were five state police cars, half a dozen from Orange County, and four ambulances. There were also five television news teams with cameras and trucks, and more than a dozen private cars bearing press identification. She could see at least a score of uniformed police, in addition to a group of still photographers who were climbing on cars, trucks, and trees to get photos of everything within ninety or a hundred yards. Journalists were pushing, shouting and arguing and reporters from seven radio stations spoke earnestly into tape recorders and "remote" transmitters in sincere but semi-informed speculation.

She saw another group of sixteen or eighteen men dressed in business suits with white shirts and ties. They might have been I.B.M. salesmen, but the shotguns and automatic weapons made that unlikely. No, they were FBI agents. Just inside the police line of wooden horses that kept the press twenty-five yards from the factory itself, one of them was standing beside a gray Dodge, speaking into a radio phone. He was a wide-shouldered man with graying hair and an air of authority.

"That's Thomson, number two in the L. A. bureau," Alison

Gordon said softly as she parked the Porsche. Thomas T. Thomson saw her step from the sports car, and glared. He hung up the radio phone as she approached.

"What are you doing here?" he challenged. Then he turned to the man beside him, a tall, rangy officer whose uniform and insignia marked him as a captain in the county police.

"What the hell *is* she doing here?" Thomson demanded.

"I'm Captain Champly. Are you Miss Gordon?"

"Yes, I am, and this is Mr. Agajanian—my associate."

"Had a call from the governor's office about nine minutes ago, miss. Asked us to extend you full cooperation. Actually, they *told* us—loud and clear. Didn't say what branch of the government you're with, though."

"She's a private investigator," Thomson said sharply.

"Oh, *that* Gordon lady. Heard about you, miss. Uh, A. B. Gordon. Well, I'm ready to cooperate."

"Thanks. I'll try not to take much of your time, captain. Maybe we'd better start with what happened here, if you can talk about it."

"Might be simpler if I just *show* you," he replied. "Watch where you step, and don't touch anything. The lab people are still finishing up inside."

He led her forward through the crowd, around two technicians finishing taking moulage impressions of tire tracks near the front door. They were almost at the building's entrance when Champly pointed at a corpse sprawled on the gravel. The body was ringed by an outline of paint, and a photographer was snapping away from various angles.

"That's number one, the first body the Feds found. Still warm when they got here. So were the others."

She decided that this was not the moment to inquire why it

was FBI men who had discovered the massacre, that it would be wiser to let Champly relax in his own pace and narration. A neat, efficient federal agent was checking the knob and jamb of the plant's front door for fingerprints. The police captain saw the look in her eyes and read her thought.

"Yeah, they've got a dozen more agents inside—and there's another crew on the way. Watch your step. Next victim's kinda messy. Receptionist named Joanne Santangelo. Must have caught half a clip."

The body was barely recognizable as the remains of a woman. Alison Gordon had seen many corpses in many lands—including bodies of those slain in battle or aerial bombardment—but she still was not used to the shock of violent death.

"Oh, my God!" she whispered.

"Looks like nine-millimeter or bigger," Agajanian judged.

"Point blank. They really chopped her," Champly said, "and the stiffs inside are shot up pretty badly too."

The production area was a shambles. Ruined machinery, spent cartridges and dead bodies were lying around the big room as if tossed there by some huge lunatic child. Blood was spattered in blotches, smears and rivulets—on the walls, floors, machines and even on the tangled reels of tape. Stunned by the devastation, Alison could only stare and wonder.

"There's seven in here," the captain said. "All multiple gunshot wounds. Some of them got a load in the front, then more in the back. Some *again* after they were dead. Somebody was either damn sore, or mighty eager to make sure there were no survivors. Feds say there must have been gunners hitting them from both ends of the plant at the same time, ripping them up in a crossfire."

"Like a military operation," she speculated.

"Not exactly. Three, four, maybe five sub-machine guns blasting at the same time—and people only ninety yards away didn't hear a damn thing."

"The Brits' L34A1 . . . our M76 . . . the Israeli Uzi," Agajanian said.

"He's saying that there are a number of nine-millimeter automatic weapons that can be equipped with silencers," she translated. Then she looked around at the carnage again. "What do —or did—they make here?"

"Cassettes and tapes of the biggest pop hits, all hot on the charts. And all illegal. This was a major operation, big-time counterfeiters. Look at those high-speed duplicators. They turned out thousands of illegal copies a day. Feds say this was one of the largest counterfeiting operations on the West Coast, a twelve- or fourteen-million-dollar-a-year ripoff."

Now Champly paused as he glanced left and right to make certain there was no one within earshot.

"It'll probably be in the morning papers anyway, so I guess there's no harm in letting you know," he said. "You probably figured it out anyway. Thomson and a dozen agents—along with four of my crew—were on their way to raid this plant when the hit team blew everybody away. If we got here twenty or thirty minutes earlier, all these corpses would be in the federal lock-up right now waiting to make bail. You didn't hear it from me."

"Hear what?" she answered as she nodded to Agajanian. "We're in on an entirely different matter, captain. Missing person. I understand his red Fiat Spider's parked here."

"There's one like that out back," Champly said.

"Show him the picture, Andy."

The captain accepted the photo and studied it.

"Hard to say, Miss Gordon. Couple of them shot up so fierce they could be anybody. Gonna run their prints and check their wallets and ID when Thomson says it's okay to move the bodies out of here—maybe in an hour or two. What's this fellow's name?"

"Sidney Adams. Can we see the Spider?"

Champly returned the picture and led them out the rear of the plant to a cluster of cars. Agajanian pointed at a red Fiat coupe, consulted his leather-bound pocket notebook and gestured at the car again.

"That's it," he announced. "The plates check."

"Miss Gordon?"

"Yes, captain."

"Mind if I ask who this Sidney Adams is?"

"No," she answered. He watched her press a gold-tipped cigarette into an expensive onyx holder and light it.

He found himself admiring her cool professionalism. Private investigators operated under a code of ethics that usually prevented them from talking about their clients and cases, so it was not surprising that she declined to identify this Adams person. However, she didn't mind if he *asked.* He could see now why she angered agent Thomson.

"Is there a want out on Adams? Criminal record? Armed or dangerous?" Champly tested.

"No to all three, and three is all you get. Thanks again for your full cooperation, captain."

"Glad I could help," he assured her. As they walked around toward the front of the building, he offered his card in case she wanted to phone the next morning about the identification of the bodies. He didn't come right out and ask her to give the governor a favorable report on his cooperation. He didn't have to; it was perfectly clear.

"If one of these is Adams," Champly said as they saw the FBI supervisor, "we're going to check him out right back to his baby teeth. Biggest mass murder in the county's history, and I'm giving it the full treatment. Nothing *personal*, you understand."

"I'm sure you'll do your usual fine job, captain. By the way, who runs Century Electronics?"

Champly shrugged and smiled, showing enough teeth to win regular work in half of this year's television series. Then he pumped her hand in farewell, and strode away briskly before she could ask any more questions.

"Baby Brother is our job," Agajanian reminded her. "What the hell do we care about some tape counterfeiting mob?"

She did not reply immediately. Instead, she puffed on the dark cigarette as she glanced thoughtfully at Thomson, twenty yards away. He was speaking with a handsome and earnest-faced man of thirty-six or thirty-eight who was obviously not employed by the Federal Bureau of Investigation. He was wearing a blue sports jacket and gray flannel trousers instead of a suit.

"I like to know what we're getting into," she finally answered.

"I say let's get into the Porsche, Al. Let's split before any of these media clowns recognize you. Come on."

As if on cue, an alert *Los Angeles Times* photographer raised his camera. She was "somebody," so he clicked off three frames before Alison and the accountant escaped in the Porsche.

"There's something funny about that business back there," she said as they headed for the Freeway.

"Funny *peculiar?*"

"*Strange* might be better, but *peculiar*'s okay."

"This is where you turn for the Freeway."

She followed his reminder, and two minutes later they were in the multi-lane flow of traffic moving toward Los Angeles.

"It doesn't add up right—"

"I'm not counting. It isn't our thing, Al."

It was as if he had not spoken.

"—nobody kills nine people either to protect or to wreck a tape-counterfeiting operation," she continued.

"Somebody just did. We both saw it, Al. World War Two-and-a-Half not ten miles from Disneyland."

He turned to look at her and recognized the expression. She was looking straight ahead and driving skillfully, but her inner eye was not on the highway. He sensed that she had seen the slaughter, but there was something about it that she did not accept. She was right, of course. From a logical point of view, wasting nine people in connection with this kind of racket made no sense. Mad-dog Colombian cocaine gangs routinely cowboyed the opposition with machine guns, but criminal organizations in California did not engage in mass murder.

"Maybe it's an act of terror to scare people," Agajanian speculated.

"I'm scared."

"For Chrissakes, Al, we've coped with the worst monsters for years. Why should this gang of crazies shake you up?"

"It's the possibility they're not crazy that shakes me," she replied. "Maybe *ruthless* is the operative word, and if that's it—"

"So there'll be more work for the cops and coroners—not for us. Listen, that probably isn't Baby Brother back there anyway. He could have lent the car to a friend, or maybe somebody heisted it."

She turned to him with a look of annoyance. "You expect me to *believe* that?"

"I thought I'd try. Sorry."

She shook her head again, then turned on the radio and put her foot down on the accelerator. With music blaring, they rode all the way back to Beverly Hills in the fast lane. As she drove, she considered the trouble ahead. The FBI was an efficient and persistent law-enforcement outfit, and there would be a lot of pressure on Tommy Thomson to solve the mystery of the massacre before the local police did. Thomson would insist on knowing why she'd come to the factory, the name of her client—everything. Alison Gordon would have problems with the FBI, all right. The only question was how soon.

# 6

SITUATED AT latitude 22 north and longitude 114 east, Hong Kong is not a very comfortable place to visit in June. It is not merely a question of the seasonal crowding caused by throngs of summer tourists; Hong Kong Island and Kowloon across the wide harbor and the adjacent New Territories on the Chinese mainland are always seething with people—4,500,000 of them within 403.7 square miles. The effect is most acute in June when the humidity and temperatures are high.

June was still two months away, but the plump Eurasian was sweating. Thanks to time zone changes and the international date line, it was only the last day of March here, so the weather was not the reason for Edwin Wolcott's perspiration—there was little moisture in the air and the temperature was a relatively pleasant 70 degrees Fahrenheit.

The Royal Air Force armorer who had fathered Wolcott would have been proud of his son's efforts to remain cool, behave sensibly and keep the situation in perspective. As a practical Yorkshireman, he would have understood that one sweats in times of acute danger. While he might not have been too enthusiastic about his twenty-eight-year-old son working as a stringer for one of those odd and nosy U.S. Government units, nobody could dispute the fact that the bloody Yanks paid top wages. Money was what Hong Kong was all about. One could buy or sell anything at almost any hour of any day. Cameras, clothing, electronics gear, gold, drugs, gems or information were all available.

Right now Edwin Wolcott needed a double Scotch and a woman. He had a strong sense that he was being followed. He had checked around him several times, when he walked through the Peninsula Hotel out onto Nathan Road, then as he strolled past the custom-made shirt and suit tailors on Kimberly Road and again when he boarded the Star Ferry for the short journey across the harbor. If they were watching him, it would be suicide to make the call. He would not even approach a telephone booth until he was certain that he was free of surveillance.

When the ferry docked on the Hong Kong side, he looked around again and felt better. There was no one following him. It was his nerves. Shortly before returning to Yorkshire, Harry Wolcott had confided to his Chinese wife that their boy Edwin seemed "a bit wonky"—a comment she had never passed on to anyone. Still, Edwin Wolcott had managed to live by his wits and contributed three hundred Hong Kong dollars to his mother's support most weeks. He did, however, have this problem with his nerves. As soon as he made the call, some good sex and a little number-four opium would help him feel better.

He walked out of the ferry terminal, made his way through the knots of people waiting for taxis and smirked at a couple of tourists climbing into one of Hong Kong's few remaining rickshaws. He zigzagged several blocks until he saw a public telephone. His heart was pounding as he turned the corner. After another glance around he put the coin in the slot and dialed the number.

"Yes?" the flat, familiar, midwestern voice asked.

"Extension twenty-one," Wolcott said.

"Go ahead."

"It's big, a lot bigger than I thought. They paid a deposit of $700,000, with another $4,200,000 on delivery," he reported. The perspiration trickled down his back.

"Lot of money."

"Not for this load. M-16 rifles, twelve thousand of them. Three hundred rocket launchers, seventy-two armored personnel carriers, mortars, machine guns, flame throwers."

He heard the American suck in his breath. Good, he was impressed. He'd pay more.

"You're *sure?*"

"Absolutely. Millions of rounds of ammo, thousands of rockets and mortar shells, two hundred and eighty field radios. Cleared Haiphong harbor yesterday, heading east."

"Where?"

"This is worth a bonus."

"Great work. What's the destination?"

"Fifteen hundred?"

"Wish I could. A thousand anyway," the man said, with no idea where he'd get the money.

"This is worth fifteen hundred," Wolcott insisted. "The shipment is big, and it was dangerous for me."

"I'll lean on them. You've got my word. You deserve it. Where's the ship going?"

Wolcott recited a latitude and longitude, and explained that he had not had a chance to check these coordinates on a map.

"We'll do that. Did you get the ship's name and registry?"

Fifteen hundred dollars! He would give his mother a quarter of it. Well, at least a fifth. She would be very proud.

"Liberian registry," Wolcott said and then paused to pat a

47

handkerchief to his dripping face. For a moment he wondered whether he had made a mistake. Maybe he could have wangled two thousand for a major coup like this . . .

"And the ship?"

Wolcott opened his mouth to tell him the name, but only a choked scream emerged. The pain of the dagger in his back was awful. He managed to turn halfway around and look into his assassin's face. So they *had* been following him after all. The man pulled out the blade and rammed it into Wolcott's throat. Then he stepped aside to avoid the spout of blood, watched Wolcott hit the pavement and walked away at a pace that would not attract notice.

"The ship? . . . What about the ship?" the voice on the phone asked.

There was no answer. He repeated the question twice more, annoyed by the thought that Wolcott might be holding out for more money. The fat little bastard was capable of that kind of crap. There was also the *other* possibility. There always was in this business.

"Is something wrong?" the voice asked.

There was no reply, but after a few moments he heard a shriek. It sounded like a woman. He waited several seconds more before he decided that it probably was the other.

He would know within four or five hours. Then he hung up the phone and went to the wall map to check those coordinates.

It was a point two hundred and ten miles due west of Ensenada, Mexico.

# 7

THE SLAUGHTER at Century Electronics made the front pages of just about every daily newspaper west of Denver. Many eastern papers ran the Associated Press report on the massacre with a photo of police loading the body bags into ambulances. The networks carried the story on both their late-night and morning news, capsule sagas that combined summaries of the bloody violence with speculation about a possible gang war. Ever vigilant for events that would reassure their readers that life in America was really lousy, the British and Russian papers played it big. At social gatherings in Beverly Hills, it was discussed as much as the imminent Oscar awards.

Waiting for word from Captain Champly, Alison Gordon focussed her attention on other cases. When she reached the office at 9:40 the next morning, she dictated a memo covering everything that she knew about Sidney Adams, and started returning phone calls that had come in on the previous afternoon. She was just finishing when Don Hovde, a former CIA colleague who'd been with A. B. Gordon Investigations since he left government service five years ago, put his head into her office.

"You were right about the Buddhist temple case," he whispered in the odd voice that memorialized a bullet through his throat in Vietnam.

"The assistant controller was siphoning off three or four grand a week—for religious purposes," he said. She gestured for him to come in and sit down.

"Must be terribly devout," she replied.

"A born-again Buddhist. Temple never suspected the money was stolen, you understand. They're a very honorable crowd."

She smiled and flashed him a thumb's-up salute as she started to examine the heap of letters and telegrams.

"That means *well done*," she translated. "Go break the news to our client."

"I think you ought to, Al. You're better with clients, and you're the one they hired anyway."

He was still shy about his injured voice and still uncomfortable with business executives—even the California breed.

"Sure, Don. Anything else?"

"Andy said we're looking for Baby Brother, huh?"

She didn't usually feel irritable this early in the day, but she was this time. Even as she spoke sharply, she was not quite sure why.

"His name is *Sidney Adams*, so let's knock off the cute crap." She thrust the tape at him. Puzzled, Hovde took it and blinked.

"That's all we've got," she announced. "It's a very *minor* and very *routine* case. The fact that his sister is an obnoxious star is irrelevant. We're supposed to find him. If he's not in the Orange County morgue right now, maybe you will track him down."

"Sure."

"Thank you," she replied and instantly regretted her tone. "Did I congratulate you on nailing this . . . uh . . . disturbed Buddhist?" she asked in apology.

"Sure," he answered and departed with the tape.

She took refuge in the mail, found a little comfort in a $16,000 check from an insurance company and went to lunch at the Polo Lounge with a trendy art dealer who wanted to sell her sculptures at his gallery. By four o'clock, she was glancing at her watch every fifteen minutes. At ten to five she phoned Champly.

"Just about to call you," he said.

"All identified?"

"No, but I have some news. One of the victims is your Mr. Adams. We're releasing the names in an hour, but I wanted you to get it first. By the way, your friend—that fellow with the funny name—was right. Slugs were nine-millimeter."

"Thank you, captain. I appreciate everything you've done." She knew it sounded mechanical.

"Glad to *cooperate*," he assured her. "FBI agrees it had to be some organized-crime thing."

"Didn't sound like a lover's quarrel," she answered as she stared at Adams' snapshot. The conversation ended with a few pleasantries, leaving her with a sense of how depressing it must have been to live in Lauri Adams' shadow, to have no identity but that of little brother to an ego-crazed superstar. Had Sidney Adams ever been happy at all? The answer didn't matter now. She had to inform Lauri Adams that her brother was dead, and that wasn't something done over the phone. Even The Bitch deserved better than that. Alison dialed the estate she had visited thirty hours earlier.

"She's kind of busy," the maid announced.

"It's important. I have to talk to her."

"She's got a whole crowd of—"

"Tell her I'm on my way."

She hung up, and at 5:25 Lauri Adams' security guard waved her through the gate and up the driveway. The number of

Mercedes, Rolls, Ferraris, Maseratis and Jaguars made it difficult to park anywhere near the front door, but the adroit detective found just enough space to park her Porsche without injuring the lavish flower beds. She heard voices coming around the corner of the house, and guessed that there was a party in progress at the patio beside the pool. She rang the doorbell, and told the maid to inform Miss Adams that she had arrived and wanted to speak to her—in private. Then she lit a Sobranie and thought about how she'd break the news. She had almost finished the cigarette when Lauri Adams rushed out, indignant.

"Listen, Gordon. You can't just barge in here. I've got some of the biggest people in the industry here, so whatever it is better be goddamn important."

"It is. I have some news about your brother."

"What the hell is it?" the entertainer said impatiently as she glanced at her diamond-studded wristwatch.

"I'm sorry to say that Sidney is dead."

Lauri Adams flinched, and for a moment her face twisted in pain. She grunted like a boxer who has been hit, then gulped as her eyes widened. Alison Gordon thought that she was about to cry, but her control returned almost immediately. It was to be expected. Superstars don't cry, except on film or tape.

"Was it an accident?"

"No. Did you read about the nine people shot at the recording factory near Disneyland?"

"Saw it on TV."

"I'm afraid he was one of them. I think his body's down at the Orange County morgue. You might call Captain Champly," Alison Gordon suggested and handed her a slip with the phone number.

"Do they know he's my brother?"

"Not yet."

A loud burst of laughter sounded from the back of the house.

"What was Sid doing at that plant? Why was he there?" Laurie Adams asked.

"Maybe Champly knows."

A limousine pulled up to discharge the gifted woman who ran 20th Century-Fox and a famous director. Both had bought sculptures from Alison during the past year. They waved in greeting and started toward the two women in the doorway.

"I want to know who killed my brother."

"The police will find out. We don't handle murders. I'm very sorry. Goodbye Miss Adams."

As she walked to her car, Alison Gordon was oppressed with sadness. All these glamorous and high-powered people must have overwhelmed Sidney, she thought. When she reached the Porsche, she looked back at Lauri Adams throwing her arms wide in greeting. She seemed splendid in the chic gown; there wasn't a sign of grief in that internationally beloved face. The superstar was grinning as she led her guests to the party. She had her responsibilities as a hostess, and these celebrities were the "A" list. Lauri Adams, she hoped, would mourn her brother later, when her guests were gone.

What *had* Sidney Adams been doing there, Alison wondered as she started her car. Who the hell was he anyway? Did anyone know, or care? Suddenly, Alison wanted to get away from this estate and these clever, talented people. She stepped hard on the accelerator and escaped into the dusk.

The slaughter was still on the front page of the *L. A. Times* the next morning. The following day it was pushed back to page three with the stories of a San Francisco jetliner disaster that killed a hundred and three and the outbreak of another war between two North African governments. The list of victims in the Orange County morgue did not identify Sidney Adams as Lauri's brother. By April 7th, the news broadcasters had forgotten the massacre and were concentrating on the tragic fire at the Pasadena mental institution and the arrest of the senator's daughter who was caught smuggling a pound of cocaine in a "body cavity." The afternoon paper did its best to keep the Century story alive with an account of the FBI's refusal to comment on rumors that arrests were imminent. There was also a statement from the head of the Recording Industry Association of America that counterfeiting was "a major problem and a billion-dollar-a-year global racket." Two days later, the murder disappeared from the local media.

That was April 9th.

It was on the morning of the 10th that Alison Gordon got the phone call.

# 8

"I DON'T like it," Agajanian told her as the traffic light changed and she stepped on the accelerator.

"You don't like pianos?"

"No, just the pianist," he replied. "You say 8162?"

"8162 Beverly, between Fairfax and La Cienega."

"He's bad news, Al, and his friends are worse. Strictly trouble."

"That's our business. *Bastard!*" she said as she braked to avoid a Ferrari that had knifed in ahead of her. "Didn't mean you, Andy."

"Let me lay it on you in numbers," he said. "The odds are nine hundred and sixty-four to none that he's got something terrible for us. I don't believe he's retired. I think he's still one of the top gangsters in the country. If he really was a gentle old dude, he wouldn't live on a mountain protected by barbed wire and machine guns. And why would any respectable person need radar to detect approaching aircraft?"

"I think it's in the next block."

"Stuff the next block, I'm telling you Spinoza is bad business.

Don't let that Old World charm fool you, Al. His crowd are the sort that blasted Century Electronics."

She nodded, and then he understood.

"You aren't thinking of asking him about *that?*"

"The idea crossed my mind."

There it was—an ordinary-looking building for the home of a very special establishment. Though the store was not very well known to the public, its customers were. Top musicians bought the finest-made organs, pianos and instruments here. A dark gray Cadillac limousine was parked in front, and two sturdy men in their twenties lounged near the door.

"He's here," she said.

"Who else has wheels with armor plate and bullet-proof windows?" Agajanian asked.

She parked the Porsche, and he followed her to the shop under the wary scrutiny of the bodyguards. There was another escort inside holding a black leather attaché case, standing respectfully a few yards from a slim, gray-haired man in a dark suit —Joseph Spinoza. The older man was admiring an enormous piano, while a dignified-looking salesman hovered discreetly nearby. Spinoza leaned forward, hesitated and played a few notes.

"Beautiful," he sighed.

"There's nothing like it," the salesman confided. "The inner rim—you might say the *skeleton*—of most pianos is made by compressing fourteen or fifteen sheets of a pliable wood such as poplar or mahogany under heat for an hour and a half, then shaping it into laminated rims in the form of a piano. The Bösendorfer inner rims are made of *solid* blocks of spruce, a resonant wood generally used for soundboards. Outer rims are solid spruce panels, with grains matched for maximum transmission of sound. This makes the whole frame something like an extension of the soundboard. There are many other refinements . . ."

Spinoza played another chord, and smiled.

"Each string is individually hitched to permit easier tuning, and the soundboard ties into the case directly. It is made with almost infinite care, Mr. Smith," the salesman said. "Most pianos are completed in no more than fourteen weeks. The Bösendorfer requires more than three *years,* including at least two for open-air seasoning of the wood to reach a properly low moisture content."

Spinoza nodded, and then he glanced up and saw her.

"Miss Gordon! Thank you so much for coming on short notice. I apologize, but it wasn't until yesterday that I heard this splendid piano was available. The company makes less than one thousand a year."

"Six hundred," Agajanian said.

"This is Mr. Agajanian, my friend . . . my associate . . . and my accountant."

Before she could complete the introduction, the older man stepped forward with outstretched hand.

"My name is Joseph Spinoza."

"I know," Agajanian said as they shook hands. The salesman was surprised to hear that Mr. Smith had another name, but said nothing. Spinoza stepped back, studied the accountant from head to toe and turned to Alison.

"Think I should buy the piano?" he asked. "I'm only an amateur, and I might deprive some very gifted professional of the opportunity to play it."

"There are others."

He stared at the Bösendorfer for several seconds and caressed it. Then he pointed his index finger at the man with the attaché case. The aide went to the salesman, who waited hopefully.

"How much?"

"Uh . . . forty-one thousand fifty . . . That includes tax and delivery."

The salesman gaped as the aide opened the attaché case. He had never seen that much currency before. Dozens of neat packets of used fifty-dollar bills, each clump secured by rubber bands, filled the case. Each small bundle contained two thousand dollars.

"Thirty-two . . . thirty-four . . . thirty-six . . . thirty-eight . . . forty. There a discount for cash?"

"I don't . . . I'm afraid not, sir."

Spinoza smiled. When the rest was counted out and added to the heap, the salesman opened a desk drawer and took out an invoice pad.

"I'm sure you want a receipt, sir," he said in awe.

"No, thanks."

"Of course, the instrument is in perfect condition—but for your records, sir, you'll want . . ."

"Don't need it. If there's any problem . . . we know where to find you."

There was nothing menacing in the tone of voice, but the salesman froze in fear. He was rigid as Spinoza's aide explained how and where to deliver the piano while Spinoza drew Alison aside to speak confidentially.

"Sorry to waste your time. I didn't ask you here to help me pick out a piano," he assured. "It's something a lot more . . . well . . . sensitive. After the fine job you . . . you and your people . . . did in Vegas, I thought you might help with another problem that's just come up."

Agajanian scowled.

"Is something bothering your friend?" Spinoza asked.

"A lot of things. Please go on."

"Well, my friends are being bothered too. You might say *harassed*, and unjustly. Certain well-meaning but misguided law-enforcement officials are obstructing normal business operations. You could say they're becoming part of this problem instead of solving it."

"Federal heat," Agajanian translated. Now Spinoza noticed the bulge under the accountant's armpit. His eyes narrowed.

"No, he's not wired," Alison said. "That's a .357, not a tape recorder. What's the problem?"

"That Century incident down near Anaheim . . . that *terrible* incident . . . They think my friends might be responsible."

"Were they?" she asked. Spinoza glanced at Agajanian, who had opened his jacket to show he was only carrying a gun.

"Miss Gordon," Spinoza said bitterly, "those nine people were *our* people. My friends *own* Century Electronics, and they don't *do* that kind of thing. That was the work of animals, beasts that belong in a zoo."

"The FBI will put them there."

Spinoza shook his head in frustration.

"The damn FBI thinks *we* did it. They don't know who's behind the three layers of holding companies, and my friends obviously can't tell them that it was their business that was wrecked."

"Why were those people killed?" she asked.

"If I knew that, I'd have an idea as to who did it. We've been checking for days, and we've got nothing. Do you have any leads or hunches?"

"Me?"

"You were out there that afternoon—on some business, I figure."

"My business. Nothing to do with your friends' tape business. Routine missing-person investigation. It's finished now."

Spinoza's aide tapped his wristwatch. It was time to leave for the doctor's office. Spinoza ignored him.

"I'd like you to help the FBI, Miss Gordon," he said.

"They don't need my help. They wouldn't accept it anyway, and they'd probably be right."

"They will if you discover who killed those people. They'd have to."

Spinoza was right, but she didn't care.

"You think we're after *vengeance*," he guessed shrewdly. "We'll settle for *justice*, but we're in a hurry. The FBI will lose weeks on the wrong trail."

"And bother your friends."

"That's a factor," he admitted. "All I'm asking is that you find out who sent in the hit squad and tell the FBI immediately. Tell them, not us. You get five hundred dollars a day, right? We'll pay five thousand a day . . . fifty thousand right now. The cash is in that case."

"Murders are police business, Mr. Spinoza."

"They're everybody's business. It's a citizen's duty to help the cops. We've got to stamp out violence. What's this country coming to?"

"*If* I find out, I'll let you know," she promised, "but I'm not taking on a homicide case. Not yours or anyone else's. Still, I'm glad it wasn't your people who did the killing."

"Maybe it was foreigners. Nobody in the U.S. of A. operates like that anymore." He patted the extraordinary piano again.

"Sinatra has one," Agajanian announced suddenly as Spinoza turned to depart, "and so does Victor Borge. I saw it in *Contemporary Keyboard.*"

"He reads a lot," she explained.

"Trying to improve myself," the accountant said.

Spinoza nodded and shook Alison's hand in farewell.

"Wish you'd think about my friend's problem, Miss Gordon."

"Thinking is all I can do. Enjoy your piano."

Spinoza smiled. His aide walked to the door of the store to warn the bodyguards outside that they were ready to leave. One swung open the right rear door of the armored limousine, and then both scanned the street. When they were sure that it was safe, they nodded and the aide went into the shop to escort Spinoza to the Cadillac. Alison Gordon and Agajanian watched it roll away up Beverly Boulevard. Neither of the private detectives noticed the gray Pontiac passing moments later.

"That was a dumb thing you did in there," she said reprovingly.

"And a smart thing you did. That bloody bit down at the tape plant was only the beginning, you know. There's going to be more killing. I can smell it. I'm glad we're out of it."

She nodded in assent. He would have felt better if he hadn't seen the brooding look in her eyes.

"We *are* out of it, aren't we?" he said.

"You heard what I told him."

"Yeah, but I didn't hear you answer my question. That's not like you, Al."

She lit a cigarette.

"I was just thinking about Sidney Adams—in the abstract. Of course, we're out of it. That's definite. You send the bill to her business manager?"

"Three days ago."

"Then we can forget about it and go on to other cases," she

said. As she drove back to the office, they discussed other assignments the firm was handling and Agajanian felt better. Unfortunately, the feelings would not last all day.

Nine miles away, Colonel Roger Halleck (U.S. Army, retired) stood with a 30.06 rifle at his shoulder and took careful aim. Though he was no longer on active service, he was still a crack shot who practiced every week. He could still kill a man at a hundred and fifty yards if he had to, a skill that he expected to use very soon. He squeezed the trigger. Another bull's-eye, the tenth consecutive one this afternoon. It came as no surprise to the "regulars" here at the Valley Gun Club range, for they had witnessed his marksmanship many times in the past two years. Though he was fifty-seven, he had the trim physique, keen eye and trigger touch of a much younger soldier. The civilian clothes and pension meant nothing. Roger Halleck was still an infantryman, ready for battle.

He collected his empty shells, slid the rifle into its nylon bag and walked back to the parking lot. He nodded politely to a few men on the way, but said nothing. Halleck was not a gregarious sort. Indeed, he spoke so little that the other members of the club didn't know what he did with his time. There was talk of a book being written, of profitable stock market investments, of running and calisthenics every day. He traveled several times a year to veterans' reunions and conventions, but most of the members paid almost no attention to him. That was what he wanted.

It was as he reached his jeep—a commercial/civilian edition of the military vehicle that he'd known so well in thirty years in the U. S. Army—that he saw Officer Carl Zelner of the Narcotics Division of Los Angeles Police Department. Zelner was trying to find something in the trunk of his Ford as he waited to report to his superior. He did not look at Halleck as he spoke.

"Looks good, sir. FBI has no idea we did the job at Century."

"Or that we exist."

"They think it was a Mafia job. They'd go crazy if they knew it was six cops."

"What's the FBI doing now, sergeant?" Halleck had known Zelner by that rank through most of the Vietnam War.

"Pounding the top syndicate bosses. Round-the-clock heat and surveillance, our friend at the Bureau says. He thinks it's funny, sir."

"Nothing about Operation Lexington is funny. It's crucial. It's our last chance, and it's going to work. In less than three weeks, we'll be running America."

"Yes, sir. Is there any message you want me to relay?"

Halleck paused.

"Tell them the weapons will be here in thirteen days, and we've got to have that money by then. The assault teams must not fail."

"They won't, sir."

"All our other units are depending on them. They're all in position, all ready. The Panama detachment hits first, and that's the signal. This government of weaklings will drop like a corpse once we sever the head. Our attack will accomplish that with minimum casualties—a quick surgical procedure." Halleck put his gun bag in the jeep.

"A strong new America," Zelner said.

"The only threat now is a leak. If there's *any* sign of another weak link . . . take him out. We're too close to victory to lose it all. A spy or a traitor, kill him instantly. That order comes directly from 'Caesar.' He's sent the same message to every detachment."

"There won't be any leak from *here,* sir."

The sergeant was a good man, Halleck thought, as he drove out of the parking lot. There were a lot of fine men—first-class patriots—committed to Lexington and ready to die for it. A strong new America—it was more than the secret army's slogan. It was a promise, and on April 27th that pledge would become a reality. With "Caesar" in command, it had to succeed. By the end of the month he would sit in the White House. The nation would be free of those phony politicians and liberal hypocrites who controlled the media. America would be great again—and Halleck would finally have the star that he'd been cheated out of by the Pentagon. "Caesar" had given his word.

# 9

At 4:55 that afternoon, a well-known and respected Hollywood "business manager" named Max E. Shimmel entered the offices of A. B. Gordon Investigations. He had no appointment, but he did have a check for $1,029 to pay for services rendered to Lauri Adams. At 5:02, Alison Gordon told him he was crazy and to leave her office immediately.

The conversation had not begun on such an acrimonious note. Max E. Shimmel—Maxie to three generations of top performers, directors, executives, agents and entertainment lawyers—was a pleasant man who was widely admired for his honesty. His balding pate and the bags under his eyes were landmarks of a thirty-six-year career. He worked hard for his clients. He was a worrier, a diabetic and a religious man who took an active role in the Sinai Temple in Westwood. He was one of the few real gentlemen in show business.

He seemed even gloomier than usual as he gave her the check, but Alison Gordon was not the sort who pried. She thanked him for delivering it personally, suggested that he sit down, and asked him about his family. She pretended surprise when he told her that his daughter was in the midst of her second divorce. Half of Malibu had long known about that mess. She decided that talking about his clients would be safer.

"And what's happening with your beautiful people, Max?"

"Don't ask. They're supposed to be stars, huh? The people I used to work for had class; now it's brass and money. The numbers are huge, but the people are midgets."

"Not everyone."

"Would you believe that some of these so-called superstars ask me to handle their dope-buying? Me, a grandfather?" He automatically opened his wallet to show a photo of his grandsons.

"Nice boys," she complimented.

"Thanks. Did I tell you that Lauri appreciates your efforts?"

"No."

Whatever it was he wanted was coming now. He put away the wallet and braced himself.

"This thing has really torn her up," he said. "She's a very sensitive person, especially about her family. She's crying blue murder."

"Give her my condolences."

"Please, she's got to know what happened to her only brother. Is that so much?"

"Maxie, you're *crazy* if you think you can talk us into this. I already told her that."

"How long have we known each other?"

"I'm very fond of you," she said, "but you'd better go now before this turns unpleasant."

"This is important."

"*Crazy* doesn't suit you, Maxie. As for her, I don't care."

He stood up and walked over to her desk.

"I don't believe this. You're a caring person," Shimmel said. "Is it so terrible that this woman wants to understand what happened to her flesh and blood? Why was he there? What did he do during those blank ten weeks?"

"You mean she's afraid that she was somehow responsible. Maxie, I don't care about her guilt trip."

"Care about Sidney."

It hit home. She did not reply for several seconds.

"Not who killed him? Just what he did and where he was?" she asked slowly.

"That's all."

"I don't know. You don't need an expensive firm like ours for that."

"You're the best, Alison. I know it, Lauri knows it—and certainly so do you."

Agajanian and Hovde would be furious, and they'd be right. From a business point of view, such a case made little sense. There was sure to be trouble with The Bitch, the FBI and God knew who else. It had to be ugly.

"It's not your job to hire detectives. Why are you pushing so hard, Maxie?"

He looked embarrassed.

"You'd be doing me a personal favor," he said. Then she remembered the rumor that another one of Hollywood's biggest agencies was wooing Lauri Adams, his most important client. He was afraid to lose her.

"I must be as crazy as you are, Maxie."

"You'll do it?"

"For Max E. Shimmel, a very classy guy. Tell her that."

He beamed as he thanked her. The mixture of joy and relief was still on his face as they walked to the elevator.

"I don't mind telling you this, Alison, but if you hadn't—"

"I don't want to hear, Maxie. You don't have to explain things to friends."

Maybe Maxie reminded her of her father. Perhaps it was

something else. Whatever the reason, she found herself hugging him. When he was gone, she returned to her office with a lump in her throat. The ringing telephone helped bring her back to reality. It was Agajanian reporting in on a stolen Utrillo case.

"Sounds fine. By the way, Andy, Maxie Shimmel brought in the Adams check."

"What else?"

"What do you mean?"

"There's more, Al. I can hear it in your voice."

"He . . . ah . . . asked us to find out where her brother had been and what he'd been up to since he vanished. I told him he was crazy, of course."

*"Jeezus Christ!"*

"What's the matter?" she asked defensively.

"What else did you tell him—as if I didn't know?"

"Well, I made it clear that we don't handle murders. He was scared, Andy. I think she threatened him. He's an old friend . . ."

"So we're in the fucking sewer. That's what it's going to be, Al. With sado-masochism and the other garbage we're sure to find, it's got to be a sewer."

"I had to do it, Andy. I'm sorry."

"That kid got to you days ago. Okay, okay, you're the boss."

"We're not touching the murder," she insisted.

"Sure. See you in the morning."

The special agent tapping Alison Gordon's phone conversation delivered the cassette to Thomson at seven that night. Word that she was investigating the final ten weeks of Sidney Adams' life reached the Lexington organization early the following day.

# 10

A. B. Gordon Investigations had a lot of experience in finding people, all kinds of people—both those who had just wandered off, and those who were hiding. The firm had located the nymphomaniacal girlfriends of rock stars, executives dodging subpoenas, blocked screenwriters who had fled without finishing scripts, vengeful ex-husbands trying to avoid child-support and alimony payments, embezzlers, amnesiacs, emotionally disturbed psychiatrists, witnesses who would rather not testify, even teen- and middle-aged runaways.

There are ways of finding people, techniques and routines that detectives—public and private—have used for decades. Some methods are entirely legal, while others involve minor deceptions, cash payments, or old friends.

"Old friends are the best friends," Agajanian said as he entered Alison Gordon's office and waved the slip of paper.

"How old?"

"She's about thirty-three, and adores Margaritas. I've known her at least fifteen or sixteen months. In California, that's a lifetime."

"Can we skip the social commentary?"

"You're the boss. The late Mr. Adams lived at 1521 Twelfth Street in Santa Monica for the past two months. I found that out by touching base with Maxie. He keeps Lauri Adams' financial records and has all this year's canceled checks. Sidney Adams used to deposit some in the Third Federal."

"And your Sybil works there?"

"Bulls-eye. A man may not tell his sister or the post office where he's moving, but he's got to notify his bank. So much for the American family," the accountant concluded.

Alison shook her head at his archness, and held out her hand for the piece of paper.

"I'll check it out in the morning, Al."

"Don't bother. I could use a drive right now."

Agajanian shrugged, and followed her out to the door.

"I won't be back tonight," she told her secretary. "Got a stop in Santa Monica. Be home around a quarter to seven."

"Me too," the accountant said briskly.

"You're coming too?" asked Alison.

"You could also use some company," he answered.

There had to be a reason for this generous offer. She had figured it out by the time they entered the elevator.

"You're riding shotgun," she accused.

"Don't get dramatic, Al. I need some fresh air."

"On a smoggy day like this? Let's have the truth."

"When the guy we're investigating has been blown away by machine guns, I figure shotguns are in order."

"You're getting paranoid, you know."

"No, I've been paranoid for years."

Though there was a fair amount of traffic on the winding road out to Santa Monica, the drive took only twenty-five minutes. Then they headed south along the highway that bordered the Pacific. Expensive beach houses were on their right and a series

70

of less costly homes on the cliffs across the road. 1521 12th Street was not in the most chic section of Santa Monica, but at the southernmost end, closer to Venice. The street was quiet with attractive shrubs and trees, a dozen blocks in from the ocean. The house itself was a two-story building, with an exterior staircase leading to the upper floor.

"Five bucks says he lived up top," Agajanian offered. He was right. When they found the woman who ran the small apartment house, she confirmed that Mr. Adams had lived in Apartment Nine.

"We'd like to see it, please."

"It's a nice little apartment, with plenty of light," replied the superintendent and led them up the stairs. She unlocked the door, swung it wide. The apartment was empty. No furniture, no pictures, no plants.

"Two ninety-five a month," the building manager announced. "You won't find a better deal in town."

"What?" Alison Gordon asked.

"You're here to rent it, aren't you?"

"No, we're friends of his sister," the accountant improvised.

"He never mentioned a sister. If you're not here for the apartment—"

"She wanted us to see about his belongings," Alison said. It was strange to look at this empty, naked place. There were no clues to be found here.

"What happened to them?" she asked.

"You just missed them. Movers hauled them away not twenty minutes ago."

"What movers?"

"Four big fellows with a truck. His father sent them to pick it all up. I guess he forgot to tell this sister he was taking care of it. Say, that was *terrible* the way he died."

71

"Terrible," Agajanian agreed. They promised to pass her condolences on to "the family" and descended to the street.

"What moving company was it?" Alison asked the woman.

"Didn't notice. It was a green truck—dark green. His father knows."

They thanked her for cooperating and were in the Porsche half a minute later.

"I'll phone the father in the morning," Agajanian promised. "Have we got his number? Wait a second, how come he knew where Baby Brother was and The Bitch didn't?"

"The only number Sidney Adams' father has is on his cemetery plot, Andy. He's been dead for three years."

"Then who sent the moving van? I think we've got a problem, Al."

"Two," she replied.

He saw her eyes flick to the car's rear-view mirror, and he stiffened. "Yeah," he said.

"Any special reason you didn't mention the tan Mustang that's been tailing us since we left the office?"

"I figured you'd bring it up when you were ready to talk about it.

"You used to lie better, Andy."

"I'm out of practice. All right, I thought I'd check it out and give you a full report tomorrow. Hell, I didn't want to bother you."

"I'm a big girl. This doesn't bother me. As a matter of fact, I like it. It could be a lead to whoever or whatever Sidney Adams was doing. Get their number."

She pulled the car to the side of the street suddenly, and they both watched the Mustang as it rolled past. Agajanian noted the license plate. Then she drove back to Beverly Hills—with the Mustang following all the way.

72

When she reached her office the next morning at 9:40, Agajanian was waiting to report what he'd learned.

"This is a little weird," he announced.

"The Mustang?"

"Yeah, it's hot. Stolen three days ago from a parking lot off Pico. That's not the weird part."

"I'm listening."

"An hour before we spotted it, the LAPD found it. They told the owner to pick it up this morning at eight, and he did. You know what that means?"

"It means that somebody stole it from the police car pound, used it to tail us and put it back."

"Don't you think that's weird?"

"It's weird," she agreed. "Now let's get back to Sidney Adams. Maybe your Sybil can help us look over his canceled checks. Banks keep microfilm records of that sort of thing. Go rub her tummy or buy her a gallon of Margaritas."

"Sybil's no dummy," he protested. "She won't let us see bank records of confidential stuff like that. It would be unethical and illegal."

"Then do it legally. Lauri Adams is Sid's closest surviving relative. Maybe Maxie or her lawyer could get us a nice, official, notarized letter requesting access to those checks. If you need a court order, her lawyer plays golf with half the judges in town."

"Anything else?"

"Don ought to drop by The Steel Cellar tonight with Sid's picture," she suggested.

"The s-m crowd isn't very chatty. It's what you might call an *in* group, very private."

"And weird."

"This whole case is weird," Agajanian said again. "Wiping out nine people with machine guns at a tape plant is weird.

Heisting all the brother's stuff is *very* weird, and so is being tailed by guys in a hot car that's supposed to be in a police lot."

"There are thieves who specialize in taking dead people's property, Andy. We don't really know who emptied that flat, or why."

"What about the Mustang, mom?"

"It could be some other case we're on. Anyway, it's been returned to the owner."

There was no point in arguing with her, for she knew as well as he did that the real issue was not the vehicle but the people in it. Agajanian left to phone Sybil, hoping that her memories of their hot-tub experiences would prevail. Alison sat at her desk staring at a small bronze sculpture on the end table. None of their other investigations involved the theft of a car from the Los Angeles Police Department.

She was still thinking about it when she left for her 10:30 appointment at MGM. The car that trailed her this time was a black Buick.

# 11

AFTER MILITARY police twice stopped José Garcia from entering the psychiatric ward, he decided not to push his luck. A third attempt at "accidental" entry could well be hazardous to his health. These guards seemed meaner and grimmer than any he'd met since he put on the U. S. Army private's uniform. Unlike the ordinary MPs, these men radiated aggression and an angry sense of mission.

There had to be something unusual and important going on in the mental facility—something secret. Garcia circled the ward carefully, searching for some other way in. There was a rear door that led to the hospital's laundry but was protected by a pair of locks and more armed guards.

Garcia would not give up so easily. He had his pride, part macho and part personal. If he could not get in, he would try to make contact with someone who came out. It would be difficult to wait around for such a person near the front door, but he could hide in the laundry room where his presence was much less likely to raise questions. If worse came to worse, he would pretend that he had sneaked in for some rum. A long swallow would taint his breath nicely.

By ten P.M. he began to wonder whether he'd made another mistake, and by 11:30 realized that he'd have to write off tonight's vigil. No one had come in at all. Stiff and tired from crouching behind a laundry hamper, he yawned. He stood up—for only a second. Then he dropped as he heard the noise in the corridor. The door swung open abruptly.

Four men pushed a pair of cargo dollies inside. Two were MPs, while the others wore patients' gowns. The wheeled platforms were heaped with boxes.

"This is what we've been waiting for," one of the patients said.

"Shut up. Get some sheets to cover everything," the other commanded.

"Yes, sir." The MPs pulled clean sheets from a shelf almost directly over where Garcia crouched, draped the white cloths over the boxes and pushed the dollies out into the corridor. Garcia could hear the twin locks being opened and the dollies being rolled into the psychiatric ward. Tense and puzzled, he lurked in the semi-darkness of the laundry room for another forty minutes before escaping through a small high window.

He had recognized the markings on those boxes from his work in the supply section. Body armor, M-16 rifles, gas masks and cannisters filled with nauseating gas stockpiled for riot control. Who was smuggling it in to the mental patients? Why did MPs take orders from the psychos?

What the hell was the U. S. Army up to anyway? Garcia would leave a report for his photographer friend in Panama City, but he'd still have to get the answers. Someone outside those rings of armed MPs must be running this covert operation. It was up to Garcia to identify him and monitor his activities. There was no telling what they'd do if they discovered that he was spying on them. After all, everyone in the lockup was supposed to be officially and certifiably insane. . . .

# 12

SOME FOUR thousand miles north and a bit west, Don Hovde parked his car across the street from The Steel Cellar. Alison Gordon's instructions had been brief and clear as usual. Get in, ask your questions and get out. He tried to remember what Agajanian had said about what the members would be wearing, chains, steel-studded wristlets and leather jackets, color-coded kerchiefs. Agajanian associated with people who knew such things. All Hovde could remember was that if a man wore kerchief or keys from the left side of his pants it meant "I do it to you," while the right signaled "You do it to me." The "it" varied in meaning, but Hovde had never gotten that far—and didn't want to.

Outside was a small sign and no windows. Inside it was all black, with the exception of the cobblestone floor, metal beams and mirrors. The bar—and many of the patrons—were done in black leather. Some were dressed as cowboys, others as miners, motorcyclists or alumni of Hitler's military. There were swastikas, chains, big belts with large buckles, and tattoos, along with an assortment of earrings and bulky jewelry. Men with mustaches, men with shaven heads, men of all sizes and colors. Two wore dog collars.

"Don't let their gear bother you," Agajanian had advised. "It's a costume party—kids of all ages playing out their fantasies. Hardly any of them are really tough. They're like the Mafia— they only hurt each other, and by set rituals. Pain by permission."

Hovde guessed that some underworld group owned the place. Burly and businesslike, the bartenders resembled those in a hundred other Syndicate joints that overcharged homosexuals across the country. Hovde made his way through the throng, avoiding eye contact. A few were puzzled by his drab attire, but they either ignored him or assumed that he had not come out of the closet far enough to put on his s-m regalia. The jukebox was blaring some lonely trucker's lament. Inching past two neo Nazis and an imitation sailor, Hovde squeezed through to the left end of the bar.

"Johnny Walker and water," he said.

The bartender nodded, poured the drink and held up three stubby fingers. Hovde found himself sipping some cheap bar Scotch. He did not protest. He downed another swallow before he took out the photo. When the bartender returned a minute later, Hovde asked the question.

"You know Sidney Adams?"

A shrug was the reply. Hovde showed the snapshot.

"Don't think so," the bartender said.

"He was in here a lot."

"I'm busy, chum."

"I'm looking for a friend of his, big fellow. Rode a heavy bike. Good-looking, mustache."

"We get fifty guys a night like that, chum."

The bartender walked away. Hovde finished his drink and

signaled for a refill. When it was put down before him, he tried again.

"It's important. I've got to find his friend. There's money involved."

"Nah."

"Try to remember," Hovde appealed and placed a twenty-dollar bill on the black leather counter.

"This kid's dead," the bartender said.

"It's his friend I want to reach. Try."

"Big Ed. I think they were in a couple of times," the bartender said as he pocketed the money.

"I've got to reach him. Big Ed who?"

"No last names in here, chum. You better split."

"Is he here now?"

Something flickered in the bartender's eyes.

"You a cop or something?"

"Just a friend of the family," Hovde replied and laid down another twenty. The bartender took it. Then he gestured to a T-shirted man who weighed at least two hundred and fifty pounds.

"Maybe he's in the back room where the action is. Freddy, show him the way."

The heavy man smiled, and Hovde followed him in a zigzag route through the clusters of customers to a rear door at the far side of the room. There were two doors side by side. One opened for a moment. A nude man in a leather mask was inside, hanging from manacles cemented into the wall.

"Not that door. This one."

Then he opened the other portal, and roughly shoved Hovde out into the alley.

"Get lost, jerk," he ordered.

"Wait a second."

The beefy bouncer pulled a blackjack from his pocket, grinned and swung it savagely. But Hovde had been trained well. He dodged the weapon, released the commando knife hidden in the wrist scabbard under his shirt and kicked his attacker in the groin. The bouncer doubled over. Then Hovde threw him against the wall. He resheathed the knife and started back to his car, glad he didn't have to use it. He felt sorry for anyone who had to deal with such thugs. What was worse, he couldn't even be sure that his efforts and forty dollars had secured the truth. Alison Gordon might well get angry. Without a family surname, "Big Ed" was useless even if it was correct. Hovde had nothing meaningful to report, and they still didn't have a goddamn clue as to the final ten weeks of Sidney Adams' life.

As he drove away, he told himself that Agajanian was probably right—this case was a waste of time. He arrived at his home in the valley at 12:40 A.M. on April 13th, eleven days before the Lexington organization would execute its plan to take over America.

# 13

WITH THE worst smog alert in five years over, the morning news broadcasters concentrated on the White House announcement that President John L. Walker would meet the Soviet premier in Paris on the 26th to "explore new steps in arms limitations." Several senators, the recently retired chief of naval operations and three governors who thought that Walker was much too liberal for a Republican, denounced his thinking as "mushy and dangerous." The vast majority of Southern Californians paid little attention to this all-too-familiar disagreement.

More important items held their attention as they drove to work. The Dodgers had signed a new pitcher, and it was a bright, warm day—the sort that was good for real-estate values. The 10 A.M. sun poured into Alison Gordon's office as she listened to Hovde's report on his visit to The Steel Cellar.

A blimp was visible from her ninth-floor window. It circled lazily a mile west, but there was no reason to pay any attention to it. The light aircraft had been flying over the greater Los Angeles area for almost two months, advertising an assortment of products via the flashing electric sign attached to its gondola. A recent item in the *Times* media column identified the operators as a new firm named Blue Sky Promotions, and explained that they had high hopes and a three-year lease on the airship. The brief paragraph had appeared in the paper before the mounts for the television cameras had been attached to the gondola.

Three of the cameras had actually been installed, and were now transmitting pictures of the city below. The images were electronic garbage to anyone whose receiver was not equipped with unscrambling equipment. The nine TV sets in the offices of Blue Sky Promotions had such gear. The four men seated in the firm's viewing room appreciated the excellent reception and sharp pictures.

"Very good, Commander Farrow," Halleck said. "I knew the Navy wouldn't let us down."

"We'll do our share, sir," the electronics specialist said. "We'll get those other cameras operational by the sixteenth, which should allow a full week for testing and adjustment."

"Excellent," Colonel Halleck told him. "The dry run's on the twenty-second. We've just had word from . . . *our friend* at the armored car company that the pickup schedule has been confirmed. Right, sergeant?"

"Yes, sir," Zelner confirmed. He admired Halleck's prudence. There was no reason for Farrow to know the name of Lexington's key agent at Pacific Coast Security. "I spoke to him this morning, colonel. All systems are go."

"There'll be no naval or Coast Guard problems when we land the weapons?" Halleck asked.

"The admiral guaranteed that, colonel. We're fully prepared to jam the frequencies to block any alert. The only problem might be Air Force patrols."

"That's being taken care of by our people. We'll have a fleet of trucks to handle West Coast distribution, and we've laid on a special freight train to move some of the heavy stuff east. Railroad's been told it's a regular army shipment. We'll have men aboard in army uniforms, full combat gear."

Then Halleck gestured, and the screens went dark. "Your communications system here all set, Parks?" he asked. The ruddy-faced head of Blue Sky Promotions nodded. The four men rose, and Parks unlocked the door to show Farrow out.

Farrow departed to return to his car parked in the lot several blocks away. It was one of Lexington's routine security procedures—designed to protect this vital headquarters.

Halleck turned to Zelner again.

"It's looking good. Caesar will be pleased. Anything else, sergeant?"

"Maybe, sir."

"What does that mean?"

"Might be a problem with *our friend* at Pacific, sir. Seems he heard that somebody's checking on him."

"Checking?"

"Looking for him. Asking questions last night at a certain club —the place *our friend* met Adams."

Halleck looked at the map of Los Angeles that covered half a wall, sighed and shook his head.

"The creeps we've had to use for Lexington," he said. "Such low people for such a high cause. What else, sergeant?"

"This man had a picture of Adams, sir. There was some trouble with a bouncer, who's now in the hospital himself. Same guy's been seen with that woman detective. He could be trouble, colonel."

"*Our friend* has been extremely helpful, and I wouldn't want to do anything hasty."

"Yes, sir," Zelner said as he waited for the decision. "This man was specifically trying to locate a biker with mustache who was a buddy of Adams. That's our Jerry, sir. The guy looking for him sounds tough, colonel. Not the kind who gives up easy."

"A preemptive strike may be necessary." Halleck checked his watch and considered his next appointment. "Necessary for all of us, for Lexington. Now that the schedule has been re-confirmed, is there anything at Pacific that our other people there couldn't handle?"

Zelner shook his head, knowing what was coming.

"Unacceptable risk, sergeant. Military necessity. Too damn bad but Jerry really brought this whole thing on himself, you know. If he hadn't been playing with that Adams runt, none of this would have happened. He's caused nine deaths so far. We can't risk any more."

"Those motor bikes are dangerous," Zelner observed softly.

"Good thinking. After all that Orange County slaughter, an accident makes more sense. No real press or heavy homicide attention. The sooner the better."

Halleck left Blue Sky Promotions through a rear exit, walked two floors down the fire staircase before he got on the elevator. He had always been obsessive about security. He had several errands and meetings before he returned to make his 3:30 P.M. call to Washington. It would be on the scrambler phone, and it would be brief. Caesar was compulsive about security too.

# 14

AGAJANIAN PHONED from the bank at 4:50 the following afternoon.

"We may have something, Al."

"Something or someone?"

"Jerome F. for Francis Otto. Got the court order just before noon, and hustled over to the Third Federal on the double. It took a while to locate the microfilms. Most of the checks are routine crap—rent, phone company, that sort of thing. But there are four made out to Jerome F. Otto, cleared through the Vernon branch of the Crocker National."

"Does he live in the bank?"

"How about four blocks from Sidney Adams? You like that?"

"Not bad."

"That's not all. For a change, we've got a guy with a listed phone. I called. Nobody home yet, but I figure he ought to be back from work around six or so. When he gets there, I'll be waiting."

"Me too." Alison Gordon hung up before he could debate the question.

When she reached Otto's apartment house in Santa Monica at a quarter to six, she saw a two-story building much like the one that Sidney Adams had lived in—and Agajanian watching stoically from his Triumph convertible nearby. He nodded. She nodded back and parked the Porsche.

Neither of them noticed the man in the wood-paneled Ford station wagon halfway down the block.

She walked to the apartment building, rang Otto's buzzer several times and turned.

"He's not in," announced a thin young black woman entering the building. Then she pointed at the curb. "If that big green Harley's not here, neither is he."

The detective thanked her, and as the slim woman entered the building, Alison walked over to Agajanian.

"He's a biker. Big green Harley."

"Wonder if his plate number ends in seven-seven," the accountant replied. Alison returned to her own car, lit a Sobranie and settled down to wait. Perhaps it had been impetuous to come here without an appointment. She should have called. Well, if he didn't show by seven, they'd leave. She puffed on the black cigarette, wondering why she had such a . . . sense of urgency in her gut.

She finished the cigarette, tried not to light another for ten minutes but succumbed. The minutes crawled by. Then at half past six she heard the roar of a big machine. She glanced into her rear-view mirror at a Harley, loud and macho. The cycle was only forty yards away, slowing noisily, when it happened.

The Ford station wagon swung out abruptly. As the cyclist stopped, swept off his helmet and climbed down, the driver jammed his accelerator to the floor. The heavy Ford threw the cyclist through the air like a doll. Before Alison could consciously plan anything, she had started the Porsche and begun the chase.

86

"Son of a bitch!" Agajanian called out to no one in particular. Seconds later, he had joined the high-speed pursuit. The station wagon raced three blocks, made a sharp, screeching right turn, burning rubber, and roared on at mounting speed. Skateboarders, bicyclists, pedestrians, roller skaters, drivers of other cars and startled truckers barely managed to avoid the three-car juggernaut. The station wagon turned right now at sixty miles an hour and struck a glancing blow to a small Toyota that sent it spinning.

The man at the wheel saw daylight ahead. Suddenly a large truck loaded with cement sewer drains rolled slowly in front of him from a cross street, and he slammed on the brakes. The Ford bucked and shuddered under the strain, slowed and skidded—but not slow enough. The station wagon hit the truck's right rear, snapping several chains that held the massive pipes in place. The impact of the collision turned the Ford around completely, and when the bleeding driver stepped out of the car, he was facing the pursuing Porsche. Hurt and raging, he pulled a .38 automatic and fired.

Alison Gordon swerved the Porsche, braked it to a miraculous halt between a van and an aged Buick. Even as her car halted, she rolled out the door and drew her own weapon. She could hear the screech of the Triumph behind her, but her attention was on the assassin.

Her first shot knocked him back against the badly damaged Ford. Her second killed him. Agajanian was out of his car, down in the shooter's crouch with his own .357 magnum in both hands. Agajanian watched as the hit-and-run driver's gun fell, and kept him covered until he was close enough to the sprawled body to be certain he was dead.

People were screaming. The sounds of sirens from two directions signaled that police were not far away. Agajanian walked to Alison, reached down and helped her get up. She sheathed her gun, straightened her skirt and brushed a gum wrapper from the hem. The sirens were getting louder.

"You okay, Al?" he asked. She nodded, staring at the body fifteen yards away.

"Was that Otto on the Harley?"

"I think so," she replied. A crowd was gathering. Some people were circling them at a distance, afraid to come too close lest more violence explode. Others were leaning out windows and pointing at the body. As Alison lit a cigarette, a police car pulled up and stopped ten yards away. Two uniformed cops emerged. They scanned the scene, and pointed their .38s at Agajanian.

"Drop it!"

He laid his weapon down on the fender of the Porsche and —slowly and ceremonially—retreated several steps.

"I've got a license for the piece," he announced, but they were not impressed.

"Why'd you shoot him?" the blond-haired cop demanded.

"I didn't."

That was when the cement pipes broke loose and fell from the truck onto the corpse. The noise and sudden movement made both officers jump, but they kept control of their trigger fingers. One of them walked to the truck to look into the cab.

"Driver's out cold," Agajanian reported.

"Call an ambulance," Alison Gordon advised.

"Who's she?" the other patrolman asked.

"My boss."

The yellow-haired cop took possession of Agajanian's gun.

"What's your business, lady?"

"Private investigator. I'm the one who shot him."

"With what?"

She flipped open her jacket to reveal the .357 in the belly

holster. Then she tapped the ash from her cigarette.

"*You* wasted him?"

"Self-defense. He'd already killed one man about a couple of minutes ago and was pointing his gun at me when I fired."

The police exchanged glances.

"You mean there's *another* stiff, lady?" the blond asked.

"Five or six blocks from here. I can show you."

While the other policeman radioed for an ambulance, the younger cop politely instructed her to draw her gun slowly, since it would be needed for evidence in a homicide. Three more patrol cars arrived. After both private detectives showed their gun permits and other identification, the police drove them back to the motorcycle. As Alison Gordon stepped out, she pointed at the Harley's license plate.

"Seven-seven. Paydirt," Agajanian said. He turned to point at the corpse of the leather jacketed cyclist fifteen yards away.

"Who is he?" a policeman asked.

"Probably Jerome F. Otto," Alison answered.

"You know him?"

She shook her head.

"Or the man you shot?"

She shook her head again.

"Or what the hell this is all about?"

"Not really," she admitted. "We were waiting to talk to a man named Jerome F. Otto, who lived across the street there, about a rather routine investigation. When that bastard in the station wagon smashed into him, we automatically went after him. That's what led to the shootout."

"That's *it*, miss?"

"All I've got, officer. We were told that Otto drove a green Harley like that one, but I'm not even sure that he's Jerome Otto at all."

She took a final puff on her cigarette and looked around for a place to drop it.

"What's the matter, Miss?"

"I don't want to litter."

The policeman walked over to examine the cyclist's papers.

Jerome Francis Otto was thirty-six years old, a member of the U.S. Marine Corps Reserve and an employee of Pacific Coast Security Incorporated. This was the handsome mustachioed cyclist whom the transvestite had described, someone who could have answered their questions about Sidney Adams. Now he was another corpse, silenced by a killer Alison didn't know for a reason she couldn't imagine. It was depressing, disturbing. The only lead into Sidney Adams' life was dead at her feet, and she had no idea where to start over again.

# 15

"Miss Gordon, I'm not sure about this," Lieutenant Philip Dykstra said as they faced the door of Otto's apartment.

"It's a homicide case and you're the senior homicide detective in the Santa Monica P.D.," Alison argued. "Seems perfectly logical to check out the victim's residence."

Dykstra looked at his watch. It was 7:10 P.M. His wife would be angry if he showed up late for dinner again. There was little chance he'd find anything significant in here, damn it. Why was this pushy woman detective pressing him? Who the hell was she to tell him how to do his job?

"This isn't necessary," he protested. "We know who killed Otto, and the perpetrator's dead. There isn't going to be any trial, you know. We don't need evidence."

"How about a motive? Can you file a complete report without explaining why Otto was hit? What's your chief going to say on that? What about those nosy reporters, lieutenant?"

She was a pain in the ass, Dykstra thought, but she was probably right. He was up for evaluation and pay increase in June. Maybe it would be safer to touch all bases and fill in all the blanks. He tried three keys before he came to the one that unlocked the door.

The living room was small and crowded. In addition to a red leatherette couch there were a wooden rocker, a metal-topped table and three black plastic dining chairs. There was a stainless steel armchair with manacles attached to both the arms and legs. Daggers, spears, swords, rifles and hand guns covered the walls. Dykstra froze for a moment.

"Lieutenant?"

"Yeah, you can come in, Miss Gordon. Don't touch anything."

He studied her face as she stepped through the door. There was no surprise in her eyes.

"You knew he was—uh—into this?"

"Heard he might be," she replied cautiously. There was a human skull—probably fake—on an end table, with a framed photo of Otto in Marine uniform beside it. Dykstra scanned the room as if it might be booby-trapped. Then he made his way across the imitation tiger-skin rug to open the two locks on the bedroom door.

"Holy shit!"

Chains, whips, manacles, clubs, leather and rubber garments, masks, gags, pincers and a large wooden cross of rough timber —the room was jammed with them. There were blowups of pictures of bound and battered men tacked to the walls. Three were of the late Sidney Adams, bleeding and covered with welts.

"I hate this sick stuff," Dykstra said. "I've seen it before. When I was on Vice, we raided a joint where some two-hundred-pound Kraut woman used to beat up guys for money. The guys *paid* her. She used to tape the screams and sell the cassettes."

"I don't like it either," she told him.

92

He looked at her again. This woman had just killed a man swiftly and professionally. From what people said, she'd killed before—so why was there hurt in her wide blue eyes?

"You figure this had something to do with the hit-and-run?" he asked.

"No idea."

"Going to be messy," Dykstra predicted, irritably. "You never can tell who's involved in this kind of crap. Could be a senator or a doctor or the head of some bank, people with heavy money. Maybe we find a list of names, and all hell breaks loose. Powerful connections, lots of heat to keep them out of the papers. Shit, I don't need this."

"It may not be that bad."

"I'm telling you one thing, Miss Gordon. I'm working on a homicide—period. Digging up dirt is not my job. We'll search this place for any connection with the guy you shot, and that's goddamn all. I'm not on Vice anymore."

"Of course," she agreed. "I'm not interested in the s-m thing either. I'm trying to wrap up an investigation of . . . well, a missing-person case."

She turned to look back at the pictures of Sidney Adams again, and she wanted to cry. Why should she feel so sorry for a man she never knew?

"Let's get out of here," Dykstra said. She followed him into the living room, and found herself facing a small kitchen alcove. A few shelves with dishes and cheap glassware, half a dozen pots and pans, a closet over the sink—probably canned goods, a two-burner stove and an eight-cubic-foot refrigerator; that was it.

The only touch of color in the kitchen was in the photo of the Rockies on a page of an airline calendar. Someone had circled two dates with a red felt-tipped marker. April 24th and 27th. Dykstra saw the markings too.

"Birthday? Dental appointment? World War Three?" he wondered aloud.

Alison Gordon shrugged.

"Whatever the deal was," the homicide lieutenant said, "they'll have to go ahead without him."

"Guess so."

Then Dykstra gestured toward the front door and she followed him out of the apartment. He locked the door behind them before calling a patrolman to stand guard until detectives arrived to search the flat thoroughly. There probably wasn't anything for them to find, but one could never tell. The only sure thing about this whole mess was that his wife would be annoyed when he got home late.

"Caesar" was in much better spirits. Each of the reports that had reached him here in the District of Columbia during the past day was encouraging. The commanders of the units in Boston and Los Angeles, Chicago, Atlanta, Dallas, New York and Washington confirmed that they were proceeding on schedule. Once the weapons arrived to provide that extra fire power, they would overrun their objectives according to plan. Lexington would seize control in hours. Casualties would be minimal; if the coordinated blitz was carried out properly no more than six or seven thousand people would die.

It would be swift, savage, surgical, he thought confidently, as he poured three fingers of Jack Daniels. There was no question of choice anymore. It was simply too dangerous to let the politicians, intellectuals, assorted leftists and pacifists continue in power. Their time was over. Now it was Lexington's turn. In eight days, they would have secured the money. The weapons would be unloaded thirty-six hours later. Then Phase Two would take place on the 27th in Panama. Phase Three—the attacks on

94

the U.S. cities—would follow at once. Surprised, confused and leaderless, the defenders would collapse under Lexington's sledgehammer blows.

The media would have no opportunity for rabble-rousing, since Lexington would shut down all the newspapers and flood the airwaves with its own message. The audio and video tapes were already in the hands of Lexington officers at network headquarters and a dozen other key cities, ready to be broadcast. After three years of planning, the time was very near at last.

Caesar pressed a button on his calendar watch. It was 12:05 A.M., April 16th. At 3:40 P.M. on the 24th, the attack would begin.

# 16

BECAUSE OF the four Rémy-Martins, Alison Gordon slept heavily, and she awoke with a minor hangover. She found little comfort in the shower; despite ten minutes of that usually effective hydrotherapy she felt lethargic, uneasy and defensive. Agajanian had predicted that they would gain nothing from this venture. Now there were two more people dead, and no facts about Sidney Adams on which to build.

Three glasses of water, some chilled grapefruit juice and two cups of coffee helped a bit. The toast tasted like cardboard, so she threw it out. She took off the silk robe to get dressed. The six-foot mirror showed that she still had a firm and splendid figure, but that hadn't seemed to matter much lately. Many men were attracted to her shapely body; Alison Gordon was not interested in how many, though. *One* was what she needed. She was a sophisticated, independent, self-supporting and thoroughly modern woman . . . who was also old-fashioned enough to believe that there was *one* special man out there for her.

She had been looking for him since her husband had vanished on a CIA mission and been pronounced *legally* dead. What the hell had "legally" meant, she wondered as she wiggled into green bikini panties. Half the country no longer trusted the Agency, the courts or the rest of the government. State and federal legislators had little credibility after the recent scandals, and there were people convinced that the President was either a secret Red or a Communist dupe. Should she believe that Mark was dead? How else could she live?

The special man would have to be durable. The fast and transient sex in this town did not suit her, she reflected, as she secured the hook on her flimsy John Kloss brassiere. It was more than a question of morality. She was neither prudish nor celibate, but she knew herself, and she liked her standards. Neither glib Don Juans nor feminist extremists had been able to shake them. She found promiscuity as stupid as sexual hostility, and she could abide neither the cliché slogans nor the smug mediocrities of those who mouthed them. Buttoning her blouse, she realized there were only a few people who believed in the same things she did.

It was time to get on with her day, which was sure to be difficult. The shooting of the hit-and-run driver was certain to create attention, phone calls and problems. She reached for her gun, remembered that it was in police custody and told herself that she didn't really need to carry it today anyway. Still she felt half-naked as she drove the Porsche toward her office, uneasy as she checked the rear-view mirror.

"Once the crane arrived it was easy," Agajanian said cheerily as she dropped into her chair.

"No games today, Andy. *What* was easy?"

"Identification of the evil chap who ran down Jerome F. Otto. Those cement drains mashed him some, but the cops found a load of ID in his wallet. Thomas Wilhite of West L.A., gray eyes, brown hair, .38 Smith and Wesson. Would you believe that he had a valid permit for it?"

"Then why didn't he shoot Otto?"

"He needed it in his work. Thomas Wilhite is an armored-car guard employed by—"

"Pacific Coast Security," she guessed.

"Give that lady two Alka-Seltzers and absolution for her many sins," Agajanian said. "Yes, ma'am. The very same Pacific Coast Security where the late and creepy Mr. Otto was deputy supervisor of all the guards."

She closed her eyes to think for several seconds, trying to make some sense or pattern out of it.

"That was in the morning paper—on page three. In today's busy homicide market, two stiffs don't make the front page anymore," the accountant explained.

"This Wilhite. Was he into s-m too?" she asked.

"I don't think so. Wilhite was married for nine years, had two kids and taught Sunday School. Pillar of the Presbyterian church in Glendale. His lovely wife, who sings in the choir, is completely *stunned by this baffling tragedy.* That's a quote."

Alison opened the center drawer of her desk to search for cigarettes, found only an empty black box and closed the drawer in defeat.

"You wouldn't happen to . . . ?"

"Negative. Gave up the filthy habit six months ago," he boasted.

"Don't be virtuous. It doesn't suit you. What else do we know about Wilhite?"

"He's Mr. Clean. Not even a traffic citation since he got his very honorable discharge from the Green Berets three years ago. Perfect attendance record at Pacific too. Not a single sick day in twenty-seven months. Didn't gamble, do drugs or hard liquor."

"You're saying he was a saint?"

"Not exactly, Al. The station wagon was hot. Heisted three days ago in Bel Air." He paused. "Say it. I can see what you're thinking. It was a deliberate and carefully planned hit that was tailored to look like an accident."

She hesitated for ten seconds before she answered. "Lieutenant Dykstra will figure it out."

"*Very* good," Agajanian said. "It's another homicide, and we don't touch those with fifty-four-foot poles—right?"

"You'd better get back to Sidney Adams' checks," she replied coolly, "and also look into his credit-card receipts. You may be able to work out some picture of what he did and where. See if you can get a log of his phone calls too."

"I didn't mean to offend you."

"We'll talk tomorrow. Goodbye, Andrew."

He knew better than to argue. He was halfway out of her office when the intercom on her desk clicked on abruptly.

"There's a Mr. Latham on line three, Miss Gordon. Says he's with the Treasury Department, and wants to make an appointment."

"Probably a tax thing. Let him speak to Mr. Agajanian."

Subduing her irritation with the petty nagging of the Internal Revenue Service, she thought about the man who had murdered Jerome Otto. It wasn't that she wanted to meddle in Lt. Dykstra's case, but she could not help wondering. The intercom broke in again.

"He doesn't want to talk to Mr. Agajanian. He says he's not with the IRS but something called ATF, Miss Gordon."

Why would anyone in Alcohol, Tobacco and Firearms want

to see her? None of her firm's cases were even remotely relevant to that federal unit's work.

"He says he wants to talk with *you,* Miss Gordon."

"Tell him I'm out of town until Monday. He can call me then."

She forced herself to concentrate on a list of jades stolen from the Fingerhuts. Mrs. Rose Fingerhut, who had a good face lift and a husband whose burglar-alarm company earned him about a million two annually, had insisted that the insurance company retain A. B. Gordon Investigations. After all, Alison Gordon was the only private detective in town who knew the difference between a Six Dynasties piece of the Three Kingdoms era, a work from the T'ang time four centuries later, and a more recent Wan-li creation of the sixteenth century. It was difficult for Alison to turn down Rose Fingerhut, for while her voice could shatter window glass, her taste in art was good—she owned three of Alison's sculptures. The insurance company was willing to pay the entire value of the stolen jades, but feisty Rose Fingerhut wanted her treasures back.

"You can shove your money" was what she'd told a startled insurance executive, who wasn't used to dealing with Beverly Hills art lovers.

Alison Gordon was actually rather fond of the woman's loud and lusty life force; despite that, she had trouble focusing on the recovery of the jades. When she finished looking over the list, she turned her attention to some counterfeiters who were ripping off another client's "designer" jeans. Then her mind drifted to Lauri Adams' sad, dead brother.

Yielding to an idea that was at least half impulse, she reached for the telephone. There were times when it was useful to be well known; this was one of them. Mr. Desmond Carew III gave her the precise location of Pacific Coast Security, the armored car company five blocks from the MGM studios in Culver City —plus an assurance that he'd see her at a quarter to three.

The three-story home of Pacific Coast Security Service, Inc. resembled a warehouse. There were very few windows—all heavily barred by thick wire and steel rods, massive walls and doors that combined two-inch-thick metal plates with panes of bulletproof glass. As she swung the Porsche around to the parking area, Alison Gordon saw uniformed guards with machine guns on duty at the entrance to the garage. When she entered the front door, she found herself in a small reception room—under scrutiny of a closed-circuit TV camera. Pacific Security was a firm that clearly took its name seriously. She had to pass through two other checkpoints before she faced the company's president.

"How can I help you, Miss Gordon?" Desmond Carew III asked pleasantly. He was a heavyset man in his early fifties, well tanned and even better dressed. He had a rather patrician air and the assured voice of old money. Only the mottled veins on his face and nose that marked heavy drinking marred the image of corporate grandeur and executive control. He had the style down, but Alison Gordon sensed that the man was not as big as his grandiose office.

"Kind of you to see me. I'm sure you're busy." She stalled as she studied the room for clues to the man behind the big desk.

"Not every day I get a call from Beverly Hills' finest," he replied with a chuckle. Alison Gordon had never liked men who laughed at their own jokes. She suppressed her reaction and pressed on to Sidney Adams.

"I don't recognize the name, Miss Gordon. Got a large staff here. More than four hundred. Grown a heap since my grand-daddy founded the firm in the twenties."

So that was it. He'd inherited the business others had built, a typical third-generation saga.

"I'm not saying that Adams worked for Pacific," she said. "A relative of his has retained us to collect some information about him, and we've found that he was a close friend of a man who was one of your employees till yesterday. Jerome F. Otto."

Carew stiffened.

"Mr. Otto was our assistant chief of security. I've told all that to the police," he announced formally. "I barely knew the man. He was not on my executive team, but merely a supervisor. I gathered from the morning paper that you—"

"No, I never met him. Never spoke to him either. Not that it's my business, but what sort of person was he?"

Carew squirmed.

"Police asked that too, so I checked with his department head. Word is that Otto was very strict, and had reprimanded this Wilhite several times. They had a personality clash. Turned into a feud. Both were simple, uneducated fellas. You know what *they're* like."

It was no surprise that he would look down on his employees, but there was something more in his eyes.

"Seems this Wilhite chap had one helluva temper," he continued blandly, "and finally blew his stack. Went sort of paranoid, I guess. Terrible thing, huh?"

Before she could reply, he picked up the telephone and told his secretary to find out whether the company had an employee —current or recent—named Stanley Adams.

"Sidney," Alison said.

"Make that *Sidney,*" he corrected. "I'll hang on. Don't want to delay this nice lady."

His smile was affable, his voice benign and his wink infuriating. It was rare to meet such a nakedly chauvinist clod these days, she thought as she studied the photos of Carew in polo attire on the wall. Desmond Carew III wasn't any good at concealing his patronizing attitude; perhaps he wasn't trying. The complacent corporate chieftain had probably been dealing with women this way for decades. Who'd dare to criticize the head of a family-owned firm?

"Thanks," he said as he put down the phone. "Your Adams never worked at our shop. We had a Norma Adams in payroll, I'm told, but she retired at sixty-five last October. Sorry we couldn't help you, but I was glad to meet you. Heard a lot about you, miss."

He stood up, and Alison Gordon realized that she was being dismissed like some junior clerk. There would be no point in asking any more questions, for he would give nothing—not even the time to ask. He turned on that fraudulent grin again, as if to flick out the lights. She controlled her anger, mouthed the appropriate amenities and hurried from his office.

Carew was more than rude, she decided as she left the building, he was unclean. More important, the son of a bitch was lying. She had sensed it all through the conversation. His description of Wilhite didn't match what the police had found, and his whole manner had radiated uneasy lies. If he lied about the hit-and-run killer, why should she believe him on Sidney Adams? As she started the Porsche, she considered whether Hovde ought to look into Desmond Carew III and his company.

An hour and a half later, the Blue Sky blimp that usually flew over the most populated sections of Los Angeles swung off on a new course. It moved out over the shopping areas of Beverly Hills, blinking its commercial messages to the affluent pedestrians on Rodeo Drive and Wilshire Boulevard. Then it circled in a wide arc across Santa Monica Boulevard in the direction of the Hillcrest Country Club.

"Two-two-six! There it is!" Colonel Roger Halleck called out.

The others in the command post's screening room nodded at the TV screen. It had been a clever idea to park a police car across the street from Alison Gordon's house. LAPD patrol vehicles had numbers on their roofs and car 2-2-6 served as a convenient map reference and checkpoint for the aerial surveillance.

"Commence video taping," Halleck ordered. The cameras swept back and forth across her house and grounds, zooming in for closeup scrutiny of the entrances and outer wall.

"Good intelligence makes a good operation," the retired lieutenant colonel recited.

"You're sure we ought to go ahead with this, Roger?" asked George Parks, the head of Blue Sky Promotions.

"Got to. For once, that yellow bastard Carew's right. I thought we'd blocked her out when we took Otto out of the game, but she's still digging. The goddamn woman's got to go, George. Face the facts. As a former Air Force officer yourself . . . as a squadron commander, what would you do?"

Parks struggled, and grunted.

"I say *kill her,*" Halleck pressed. "What do you say, George?"

"I guess so," Parks agreed reluctantly. "What a mess! All this because of Adams. That was a mistake."

"What else could we do?" Halleck argued. "We heard from our friends that the FBI was going to knock over Century. We were lucky to get two hours' notice, and I'd say we laid on a damn good little assault in that time. We couldn't warn them, because one of the men there was a federal undercover agent. Our ear at the L. A. bureau might be endangered if the raid was tipped."

"We killed an FBI man?"

"Had to take them all. Only way to take the light off that

Adams punk. He was the whole problem," Halleck said bitterly. "If he was arrested, how long before he'd crack and tell the FBI about Lexington?"

"Did he know that much?"

"He knew Otto. Would you risk them checking on Otto and Pacific Coast Security now, so close to D-Day? Otto never guessed we zapped his boyfriend." Halleck sighed. "I say we can't count on luck anymore—not with this Gordon woman making waves."

Parks looked up at the screens for several seconds. He seemed to be studying the various views of the target, but he was actually seeing nothing. He computed and recomputed before he grunted again. "You're right, Rog. We've got to get rid of her."

"I was thinking of an armed burglar," Halleck said. "Shoots her while robbing the house. Plenty of break-ins in that part of Beverly Hills."

They began to select the right men for the mission. The trio chosen listened attentively as Halleck showed the tapes of their objective. By 7:45, they had agreed on how Alison Gordon would die.

# 17

HOVDE DID not understand why she wanted the investigation of Desmond Carew III and Pacific Coast Security to be a "black," or covert, operation, but he complied. A. B. Gordon Investigations was not to be involved officially. A dummy name or that of some friendly business willing to cooperate was to be used. Even with the assistance of a police reporter on the *Herald Examiner,* a vice president at Golden State Equities and a commodity futures broker who owed Hovde two favors, he had only a skeletal report ready when he entered her office late the next afternoon.

"No, I am still *not* in as far as Mr. Latham is concerned," Alison Gordon said into the phone. Then she slammed it down and looked up at Hovde sharply. The expression on her face and the ashtray overflowing with cigarette butts confirmed that she was not in the best of spirits.

"I am being harassed by the Alchohol, Tobacco and Firearms unit at Treasury," she announced, "and I don't like it. I don't need it. I won't stand for it. Does that sound like a tantrum?"

"Close. Want me to come back?"

She gestured to the armchair.

"No, tell me what you've got . . . please."

He sat down, studied the notes on his clipboard and cleared his throat.

"Carew is a lightweight and a boozer. Two divorces and a number of drunk-driving citations that he managed to keep out of the papers. Paying thirty-five hundred a month in alimony. Rumors he's got problems with the IRS, and his credit rating is lousy. Started out as a playboy at Stanford, was a mediocre polo player and avoided work until his older brother died nine years ago. You want to ask about his hobby?"

"I just did."

"Very young girls. White, black, latin, oriental—all jailbait. Was arrested once on charges of sleeping with a fourteen-year-old, but he beat the rap. People think he paid her mother."

"That's a *terrible* hobby."

"You were right, Al. You said he was rotten. He's not much at running the company either."

"Tell me about it," she said. Hovde shook his head and coughed.

"It isn't *his* company anymore. He's just finishing a three-year management contract that runs out in June. Trans-Global Industries bought control a few years ago. Pacific Coast Security is one division of Trans-Global. Remember, we did a job for them a few years ago. The president had the hots for you."

She smiled as she remembered the "boy wonder" tycoon. "Joshua Friedman wanted to *marry* me, Don."

"They say he wants to *divorce* Carew—from Pacific Security. That's all I got so far, Al."

"Anything to connect Carew to Adams or Otto?"

"Negative, but I'll keep trying. One more thing."

"Yes?"

"Harry Fischer says buy British pounds and sell cocoa futures." Fischer was a shrewd broker, but Alison had neither the interest nor the loose cash to take his advice.

"I'll keep it in mind," she said vaguely.

Instead, she settled for buying two pounds of dark Swiss truffles on her way home. She limited herself to three pieces before she undressed for her nightly swim. Nobody's perfect, she rationalized as she dropped her underclothes on the bed. This passion for chocolate was such a *small* vice compared to many others. It was *merely* something left over from her childhood.

One more *little* piece wouldn't hurt. With her mouth melting with delight, she wrapped herself in a terrycloth robe and walked to the pool. It and the privacy to swim in it nude were two of the rewards that working hard had given her, that helped make the hours and effort worthwhile. Enjoying the feel of the water against her skin, she completed six laps before the chime sounded.

At Agajanian's insistence, there were three separate alarm systems protecting the area between the front gate and the house. That was the first, the outermost detector that provided perimeter security. There was no reason to believe that it had been set off by a "hostile," but no way of knowing that it had not. As she reached the side of the pool, the second ring of detectors was triggered. She pulled herself up and out, seized the robe and ran. . . .

The thin-faced man walked slowly toward the house. He paused every few steps—the wary sort. The automatic in his shoulder holster did not make him any less careful. He had been told about Alison Gordon, and he wasn't going to make mistakes. He wasn't the least bit afraid as he advanced cautiously down the flagstone path, but he was in no hurry either. Some fifteen yards from the house, he stopped completely to go over his plan. Then he stepped forward again.

"Freeze."

It was a woman's voice, cool and devoid of tension.

Yes, that would be A. B. Gordon. He halted.

"Raise your hands."

"My name is Todd Latham," he said as he complied.

"Turn around—slowly."

He obeyed, and five seconds later saw a beautiful woman in a terry robe step out of the shrubbery. She had fine golden hair and an automatic shotgun.

"Latham," he repeated.

"You were talking to Champly at the Century plant," she said.

"Todd Latham. I'm with A. T. F., Miss Gordon. You can put away the shotgun."

She didn't. It was still pointed at his navel.

"*You* can get the hell out of here, Latham. You've got some nerve breaking in here. You were supposed to call back Monday."

"Don't have the time. Can I put my hands down?"

"How do I know you're Latham?"

"God, you're a jumpy lady. I didn't *break* in. I walked in to talk to you, and that's all. I'm going to lower my hands now, and you're not going to shoot me. *Artemis* was never trigger-happy."

He could see the surprise in her face.

"What do you know about *Artemis*, mister?"

"Greek goddess of the hunt, and your code name. I was with the Agency too—almost five years. Three in the Far East. I was attached to *Columbine*."

"Is that supposed to mean something?"

"I worked with your husband for eight months. He was a good man. I'm sorry he's dead."

She turned the muzzle aside, and he lowered his hands.

"You want to see my ID?"

*Artemis?* She hadn't heard that name in years. She had not spoken the word herself in ages. She had tried so hard to forget it. With memories choking her throat, she nodded.

"My wallet is inside my jacket," the stranger said. "And I've got a .38 automatic under my arm too. I don't intend to touch it."

"Don't," she replied and pointed the shotgun at him again. Following her instructions, he walked on to the patio and placed his wallet on a glass-topped table. Then he retreated while she came forward to examine his cards and papers. Among them was a plastic-covered U.S. Treasury ID with photo of Todd A. Latham. All correct.

"Who ran *Columbine?*" she demanded.

"Soloyanis. Five feet seven and mean as a chainsaw. . . . Can we talk now?"

She swung the shotgun toward the French doors and led him into the living room. It was a handsomely furnished chamber with Far Eastern touches, including the carved wooden statue of Ramayana that Mark had bought her in Chiang Mai.

"Thai?" Latham asked, putting his papers back in the maroon calfskin wallet.

Instead of answering, she strode to the liquor cabinet. "Your boss let you drink on duty?"

"Malt Scotch is okay. Ice, if you've got it."

Her stomach jumped as she remembered Blue Leader, the remarkable bomber pilot who had been her lover two years before and had died on an impossible mission. He had preferred malt Scotch too, but she didn't tell that to Latham. She prepared the drinks, handed one to the Treasury agent and sat down to face him.

"Let me start by telling you that Thomson doesn't trust you, or any other private investigators. He didn't like you showing up at Century, and he didn't buy your missing-person story. Then that business at the piano store convinced him you're with The Other Side."

"That's ridiculous."

"The FBI surveillance team covering Spinoza saw you."

"But they didn't *hear* me," she erupted. "He wanted me to *help* the FBI—that's the bloody truth—help the FBI solve the Century killings. The federal heat Thomson's applying is driving Spinoza's people crazy."

The Treasury man sipped and sighed.

"Thomson's never going to believe that," he said.

"And I told Spinoza I wouldn't touch a homicide case."

"Thomson won't buy that either."

"So the FBI believes I'm the Dragon Lady. What does your boss think, Latham?"

"What boss?"

"The clown who runs A.T.F. in Los Angeles!"

Latham took another sip of the Glenlivet before he replied.

"I'm not a clown, Miss Gordon. I'm a serious person, and I'm here on a serious matter."

"*You're* the boss?"

He nodded. She downed half of her drink.

"*I* trust you, Miss Gordon. I know who you were and what you did, and I believe in you. I'm hoping that you can help me."

There was something in his speech that signaled New England. He appeared to be sincere and he was definitely unusual. Federal police executives were not usually this good-looking, and none of them had asked for her assistance in years. The very notion of requesting the help of a private investigator—a *female* private investigator—would strike 99.99 percent of public officials as something for the comics. Of course, there was probably a catch in it—but she decided to hear him out.

"I'm listening, Mr. Latham."

"I'll start by telling you where I'm coming from. I am not in A.T.F. for that paycheck every two weeks, or the pension either. Without boring you with my life story, I'm one of those gun-control freaks the National Rifle Association despises. There are literally millions of guns out there, and less than half in the hands of responsible people. I'm not talking about hunting weapons or twenty-two-caliber rifles used for target shooting. I'm speaking about illegal hand guns and machine guns used to kill people. There's no other country in the world with so much lethal hardware in private hands. It's insane."

"I'm with you," she said—and wondered how someone who had served the Agency in an armed team on covert operations had come to this passion. There had to be something personal behind this intensity. He was talking from his gut, not his head.

"I don't think I'm the messiah, and I have no delusion that I'm going to clean out America singlehanded. I am doing what I can—with the small staff in my local bureau—to break up the gun traffic here. A.T.F. has thirty-seven hundred employees, thirty-two district offices. I'm the Special Agent in Charge at this one and gun control is just one of my responsibilities."

"The most important one?"

"In my book—my *private* book. From Washington's point of view, they're all supposed to be equal and my job is to run the office from behind a desk."

"Then what the hell are you doing here?"

"I'm trying to tell you. It's sort of like what George Orwell wrote in *Animal Farm.* 'All animals are equal, but some animals are more equal than others.' "

Another romantic, she thought, another obsolete goddamn hero like the bomber pilot who had broken her heart. There was no way this Yankee would get to her. Alison Gordon was rational enough to steer clear of an obsessed federal agent, even one this handsome. It was touching to know that such virtuous and dedicated men still existed, she thought, but let them touch somebody else.

"To get to the point, Miss Gordon, it's the machine guns. Thomson was at the plant on a counterfeiting raid, and now he's after the people who killed his undercover agent. I hear your interest is in a missing person, who was also a victim. *I* want the machine gunners, and the bastards who sold them those weapons."

"Hope you find them," she said truthfully as she rose.

"Don't hope. Help."

It was easy enough to see that he meant it; the illegal gun scourge *was* a nightmare. Cowardly state and federal legislators were doing almost nothing out of fear for their political survival. But that didn't give Latham the right to drag her into the mess. For a moment she felt a surge of guilt, and then, when she tried to resist something else.

"I'm going to pour myself a beer," she announced. "You want one?"

He nodded. Her effort to escape to the kitchen did not succeed; Latham followed her down the hall and through the swinging door—right up to the refrigerator.

"Ideally, the three of us should cooperate, but the FBI doesn't do business that way. That leaves you and me, Miss Gordon."

She filled two glasses with dark Carlsberg "Elephant" brew and put his on the butcherblock sideboard.

"FBI's a first-class outfit," she said. "They don't need us muddying up their case. Leave it to them."

"They're getting nowhere," he answered. "More than a dozen agents have been working fulltime for eighteen days, and they haven't come up with a thing. All the people they were going to arrest and interrogate were buried more than two and a half weeks ago. They're not doing any better squeezing Spinoza's crew. I'm not even sure his outfit did this job."

"They didn't," she replied and carried her glass back to the living room. He trailed her patiently. When she was seated, he savored a long swallow of Carlsberg before he spoke.

"Glad you agree. This has to be more important than a Syndicate hit. The gunners at Century used special hardware, nine-millimeter automatic weapons with silencers. In February, fifty-two Ingram Mac-10s equipped with silencers were stolen from a Special Forces armory at Fort Bragg. I think those army submachine guns chopped those people down."

"Finish your drink and go find them."

"You don't understand," he argued. "There's been a major increase in weapons thefts at army, Marine Corps and National Guard bases in the past year. None of those guns have showed up, which means somebody is stockpiling. They could have been sold for a lot of money, but they weren't. There's something spooky going on."

"There usually is, but I'm out of the spook business." Even as she spoke, she thought about the stolen cars that had been following her. Organized-crime groups didn't operate that way, and FBI surveillance teams wouldn't use such vehicles.

"Nine hundred and eighty-four weapons stolen in ten months, Miss Gordon. Not one clue to any of them, till this Century massacre. I hear you're running an investigation of a victim named Adams. Have you come across anything at all that could relate to those Ingrams?"

She shook her head as she tugged her robe closed.

"No, but I wouldn't. We're simply doing a bio for a bereaved relative. Look, I'm not getting involved in your gun case. I run

114

a quiet little cottage industry. Your problem is way out of our league. There's no way I could help you if I wanted to."

"How do you know? Maybe something you find will relate to my guns. Think about it."

"There's nothing, and if there was I'd still be bound by the confidentiality of the client relationship—"

"But that's ridiculous. You couldn't put that above the national interest. That would be immoral . . . and dumb."

He saw his mistake and said he had no intention of insulting her. "I'm sorry," he apologized.

"That I can handle. It's the self-righteous part that was too much. You were about to go into that John Kennedy bit about what you can do for your country, weren't you?"

"Maybe."

"Well, I already did it, and you goddamn well know it, Special-Agent-in-Charge Latham. You're not in charge of me. Maybe I could do more—and I might tomorrow morning, but I don't need any sermons from you. This is my sanctum here. Go set up your pulpit somewhere else."

"I didn't mean to—"

"But you did. If I think of anything, I'll call you."

Latham had the good sense to leave without further argument, but she could tell that it was not the last she would hear from him. His well-intentioned arrogance was bad enough. He *was* right, but that didn't give him *the* right to dump his obsessions into her life. She would not tolerate his effort to manipulate her with guilt, to further complicate the already disturbing case.

Latham was grasping at straws, she thought as she started back to the kitchen. It was preposterous for him to believe that The Bitch's brother could have any link with stolen Ingram machine guns, but not entirely surprising. It was inevitable that the 1980's would see the conspiracy theories of the 60's and 70's contaminate law-enforcement professionals as they had already infected the general public. Watergate and the never-fully-explained murders of the Kennedys and Martin Luther King had polluted the highest places. Corruption spread like a virus. Now it was everywhere.

When she opened the refrigerator, she suddenly remembered that she'd been invited to the first private screening of a soon-to-be-released $16,000,000 musical epic—another tendentious piece about alienated youth battling corrupt adults with innocence and rock and roll music.

She looked at a cold half-lobster, leftover slab of cheese cake and bottle of Niersteiner, and decided to spare herself the ordeal. She phoned her regrets and settled down for a quiet evening at home.

Aside from the baroque trumpet music that soared so elegantly from her stereo, the house was quiet—until shortly before one o'clock. She had turned off the machine and was lying in the darkness of her bedroom trying to sleep when the red bulb beside the door began to flash. This time someone really was trying to get into the house . . . someone skilled enough to have penetrated the outer alarms.

Naked and alert, she hurried down the stairs to get the shotgun she had left on the sideboard. Then she crouched, inhaled a deep breath and listened intently. It took a few seconds for her ears to pick up the faint scratching noise of a glass cutter. The sound was unmistakable. An intruder was taking a pane out of the rear entrance door that led to the kitchen.

Bent low, she slipped down the corridor as quietly as possible to open the swinging door. As she did, a black-gloved hand reached through the opening where a pane of glass had been.

116

The hand opened the door, and a man entered. She could not discern his face, but she caught the silhouette of the gun he held. It was a long-barreled pistol, made even longer by the silencer screwed into the muzzle. Burglars did not usually carry guns, and rarely if ever used silenced pistols. Those were the weapons of assassins.

Hovde or Agajanian would have killed him on the spot, without hesitation. Alison Gordon had shot people in self-defense before, and this bastard had almost surely come here to murder her. Still, she could not simply squeeze the trigger.

"Drop it!" she ordered.

The intruder did not obey. He swung his weapon toward the sound of her voice. That was when her training and survival instincts took over. The blast from the twelve-gauge shotgun smashed his upper right arm and much of his chest. The silenced pistol flew from his hand, then he screamed as he staggered back out into the blackness. She heard more sounds from out there, but she did not follow. If he had an accomplice, pursuing him could be fatal.

She listened in the darkness and waited. After a long minute that seemed like five, she heard the slam of a nearby car door and an engine moving away. She waited longer; it could be a trap. Several minutes later, she made her way—still in a crouch—to the ammunition cabinet and reloaded the shotgun. Despite the fact that she was nude and the night was not hot, a film of perspiration covered her entire body. Beads of sweat dripped down her face, and her hands were wet. Now the sole sound she could hear was the pounding of her heart. At 1:10 A.M., she telephoned Agajanian.

"I'm sorry to bother you," she began.

"How bad is it?" the accountant answered. He knew that she

wouldn't call at this hour unless the situation was grave.

"It's okay now, but about eight minutes ago I had to shoot somebody."

He didn't ask who or why.

"You okay, Al?"

"Yes . . . I'd like to talk to you. I think we're in that sewer all right."

"Be right over."

She sat there thinking and breathing heavily for another minute before she returned to the kitchen. Taking care not to expose herself to any marksman outside the house, she flicked on the lights. Dark red smears of blood were splashed on the linoleum floor, the door frame and nearby wallpaper. The gun lay there in a corner—a .22-caliber Margolin target pistol with silencer. To call it exotic would be an understatement, she thought, and wondered what Latham would say if he saw this assassin's tool in her kitchen.

She did not touch it, or even go over to that part of the room. At 1:14 she telephoned the Beverly Hills police. She had barely finished dressing six minutes later when the two radio cars arrived with flashing lights. The plainclothes detectives got there at half past one. They looked at the drops of blood on the flagstones, the crimson smears in the kitchen and the pistol on the floor. The silencer seemed to impress them particularly. Tape recorder in hand, one of the detectives was questioning her carefully when Agajanian hurried into the house. It was as she finished her "statement" that a uniformed officer stuck his head into the room.

"We got a Fed outside, sarge," he announced.

It was Latham.

# 18

"ARE YOU all right?" Latham asked. To her surprise, he sounded as if he cared. Before she could reply, he saw the two weapons on the table and spoke again.

"That's a Margolin!"

"Mr. Latham, meet Sergeant Garfield of the Beverly Hills P.D.," she said. "Mr. Latham is the Special Agent in Charge of the local A.T.F. bureau."

"What's a Margolin doing here?" Latham asked.

"What are *you* doing here?" Garfield countered.

Latham ignored the question.

"Haven't seen a Margolin in years," he told them. "It's a Sov-Block training piece—and assassin's gun. The V.C. used them to pick off government officials in 'Nam."

Agajanian nodded in appreciation of a fellow professional's knowledge of weapons. Then he remembered.

"*Columbine,*" he said. "Yeah, I thought you looked familiar at the tape plant. *Todd* Latham, right?"

"Don't want to intrude into your reunion," Garfield said sarcastically, "but I'd still like to know why Mr. Latham is with us."

"I was on my way home when I heard the call. I am authorized to have a police radio in my car, sergeant."

Typical federal shit, the Beverly Hills detective thought. FBI, Treasury, Secret Service—they were all the same in at least one thing. They drained information from local police and never provided any in exchange. This Treasury agent had no intention of explaining his presence to a mere detective on the Beverly Hills force, Garfield brooded bitterly. At least the woman had been courteous, much more so than most other people in this affluent community.

"Anything else, sergeant?" she asked.

"Please stay out of the rear part of the kitchen near that door until our lab man scrapes some blood samples, and don't touch these guns. He'll be taking them with him."

"Whatever you say," she promised. For a moment the sergeant wondered whether the armed intruder might have been a jealous lover or hit man hired by an ex-husband or boyfriend. Alison Gordon certainly was beautiful enough to drive some men to violence. Or it could have been some dope dealer making an example of a rich customer who hadn't paid up. Hell, a lot of these so-called "beautiful people" were snorting and shooting and smoking all kinds of drugs.

"Sure you can't think of any enemies?" Garfield asked. She shook her head.

"Probably a thief," he told her. "Lots of cat burglars working this area. We'll get him."

"What *are* you doing here?" she asked Latham as soon as Garfield departed.

"I was worried about you."

*"And?"*

"And I wanted to talk to you again."

"Never give up, do you?" she complained. "You ought to sell

pots and pans door to door. You'd make a bundle. Tell Mr. Agajanian about *that matter* you're hustling."

Latham explained his proposal succinctly.

"Too much, isn't he?" she asked the accountant. Agajanian looked at the two guns, and then he shook his head.

"Maybe not, Al. There has to be a crazy reason why somebody would send a hit man to waste you. This Adams thing is the only crazy case we're on. That bastard didn't come here with a silencer to steal your pearls or the Parrish necklace. Even Garfield knows that. You'd better face it."

"I don't see any connection with Sidney Adams."

"Feel it," Agajanian urged. "They'll send someone else to stop you, so we've got to stop them first. To do that, we've got to identify them. Al, you've got terrific instincts. What does your gut say?"

"Since when have you believed in feminine intuition?"

"Not feminine, as a class—*yours.* I'd be dead three times over if it wasn't for your instincts. As for that crap about confidentiality, I say *shove it.* There's no goddamn room here for nobility. As far as I'm concerned, I don't owe The Bitch anything. You come first in my book—first, second and third."

"Andy, I really appreciate your—"

"We'll do the hearts and flowers later. Please answer my question. What does your gut say?"

She lit a cigarette and inhaled. "I suppose he could be right," she said slowly.

"You've got my word," Latham said. "Whatever you say on this case stops with me. It won't go into any file. I won't put anything about Adams in writing. Your confidentiality is safe."

She told the story from the beginning, carefully and completely.

"There could be something worth checking at Pacific Coast

Security," she concluded, "but I can't see it relating to illegal machine guns."

"And those cars that have been tailing you?" Latham asked.

"Yes, there has to be a reason—but who knows whether it has anything to do with nine hundred and eighty-four military weapons stolen three thousand miles from here? Wait a second!"

"What is it, Al?" asked Agajanian.

"They stopped tailing me after Otto was run down—but there was a Peugeot following me home tonight. Why did they resume the surveillance?"

"You're checking on Carew and they're back-checking on you," Latham said. "Maybe that's not coincidental. You mind if I look into Mr. Carew?"

"Be my guest. I'm tired. My eyes hurt, and I want to go to bed," she said as she yawned.

Even half asleep, she was desirable. Latham realized that he had not felt this attracted to a woman in a long time. He had only met her a few hours earlier, so it had to be an animal thing —a physical pull. He reminded himself that he was one of the proper Lathams who had lived near Pittsfield, Massachusetts, for some three hundred years. Controlling impulses and appetites was one of the things they did best. Aside from this obsession about illegal guns, he had upheld family tradition.

"Get your sleep," he replied. "We'll talk tomorrow."

Finished in the kitchen, the police technician collected the two weapons in plastic bags and mumbled his farewell. Then Agajanian and Alison Gordon walked Latham to the front door.

"I suppose your wife is used to the hours you keep," she said as she stifled another yawn.

Something fierce and terrible suddenly flashed from his wide gray eyes. "My wife is dead." He looked away and strode swiftly out into the night.

# 19

ALTHOUGH HE prided himself on being an independent and creative thinker, John L. Walker was a creature of habit in several ways. This morning—as on almost every other since being elected President of the United States, he awoke at 6:30 without the aid of an alarm clock. The hour was no problem; he had regularly arisen earlier than that on his parents' dairy farm in Wisconsin during the first eighteen of his fifty-seven years.

John L. Walker—Jack to family and friends—slid his feet into black leather slippers and admired the woman who had given them to him. Deep in sleep on her side of the king-sized bed, the dark-haired First Lady looked rosy-faced and serene. Journalists often complimented her charm, grace and intelligence, and if the media didn't know about her bawdy sense of humor and sexual appetites, that wasn't their business anyway. Though every day promised problems and pressures, it was a pleasure to wake up beside this woman each morning.

It usually went downhill after that, he reflected, as he made his way across the historic bedroom. The bathroom was—thank God—modern and free of associations with any of his distinguished predecessors. He entered, stepped on the scale and ruefully noted that he was still fourteen pounds overweight. He eyed himself in the mirror over the sink and flashed the boyish grin that had become one of his political trademarks.

"Morning, Mr. President," he said to his reflection.

After he shaved, brushed his teeth and downed the multivitamin pill that Dr. Spanbock had prescribed, he put on his bathing suit and bathrobe and descended to the swimming pool. The physician had instructed him to do fifteen laps daily, but Walker generally quit after eleven.

"Don't tell the doctor I shortchanged him, Christie," he joked as he climbed out of the pool.

"No, sir," the Secret Service agent replied.

"Those medics like to order everybody around, don't they?"

"Except you, Mr. President. You're the Commander-in-Chief."

Walker laughed, and returned upstairs to shower and dress. It was as he adjusted the knot on his tie that his wife opened her eyes. She smiled, and then her small hand darted from beneath the covers to pat the mattress beside her.

"Too late," he told her.

She patted the mattress again.

"I'm all dressed, Mrs. Walker," he said.

She sat up abruptly. The covers fell away, exposing her to the hips. It was no accident, as they both knew.

"Come here."

The President walked to the bed, sat down and embraced her as they kissed. They kissed several times before he reluctantly let go.

"You're a terrific kisser," he told her.

"I'm good at other things too," she replied slyly and kicked away the covers. She had the splendid figure of a woman a dozen years younger.

124

"What do you think, Mr. President?"

"Not bad for a grandmother," he admitted, "but it isn't on my schedule this morning. The CIA will be here to brief me over breakfast in fifteen minutes, and then there's a visit from Senator Kincaid."

"He'd slit your throat for a nickel, Jack," she said as she ran her hand through her tangled hair.

"And give three cents change. He never did understand why I got the nomination instead of him."

"It's because you're better in bed, luv."

"Lot of people would agree with you. Some of them are saying I'm screwing the whole country. It isn't as if I lied to them, damn it. I ran as a liberal Republican, not a conservative hawk."

"Nobody believes politicians, Jack. Oh my lord, I'm having breakfast with those Hadassah ladies in thirty-five minutes!"

She arose from bed as her husband started for the door, and by the time he left the room she was on her third pushup. He knew that she'd complete all forty-nine—one for each year of her life, for this was a very determined First Lady. Even with a twenty-hour-a-week job, she'd been third in Vassar's class of 1952.

As usual, the CIA briefing contained few surprises but plenty of incident—most of it negative. Marxist "liberation" forces were moving toward the capital of another shaky African nation, the government of one of America's Asian allies was stealing U.S. wheat before it reached the starving peasants, accelerated Soviet production of heavy tanks would let Moscow put two more armored divisions in the field by September and the devout hysterics running Iran were trying to cause another uprising in Saudi Arabia. Bonn had uncovered an East German spy ring in its Ministry of Defense. There was also an excellent chance of a steel industry strike in Britain.

125

"Is that the good news or the bad news?" Walker asked as he stirred his coffee.

The CIA official forced a wan smile.

"Go ahead, Dietrich."

"There's some encouraging news from Japan, Mr. President. A medical team at the University of Tokyo has a very promising anti-cancer drug in advanced testing. It's done wonders with gerbils and rhesus monkeys. It could be a breakthrough, sir. They'll know in two years."

The President thought of his mother's death from cancer nineteen months earlier, and nodded to the briefing officer to continue.

"Next item isn't that positive, sir. Our French friends are selling another nuclear plant to the Iraqis. It might be used to manufacture weapon quality uranium."

"Son of a bitch! I suppose this will replace the one the Iranians knocked out last year, huh?"

"Uh . . . well, sir . . . the *official* story was that the Iranians did that. We have reason to believe that the plant was actually neutralized by an Israeli sabotage team."

Walker ate the last of his boiled egg and shrugged.

"Maybe you ought to pass that to the Israelis," he suggested. "With a little luck, they might *neutralize* this one too."

Dietrich looked embarrassed.

"Fact is, Mr. President . . . it was the Israelis who tipped us —yesterday."

Projections of the Cuban sugar crop and Mexican elections concluded the briefing. Then Walker skimmed *The Washington Post* and *The New York Times,* reading the articles that his aides had circled for special attention. He barely finished before the chairman of the Senate Foreign Relations Committee arrived to discuss the bipartisan opposition to the administration's current policies.

The 10:45 meeting with General Omar Reedy brought only more problems. The Chairman of the Joint Chiefs of Staff had a furrowed brow. He was too tactful to bring up his dissatisfaction with the arms limitation negotiations, but he did present a substantial shopping list of "essential" new weapons that needed "priority attention." Walker accepted the ninety-two-page proposal, thanked him and wondered where the hell the money would come from.

At 11:20, White House press secretary Susan Trotta entered to announce that the labor leaders, reporters and TV crews were waiting to witness his signing of the industrial safety statute. It was on his way to the ceremony that Walker saw his military aide, Major General Bradley Steele, in the corridor.

"I was just speaking with State, sir," Steele reported. "They say all systems are go for your Panama trip next week."

"And I was just talking to Reedy. Looking mighty gloomy."

"He's a good soldier, sir."

"So are you, Brad," Walker told him, "but you're not fighting me the way Reedy and some of his Pentagon buddies are."

"I'm afraid those four-stars don't pay much attention to the opinions of a two-star like me, but I think their opposition to your negotiations has peaked. I'd say it's declining. They'll go along."

"They'd better," Walker replied as Susan Trotta gestured urgently for him to keep moving. "I'm the Commander-in-Chief, so they'd damn better follow my orders. What else can they do—start a revolution?"

Then the President of the United States took a deep breath, put on his smile and walked down the hall to do his duty: appear

127

on all three networks' evening news programs. That was the name of the game. John Lincoln Walker played it rather well after so many years.

By the time the signing ceremony was completed at the White House, it was noon in Washington—and nine A.M. in Beverly Hills. Alison Gordon locked the door of her house, scanned the grounds and got into her car. When she pulled out of the driveway onto the street and saw Hovde in his drab brown Dodge, she brought the Porsche up alongside him.

"Just passing by?" she asked.

He lifted a submachine gun from the seat beside him.

"Is this a joke?"

"Was that number last night a joke?" he countered.

"Listen, Don, just because the Santa Monica cops took my gun doesn't mean I need protection."

"Course not," Hovde rasped and handed her a brown paper bag. She opened it to see a .357 magnum exactly like hers.

"Is this licensed? Where the hell did you get this?"

Hovde pointed back to Agajanian watching in his Jaguar thirty yards away. She crooked her finger, and he drove up to join them.

"Where did this come from?" she said again.

"Out of a Crackerjack box. Let's get going. The lady I work for gets nasty if I'm late."

She shook her head, put the bag down and drove off. Hovde and the accountant followed. When she glanced back two minutes later, she could not see the Jaguar. She didn't have to—she knew that Agajanian had widened the space so that he could observe any strangers without being detected himself. When she was a block from her office, Hovde tooted twice to signal that he'd be circling to go in first. He was "talking the point" with his submachine gun, just in case someone was waiting for her in the basement garage.

When she got out of her car, she could tell that the weapon was at the ready under his raincoat. They rode up in the elevator together without speaking, and neither uttered a word until they entered the reception room.

"Good morning, Ruth," she said to the Japanese-American woman in horn-rimmed glasses who sat behind the desk. Like all the other employees, Ruth Tanaka O'Brien had worked overseas for the Central Intelligence Agency for several years. The able and pretty divorcée was a friend as well as executive secretary, so Alison decided to tell her what had happened.

"Last night—"

"I heard," the woman replied and pointed to a half-open drawer in her desk. Alison Gordon looked down at the butt of a .32-caliber Beretta.

"You may be overreacting, Ruth."

"Me? Hovde's got a machine gun!"

Alison Gordon considered the weapon in the brown paper bag under her own arm, and decided not to press the point.

"I think you can put that away for the moment," she told Hovde and walked into her office. One and a half cigarettes later, Hovde joined her. Agajanian was only a few steps behind.

"I just came up to get a camera," Agajanian explained. "This time it's a woman in a Chevy two-door. She picked you up half a mile from the house. She was *waiting*, Al."

"Don't say it: It's dumb to take the same route to work every day—even in peaceful Beverly Hills."

"What kind of woman?" Hovde asked.

"Redhead in her thirties or so. She's parked out back."

"They may have someone covering the front too," Alison Gordon said. "We'll need more people, and cars. That will cost, but I suppose there's no choice."

"Not unless you like pine boxes. These bastards tried to kill you," the accountant said. "It isn't as if we're short of cash, or friends either. You'd better start calling up the reserves."

"*You* call them—from outside. We don't know who's sitting on our phones. Get as many troops as you need. It's pull-your-wagons-into-a-circle time, and we're short of wagons. Give her plenty of room, Andy. She's our only lead, so don't spook her."

"Anything else?"

"Thanks—to both of you, and be careful."

"You can bet on it, mom," he replied and left humming "This Could Be the Start of Something Big."

For years she had been pressuring both Agajanian and Hovde to modify their methods, telling them that the violent CIA tactics required for survival in foreign espionage battles had no place in peacetime Southern California. Now the savagery of covert operations and sudden slaughter was right here, and she knew the accountant was humming because he felt comfortable again in the brutal world he knew so well.

"He *likes* this," she said.

"It's not his fault," Hovde told her. "He didn't want the case. He warned you that it was a sewer, Al."

"And all three of us have plenty of experience with sewers, don't we?" she recalled bitterly.

"Look on the bright side. They're playing our game, and you know there's nobody better at playing it than us."

"You call this a *game?*"

"*They* started it."

And we've got to finish it, she thought—whoever *they* were. The sooner she started, the quicker it would be over. She col-

130

lected all the notes, tapes and facts they had acquired since the moment she first met Lauri Adams and began to go over every fragment with Hovde to search for clues to *their* purpose and identity. *They* were numerous and organized, much more sophisticated than any gangland group she knew of . . . but somehow primitive too.

"My sense is they don't have much experience at this game," she said.

"Plenty of nerve though."

"They're not afraid of anyone or anything. Their violence is almost casual, like some foreign terrorist outfit. It's as if they weren't American at all."

"But the guy who ran down Otto was Mr. Apple Pie, Al. He was a Sunday School teacher."

"And what else? How deep did the cops dig? Maybe Latham's agents can turn over a few more rocks." She looked at the wall clock and wondered about the red-headed woman nine floors below.

"Latham?" Hovde said. "What makes you think we can trust him? What's under *his* rock?"

The questions were paranoid and logical at the same time. It was that kind of case, disturbing and dangerous. Equally troubling was her visceral sense of urgency. It was more than a by-product of the attempt on her life. She stared past Hovde at the clock again. Five minutes to one. She was reaching for the bag that contained the .357 when the phone rang. It was Agajanian's voice.

"You're going to love this," he said.

"I doubt it. What's happening?"

"I'm calling from the car. You'd better hit the red button . . . now."

131

She flicked on the scrambler, turned on the speaker phone so Hovde could hear, and waited.

"First, I've got good people covering the front and back of our building, and two men are on the way to your house. You know them—Pete Wilcox and Balducci."

"Fine. What about the redhead?"

"That's the part you're going to love. At twenty to twelve, another car showed up to take over the surveillance. A green Subaru, keep your eye out for it. The redhead split, and we tailed her out here to West Hollywood."

"*We?*"

"Amos Axt is with me. I figured she'd be less likely to spot two cars leapfrogging. She drove out here, parked the car in a lot and went into a building. I'm across the street."

"So far there's nothing to love."

"Al, she's not a redhead. Just before she climbed out of the coupe, she whipped off a wig. She's a brunette, and a *cop.*"

"You're sure?"

"The building is the West Hollywood police station. Only cops can park in this lot. I had Amos call in her plate number to my chum at Motor Vehicles. Officer Elizabeth Wade. It gets better."

"It couldn't get worse. You're dead certain, Andy?"

"I phoned the station. She's with the *Sex* Crimes Unit. How about *that?*"

Alison Gordon looked up at Hovde, who shrugged.

"*Sex* Crimes?" she said.

"Fantastic, huh?" Agajanian sounded exuberant. "We've got her home address in Maywood too. Full surveillance?"

"Yes, but give her lots of room. Don't crowd her for a second, Andy. Using her own car was their first mistake, and our first break. Don't blow it."

"Soul of discretion," he pledged.

She hung up, and turned again to Hovde. "What do you think, Don?"

"It's a beginning," he said and started for the door.

"Where are you going?"

"Out to turn over Latham's rock."

"You sure he's got one?"

"Everybody does, Al. You know that."

When he returned an hour later, he found her pondering the ruins of a half eaten sandwich, a cold carton of black coffee and an ashtray filled with butts. A little cloud of cigarette smoke hovered over her desk.

"What did Latham tell you?" Hovde asked her cautiously.

"He's the Special Agent in Charge for law enforcement at the local A.T.F. bureau. Gun control is a personal crusade for him and he's worried about nearly a thousand military weapons stolen in the past ten months or so. The FBI is getting nowhere on the Century massacre, and he wants to work with us because he's got this wild hunch that our Adams investigation could help him track the gun dealers."

"Anything else?"

"His wife is dead."

Hovde waved away the acrid smoke. "He left out something. His wife was pregnant with twins when she was killed."

"Killed?"

"By a nineteen-year-old stickup punk carrying a forty-dollar Saturday Night Special."

"*Oh, my God.*"

"She was in her eighth month, Al. The babies died too," he reported in a voice even more choked than usual. "I think he's got a reason for his crusade, Al. I think he's okay."

Then Hovde left. Alison put her hands to her face. Then she

blew her nose and forced herself to concentrate on the people who were attempting to kill her. On the basis of their past performance, they might try again at any moment. This time she would be ready.

# 20

SEVEN MILES away in his fourth-floor office in the Federal Building near City Hall, Todd Latham frowned in disappointment.

"Nobody?" he asked.

"Afraid so," agent Dilchik replied. "LAPD came up dry. No civilian with a shotgun wound has shown up at any emergency room within forty miles since midnight."

"He had to have medical attention, Eli."

"Maybe some private doctor might have patched him up," the younger agent suggested.

"He lost too much blood. He needed a hospital, damn it. All right. Thanks, Eli."

Dilchik turned to leave.

"Wait a second. You said *civilian*. Was a soldier wounded?"

"No. Some motorcycle cop in Riverside was dumb enough to drop his shotgun while loading it in his garage. One of his hunting buddies brought him in."

"Twelve-gauge?" Latham asked.

"He's a *cop.*"

*"Right shoulder?"*

"I didn't ask. You really think . . . what kind of case is this?"

Traffic noise drifted up from the City Center below as Latham reflected.

"I'm not sure," he finally answered. "Find out where he was hit, whether the pellets were twelve-gauge and what time his pal brought him in."

"Yes, sir. Christ, a *cop?*"

"Just an idea, Eli. Probably nothing to it. One more thing."

"Yes, sir?"

"Phone the hospital yourself," Latham ordered, "and please don't mention this to anyone. We wouldn't want A.T.F. to look silly, would we?"

"No, sir. I'll get right on it."

As the door closed behind Dilchik, Latham looked down again at the single-page document on his desk. It was a disturbing "bulletin" from the Office of the Sheriff of Los Angeles County next door in the Hall of Justice. There was information from "reliable sources" that California motorcycle gangs had recently acquired automatic weapons. Hell's Angels units alone were armed with twenty-five Ingram Mac-10s and 11s, some equipped with silencers.

They had probably bought the submachine guns with proceeds of drug deals, Latham calculated. There were a dozen twisted reasons why barbarian bikers, confident that they were a law unto themselves, might have massacred the people at Century. A failed narcotics transaction, a ripoff raid to steal a load of meth, a feud over a woman, an unpaid debt or imagined insult to the gang's sense of honor—any one of these could have caused it.

The specific reason really didn't matter. It was the guns that counted, and nothing else. Without those weapons, the killings would be impossible. Suddenly the rage was back and he was thinking of his wife's violent death.

After a moment, he regained control and found himself thinking about Alison Gordon. If the Riverside policeman had actually shot himself and was not connected to this, she was the only key. The attempt on her life was the one solid lead. Her vague suspicions about Pacific Coast Security were being checked out by Ryer now, but there was probably nothing there. Latham sighed as he turned over the L.A. sheriff's bulletin to study the photos of recently seized weapons. That was when the phone rang. It was Ryer.

"Just finished at Pacific Coast Security. Their guns are all clean, every one properly licensed," he reported.

"What about the vibes? You get any sense somebody was nervous or scared?"

"Nothing like that. Guy I talked to was the boss of the guards, Lou Montague. Total cool."

"Did you speak to Carew?"

"Tried, but he left town this morning. Back on the twenty-fifth. Was it important?"

"Probably not. Come on back," Latham instructed. It was time to speak to Alison Gordon. He dialed her number, made an appointment to meet her at 4:30 and devoted the next hour to other cases. At ten minutes to four, he stood before the elevator door.

The doors slid open. Inside was a long-haired woman with twin daughters, perhaps seven or eight years old. He could not help thinking that his children would be that age now. The mother's tresses were the same color as Anna's. She'd been so vain about her hair. He stepped into the elevator and closed his eyes. He did not open them again until everyone got out at the ground floor. By the time he reached his car, most of the pain had subsided.

137

In Panama's Fort Amador, Private José Garcia's pain was getting worse. The military policemen who had captured him in the hospital's laundry room had stopped smashing his teeth, kidneys and feet with the butts of their guns and burning his toes with cigarette lighters. The smell of scorched flesh still lingered in the "therapy" room, but that phase of the "treatment" was over. Now an ideologically devout U.S. Army physician was directing the application of electrical shocks to his genitals.

"Again," the captain ordered. A white-uniformed technician threw the switch once more, and Garcia jackknifed in agony, screaming.

"Let me repeat the question, private," the officer said coolly. "Why did you conceal a bug in Major Bass' office, and who are you working for?"

"I didn't," the private mumbled faintly through blood-caked lips.

"You stink, Garcia. You stink of your own feces, and you're a stupid fool. You disgust me. What's more, I'm losing my patience with you, spic. Who sent you?"

More vague sounds emerged from the ruined face.

"Damn it, Garcia. Speak up. I'll help you," the irate captain announced. He jerked the captive's mouth open impatiently, and nodded.

"No wonder you're whimpering. You got a loose tooth, soldier. I'll fix that."

He picked up a pair of surgical forceps, reached in and pulled it out. Garcia howled again in agony.

"Now talk louder. Come on, Garcia. Who sent you?"

"Uh . . . uh . . . no-bod-y . . . Didn't do any-thing . . . no-body."

The doctor gestured, and another electrical jolt hurled pain into Garcia's groin. The men who had trained him to resist "intensive interrogation" would have been proud of him, but

138

Garcia felt no elation, or anything else. He had escaped into unconsciousness.

"He's out, captain," the technician said.

"I noticed, Toby. I'm not as dumb as he is, you know. All right, we'll resume out reeducation of this animal in a couple of hours. Maybe we'll give him swimming lessons in the hydrotherapy tank. Meanwhile, get him out of here, and hose down the floor."

"Where do we park him, captain?" an MP asked.

"Padded cell. This sleaze thought he could mess with Lexington . . . He's obviously crazy. Better put him in a straitjacket, Toby. I don't want this poor sick man to hurt himself."

The doctor knew that the interrogations would continue—with various methods. Water treatments that would bring the prisoner to the brink of drowning, again and again . . . more electrical shocks . . . starvation and denial of sleep . . . "truth" drugs that would dissolve his will to resist or conceal. This little bastard would surely break, and then they'd pick up his outside contact. How much had Garcia discovered? What had he already communicated to his contact?

It couldn't be much, Captain McKee told himself as he paused before a wall mirror to check his uniform for blood spots. If it was anything significant, there would be tanks surrounding the hospital right now. Since that was not so, the plan to seize the President of the United States on April 27th—six days from now—could proceed.

# 21

"I Don't *have* any problems with cycle gangs, Mr. Latham." Alison Gordon smiled and lifted another forkful of fresh pineapple to her lips.

The late afternoon sun was warm and pleasant in the garden behind the Swiss Cafe, but the agent was not enjoying either the weather or the Rodeo Drive restaurant. His focus was elsewhere. It was the guns, she guessed.

"Sometimes they do freelance jobs for customers," he thought aloud. "For a pound of meth or half a dozen weapons, they'd rape the governor's mother . . . Of course, it could be ammo."

"Is this a private conversation, or can anyone join in?"

"Sorry. I'm trying to make sense out of this." he apologized.

"Me too. Now what the hell is this talk of motorcycle goons all about?"

"Ingrams. Mac tens and elevens."

So it was the machine guns.

"Sheriff's Motorcycle Gang Unit has a pretty good intelligence operation. Their latest bulletin warns that Hell's Angels groups in this region have twenty-five hot Ingrams, some with silencers like the pieces that chewed up the people at Century."

"Long shot." she said.

"Maybe, but it could be them."

"Okay, it's a *possible.* I've got something *definite,*" she said as she reached for the espresso. "If it's any consolation, it's just as bizarre as your Hell's Angels notion. No, more."

"What is it?"

She swallowed a sip of the strong coffee and told him about the policewoman from the Sex Crimes Unit.

"Would you believe it? A cop?" she concluded. The faraway look returned to his eyes. The beeper hooked to his belt suddenly sounded, and he excused himself to telephone his office. When he returned, he stared at her for several seconds before he spoke.

"A cop?"

She nodded.

"I may have something about a cop too. Motorcycle patrol-type named Joyce. Brought into the emergency room of a hospital at Riverside early this morning with a shotgun wound. That call was from one of my agents who I asked to check on it."

"Right shoulder?"

"Right shoulder," he confirmed.

She stood up and left the table. He had to hurry to catch up with her as she led the way through the dimly lit main area of the restaurant. She stopped abruptly just inside the exit to Rodeo Drive.

"Hang on a minute. I've got a call to make," she announced. When she rejoined him, she lit a cigarette and looked at her watch.

"Can we go?" he asked.

"Not yet. Might be better if we use your car. There are some friends of our lady cop who know mine. This Joyce we're going to see? Has he got a first name?"

"Don't laugh, but it's James."

She puffed on the Sobranie, then blew a perfect smoke ring.

"I never laugh at people who try to kill me, not even literary types."

"Who *may* have tried to kill you," Latham corrected. "He says the shotgun went off accidentally while he was loading it."

"The other James Joyce told better stories than that," she said, and glanced again at her watch.

"What are we waiting for?"

"You wouldn't want to know." He was obviously smart enough to understand that she was planning something illegal, so she braced herself for the inevitable questions.

"I'll take your word for it, Miss Gordon."

*That* was a surprise.

"You can call me Alison."

"Thanks. I'm Todd. Excuse me, Alison. Have I got time to—?" he asked and pointed at the men's room.

Five minutes later she was sitting beside him as he drove his blue Cutlass up Rodeo Drive.

"Mind if we go by the County Art Museum?" she asked.

He knew it was not the most direct route to Riverside General Hospital, but he realized that she had a plan that she didn't want to discuss. In fact, she didn't say anything until they were five blocks from the museum.

"Yes, Todd," she said in reply to his unspoken question, "we are about to lose the Rambler that followed us from the restaurant. If it works right, our tail won't even know what happened. Slow down a bit so we get stuck at that next light."

The agent complied. In his rear-view mirror, he saw a Jaguar move up and take a position a few yards behind the Rambler that was in the next lane. No one saw what happened next, for Agajanian held a newspaper to mask his weapon. He raised the bulky real-estate section of the morning edition, took careful aim at the Rambler's rear right tire and squeezed the trigger twice. The silenced .32 barely made a sound, just two soft "plops" lost in the city traffic.

The light changed. It was two blocks before the man in the Rambler noticed anything, and another four before he had to pull his car over to the curb. Latham drove onto the Pomona Freeway. The Jaguar was thirty yards behind all the way to Riverside.

The hospital was eight floors high and a fine example of mediocre architecture; the style could only be described as contemporary public, she thought, as Latham parked in the very large lot at the rear. There was a sign designating the entrance to the Emergency Room, with an ambulance waiting at the nearby loading dock. When Agajanian halted the Jaguar beside her, she swung her right index finger in a wide arc.

"Cover the front," she said. "We'll take the back." Agajanian drove off to take up his position, and they began to walk to the Emergency Room door.

"You expecting trouble?" Latham asked.

"Almost always. Okay if I do the talking?"

"Be my guest."

They entered the building, stepped aside to let a balding orderly push past a blanket-wrapped patient in a wheelchair and found the admissions desk. Behind it sat a large black woman in a white uniform.

"Help you?"

"We're here to see my cousin, Jimmy Joyce." Alison lied

convincingly. "I think he was admitted early this morning."

"Joyce?"

"Is he all right?" Latham asked solicitously.

"Don't worry. I'll find out, honey." The admissions aide flipped open a loose-leaf notebook, ran her finger down a page and looked up.

"James A. Joyce? *Right,*" she said, and reached for a beige desk phone. "Hello, this is Darletta Williams down in E. R. admitting. . . . You're right, honey. Busy, busy, busy . . . Say, what's the room number for Joyce, James A.? . . . What? . . . Thanks."

She hung up the phone and smiled.

"He must be doing well. They checked him out a few minutes ago. There's an ambulance waiting to take him to a nursing home."

Latham thanked her, and they ran. They reached the rear exit just in time to see the man in the wheelchair—the one they'd passed on the way in—being helped into the back of an ambulance.

"Mr. Marks?" Latham called out.

"Nah, he's Joyce," a hospital attendant answered. They watched the ambulance pull away, and as soon as it turned the corner they followed in Latham's Cutlass. She waved to Agajanian when they reached the front of the building and he joined the pursuit.

"What do you think?" Latham asked as the ambulance moved onto the freeway.

"Your phone call spooked them."

"That's a definite *maybe,*" he admitted. The "Mr. Marks" ploy had been highly professional. She did not usually like to work with routine-ridden government agents, but this one didn't

144

seem to be the standard civil servant. Her attention shifted as the ambulance swung onto the Escondido Freeway heading southeast.

"This goes right to March Air Force Base," she said.

"Now that's a very long shot," he answered with a smile.

His expression was quite different fourteen minutes later when the ambulance turned through the entrance to the base. They saw the driver speak to the armed guards at the gate, and watched them gesture for the white vehicle to pass the check-point. Why would the Air Police admit a wounded civilian in a non-military vehicle to March Air Force Base?

"This is crazy," Latham said as he pulled the Cutlass off the freeway a hundred and fifty yards past the gate.

"There goes your Hell's Angels theory, Todd."

The accountant stopped his car five yards behind the Cutlass and walked forward, shaking his head.

"Where do we go from here?" he asked.

"In, I guess. You're special agent in charge of a major A.T.F. office, Todd. You're in the same federal family, so they've got to cooperate."

"That's definitely another *maybe*," he answered. When they pulled up at the gate, he told the Air Police who he was and asked to speak to the base security officer. Moments later, he was on the phone to a Major Satourette, a very polite Louisianan. Latham identified himself and explained that he wanted to come on-base to discuss an important A.T.F. investigation.

"'Fraid I can't help you there, suh. We're smack in the middle of a Red Dog exercise, Mr. Latham. That's a surprise see-curity alert. Whole damn base sealed tight since three o'clock. No civilians or civilian vehicles coming through till oh six hundred hours tommoruh mornin', suh."

"I've got to get inside *now,* major."

"Only person who can authorize that is the base commander, suh, and he's up logging flying time for another two hours. You mind calling back, suh?"

"Eight thirty all right?"

"That'll be dandy, suh."

Showing none of the distrust and anger he felt, Latham nodded casually to the sentries and drove off. He told Alison Gordon what the major had said.

"That son of a bitch is lying," she erupted.

"Absolutely. We saw the civilian ambulance go through, not three minutes before they locked us out. Could be this Joyce is doing something confidential for the fly-boys. Maybe a drug investigation. Who knows?"

"What the hell was he doing at my house with the assassin's gun?" she demanded. "I can't believe that I'm on some Air Force hit list, and I can't see why they're hiding this guy. Who is this James A. Joyce anyway?"

"I'll ask the general."

When Latham telephoned from her house at 8:35 P.M., he learned that the base commander was Brigadier General Milton Rust. He was not only energetic but also more than willing to cooperate with A.T.F. He would locate Joyce immediately, and arrange for Latham to continue his investigation at the air base in the morning. The general would call back with a specific time within the hour.

When the phone rang at 9:20, Latham recognized the rich Cajun tones of Major Satourette. He was calling on behalf of General Rust, who had looked into the matter thoroughly. They had made a very careful check. There was no one—Air Force or civilian—named James A. Joyce at March Air Force Base.

What's more, the personnel files indicated that there never had been.

"Then he promised to phone if they ever did find *this fellah*," Latham reported. "First Carew leaves town suddenly, and now James A. Joyce simply goes up in smoke."

"Not so simply. I wonder whom they'll 'vanish' next."

"Try Mrs. Wilhite, Al," Hovde advised as he walked into the room. It took Latham a moment to remember.

"Wilhite? The Pacific Coast Security guard?"

"The homicidal Sunday School teacher," Alison confirmed. She saw Hovde staring at the chicken quarter left on the ironstone dinner platter and realized that he hadn't eaten.

"Help yourself, and tell us what happened."

He tossed down his raincoat, and took a piece of chicken.

"I was watching the house. All quiet till just after eight, when a two-door Chevy pulled up . . . Good chicken, Al."

"Thanks."

"Get this. Red-headed female at the wheel."

"The policewoman?" Latham asked.

Hovde nodded, and swallowed another mouthful.

"You got it. Elizabeth Wade. Recognized her from Andy's pictures. Mrs. Wilhite must have been expecting her. Whipped out the door with a suitcase, and they took off."

He paused for some more chicken.

"Wade drove her to a house near Hawthorne Municipal Airport," he continued, "and then she came back alone to 6430 Sunset Boulevard in Hollywood. Big office building full of music companies."

"Who did she see?"

"Tenth floor is all I know, Al. Building directory shows ASCAP and Irving Berlin Music on that floor."

She poured him a glass of Riesling and refilled her own. "Can we get back to Elizabeth Wade?"

"In and out, Mr. Latham. She was only upstairs for three minutes. She's home now, and Pete's watching the house in Hawthorne—286 Largo Terrace, off Imperial."

Hovde drained his wine, and Latham turned to Alison Gordon.

"Maybe my agents should take this surveillance," he offered. "I can get a full team in place in two hours."

"Quick as you can. Whatever it is, my guess is it's going down soon. The hit man, Carew, Liz Wade and the widow Wilhite —all in the past thirty hours. They're moving fast, and they know we might spot them. Got to be a reason. If I'm right, we have to move fast too."

"Two eighty-six Largo Terrace?"

"Our best lead, Todd. How soon can your people get a rundown on the house and its owners?"

He stood up and looked at his watch.

"With luck, noon."

By 11:30 A.M., A.T.F. agents had discovered from county tax files that 286 Largo Terrace was the property of Tucker P. Ludlum. They followed Ludlum to the Hawthorne Airport at nine. He had been flying over Los Angeles since ten. He was the pilot of an advertising blimp operated by Blue Sky Promotions, whose offices were on the tenth floor of 6430 Sunset Boulevard.

"Your people are great detectives," Alison told Todd Latham.

"Thanks for the compliment, but I'd say what we need right now is a court order for a wire tap."

"That's your way, and I respect it under normal conditions— which this isn't. Any suggestions?"

"Only one, and it's goddamn illegal. We could both go to

jail." He looked at her. "All right, we need a first-class burglar. You wouldn't happen to know one, would you?"

"The best in the business." Now she was feeling better. After three weeks of frustration, she *could* do something. And the enemy now had a name.

Alison Gordon was ready to strike back.

# 22

THE DARK-SKINNED woman looked businesslike as she stepped briskly from the elevator, but even the tailored suit did not wholly conceal her full figure. She adjusted her rimless glasses, glanced up and down the corridor and found her way to the door marked BLUE SKY PROMOTIONS. She paused to study the lock and scan the frame for alarm wires or sonic detectors. She opened the door and went in.

She was searching, checking, computing every second. The door was just a bit heavier than most—an extra layer of steel there. Her eyes swept the reception area, registering details. She pressed the catch on her sensible black leather purse to trigger the electronic scanner and stepped forward to the blonde receptionist.

"Consumer Audio," she said.

"This is Blue Sky Promotions, miss."

"I know that," the visitor replied officiously. "*I'm* with Consumer Audio. My name is McInerney, and I'd like to speak with your sales director."

"May I tell him what you're here for?"

"Your rates and schedules . . . demographics . . . viewer impact estimates. Our marketing group wants to consider Blue Sky for a new product we're introducing in September."

While the receptionist relayed this to someone over the telephone, "Ms. McInerney" let her eyes rove down the corridor, over the ceiling, across the walls, furniture and windows. Antonia Shephard had an exceptional memory for detail, a talent she had meticulously trained and frequently used. She was an outstanding thief, married to an even more remarkable one.

"Someone will be right with you," the blonde promised. Half a minute later, a shirtsleeved man came down the hall with a smile and large blue folder adorned with the sketch of a blimp.

"Sorry Mr. Parks is out with the McCann-Erickson folks," he said pleasantly, "but everything you want is in the kit. Look it over, and give us a call."

She thanked him and left with the folder. When she reached the street, she walked two blocks, turned the corner and made her way to the gray panel truck where her husband waited.

"It's gonna be a bitch," she told him. She took from her purse what looked like a plastic compact, but which was actually a tape recorder. She began to dictate a comprehensive description of what she'd just seen—the reinforced door, the concealed television camera, the telltale burglar alarm cables, the electric eye beams, sonic alarms—everything.

"That's it, doc," she said. "Oh, *shit*. I forgot the double circuit setups on the window latches."

He waited patiently for the vital taping that had to be completed while her memory was fresh and full. She talked into the machine for another half-minute.

"This is worse than my M.I.T. finals," she said.

"No false modesty, Tony. You're very good. I'm proud of you."

She looked up at her husband. Some fourteen years her senior,

151

he was the strongest, smartest and most fascinating man she knew. At forty, mustachioed Doc Shephard was a loyal and considerate husband as well as one of the three top burglars in North America. He was also an excellent lover.

"And I'm crazy about you." she kissed him and put away the recorder as he started the truck's motor.

"There's no way an advertising or promotion outfit needs *that* kind of security," she said.

"We'll cope."

"Sure—but what do you think they're really dealing up there? What are we going to *take?*"

"Pictures." He wished that he knew more to tell her. Unfortunately, Alison Gordon had not yet explained the entire operation —but she surely would before they broke into the Blue Sky offices in just nine hours.

Three hours and five minutes after Antonia Shephard left the Blue Sky offices, almost everyone else had too. As usual, George Parks remained behind to make sure that all the alarm systems were operating. Today he had another reason. It was April 22nd, and the timetable required that he call Caesar on the special phone that he never used unless he was alone. Now everyone was gone and it was seven P.M.—four o'clock in Washington.

Parks entered the command post, slammed the heavy bolts that barred the inner metal door behind him and walked to the closet. He was the only person on the West Coast who had the key. He opened the door, and faced the ten-inch-thick steel vault whose combination was known to no one but himself and Roger Halleck. He dialed the four numbers carefully, swung the massive portal open and stepped inside.

The air smelled stale—almost dead—inside the rarely opened

152

compartment. He had once called it the most expensive telephone booth on earth. Halleck hadn't laughed, but the description was accurate. The sole contents of the drill-proof, blast-proof, torch-proof vault were a straight-backed chair, a small desk and the direct-line scrambler phone to Caesar. Parks sat down, adjusted the scrambler setting and spoke.

"Right on the money, sir," he reported. "No, that wasn't meant to be a pun . . . The dry run this afternoon went perfectly. Cameras worked—every one of them. Timing was excellent. The Midas truck actually reached the liftoff point a minute and a half early . . . Thank you, sir . . . Yes, they are an outstanding group . . .

"That's under control, sir . . . No, but she has been neutralized, maybe I should say *isolated*. We have denied access to anyone who might have information about us. They're all in secure places where she can't get at them . . . My thinking *exactly*. With less than forty-four hours to go, we've got to minimize our exposure . . . Yes, we ended the surveillance this morning just in case she might notice it . . .

"Of course . . . Yes, Popeye's courier was in late this afternoon. Our goods are only a hundred and sixty miles from the rendezvous . . . Should be in position a day early, sir . . . I'm not worried about that part of it. Popeye won't let us down."

At the U. S. Navy headquarters in San Diego some one hundred and eighteen miles south of 6430 Sunset Boulevard, another man was on the transcontinental telephone discussing the same subject.

"That's what our patrol planes report. Don't mean to reflect on the CIA, you understand. Hell, I served with the agency for three years myself."

"What are you suggesting, admiral?"

"Maybe . . . it's possible somebody sent you fellows in Langley the wrong information."

"Somebody died for that goddamn information, admiral. The freighter *has* to be there, or not far away."

"It isn't. Not within four hundred miles of the map reference you gave us. We swept that entire area carefully—twice."

"How about twice more? This might be *important.*"

"First thing in the morning, sir."

"Thank you very much, Admiral Walford." The deputy director of the Central Intelligence Agency didn't know him well enough to call him "Popeye."

# 23

AFTER AN excellent steak dinner at The Saloon on Santa Monica Boulevard, Alison Gordon and Todd Latham drove around Beverly Hills for twenty minutes to see whether they were being followed. First to the Beverly Hilton, then to Century City's towers and on in a wide loop back past the dignified headquarters of the Academy of Motion Picture Arts and Sciences—"The Academy" to traditionalists. They cruised slowly through the soft April night.

Window shoppers were out in force—mostly well-dressed couples over forty—studying the costly wares of Rodeo Drive's boutiques and Wilshire Boulevard's row of "better" department stores. Nonconformists who believed that there was life beyond *TV Guide* and organized sports roamed the aisles of the well-lit Brentano's and B. Dalton book stores.

She paid no attention to any of these people, and neither did Latham. Only when they were reasonably confident that no one was tracking them did she guide the Porsche to the large building that housed A. B. Gordon Investigations. At a quarter to ten, they emerged from the elevator and she took out her key to open the door. As she moved to insert it, her shoulder brushed the door and it moved. Surprise showed in her face, and Latham reacted at once. His hand moved to the Smith & Wesson Model 66 in the holster under his arm.

"Is it supposed to be open?" he asked. She shook her head. He drew the short-barreled gun, slowly pushed the door open and looked inside. The lights were on, and the sound of a vacuum cleaner came from somewhere beyond the reception area.

"Cleaning crew?"

"Maybe," she replied. "Could be my office."

It was. A man in gray coveralls and a woman in a matching uniform—each adorned with the patch of L. A. Services—were hard at work. He was pushing a battered Hoover, and she was dusting with a colorful handful of cloth that vaguely resembled the cheap bandana on her head.

"You know them?" Latham asked. Before she could answer, he demanded that the cleaners show their identification papers.

"He's not bad, Al," the cleaning man announced. "Of course we've got ID, but he's not bad at all."

"I know them, Todd," Alison Gordon admitted with a smile.

"They're not cleaners," Latham guessed.

"Not exactly, but they're tidy."

"Surplus property disposal is our line," the man in coveralls explained. "Could you put that piece away, mister? Guns make Tony nervous."

Latham holstered his gun and studied them.

"Todd, meet Doc and Tony. No last names and no questions. Now let's get to work."

While Antonia Shephard reached inside her blouse for the compact-recorder and a folded square of fast-burning "flash" paper, her husband urged them to listen carefully and memorize her instructions.

"I'm the box man, but she gets us in and out. Her degree's in electrical engineering," he confided.

"Come on, Doc," Tony protested, as she unfolded the floor plan that she'd sketched. While the tape was playing, she pointed out on the drawing where each alarm was situated. Then she repeated the whole process.

"Do what I tell you as soon as I say it, and we'll make it," she assured. "Trust me. Security systems are my bag. Any questions?"

There were none.

"Then I've got one," she said. "That Smith and Wesson with the two-and-a-half-inch barrel looks familiar. It's a piece Treasury agents carry."

"What's your question?" Latham said cooly.

"Are you federal?"

As Latham nodded, Doc Shephard spoke up.

"I don't care who he is. We're doing this for Al. She's the one we *owe*." He raised his left hand with the five fingers spread apart. Latham wondered what they owed her and what the gesture meant, but this was not the time to ask.

"I wasn't arguing, Doc, and I wasn't forgetting," Tony said. "It's probably just that guns make me nervous. I hate 'em."

"So does he," Alison Gordon told her with a look toward Latham. "I give you my word. He's not trigger happy. There's one more thing you ought to know."

"It's a mob operation," Tony said.

"Yes, but we don't know which mob—or what they want."

Latham shook his head in disagreement. "They want you dead, ma'am. This outfit kills people."

"Bring the piece," Tony Shepard urged. Then they went over the timetable. It had to be a rough estimate, for they could not predict what other defenses there might be in the offices—ones

157

Tony had not seen. It could be either fourteen minutes or thirty-four.

"Forty is the outside limit in a place that's got a night watchman," advised Doc Shephard, "and this building's got one."

"You're sure?" Latham asked.

"We phoned the owner to offer the low annual rates of Far West Protection, Inc., and he said he was satisfied with the guard service he had. Let's roll."

"Make the phone call," Tony reminded him. They went over the equipment and the sequence in which it would be used.

The thieves left first. At 11:30, they pulled up behind 6430 Sunset Boulevard in a gray van carrying the logo of L. A. Services. They silently unloaded their gear in the shadows and walked to the building's back door where Doc Shephard picked the lock in twenty-five seconds. The outer locks on most office buildings were no challenge to him. They descended to the basement, found the freight elevator and took it up to the twelfth floor. They stepped out and nearly collided with an Hispanic cleaning woman.

"Hey," she said.

Doc Shephard acted before any questions could form in her mind. "Exterminator. You finished in twelve-oh-three?"

"*Cucarachas?* In this building? I clean it good, señor."

"Nobody said there were any. This is to make sure they stay away. You finished? Gonna stink up the hall too."

"I finish. No *cucarachas* on my floors. This crazy."

Shephard laughed pleasantly. "It's not crazy. It's seven bucks an hour. That's what they pay me. Good night."

She shrugged, rang for the elevator and took it up to the fourteenth floor. The thieves immediately found the fire stairs and started down. At that moment, Alison Gordon and Latham entered the front door of the building.

"A whole new sound track," Latham said loudly, as he swung the large fiberboard guitar case. They walked to the guard, who looked up from the TV set he was watching as they approached.

"That was a lousy arrangement, Eddie," Alison Gordon said. "For that kind of bread, it was crap."

"Pure crap, but we're getting double time so who cares?"

"Your name Finkel?" the night watchman asked Latham.

"Sure, Eddie Finkel."

"Your wife wants you to call her. She phoned."

"*Jeeezus.* Okay. Thanks," he told the guard and signed the logbook. He jotted down that they were going up to Video Plus on the tenth floor. When they emerged from the elevator, Tony Shephard was crouched in front of the door to Blue Sky Promotions with a small piece of electronic gear in her hand.

"Jap job," she diagnosed. "Motsu sonic. No sweat."

She set some dials and flicked a switch. She had neutralized the sound alarm on the door. She stepped aside and her husband began trying master keys. She had spotted the lock as a Keffler "G" on her earlier visit, simplifying his task substantially. The seventh key he tried produced an encouraging click. He held the knob in his gloved hand as he pushed the door open very slowly —but only two feet. Tony dropped to the floor, rolled onto her back and inched in warily under the first photo-electric beam.

She listened, her ears straining for any sound that might signal someone was in the office. She kept her eyes closed to shut out distraction and sharpen her hearing. After twenty-five seconds, she sat up and waited for Doc to slide in her plastic tool box. He pushed it under the photo-electric ray, and she pulled it between her knees. After she put on the infra-red goggles and donned the infra-red headlamp, she hooked the tool box to her belt. Then she took out the wide-frequency electronic scanner to sweep the area around her.

The miniature transmitter in the tool box, blanketing the room with neutral "white" sound, was one she had built herself. She had worked with it a dozen times successfully. Using the headlamp as a flashlight, she eyed every inch of the reception area and corridor slowly—then a second time. Proceeding with extreme caution, she began to deceive and disable each of the alarm devices. She bridged circuits, put up reflectors and blocked frequencies in an exact sequence. Only when that was done did she stand and invite her companions—by silent gesture —into the suite.

They were all wearing the special goggles and headlamps that would permit them to operate in the dark. Latham opened the carrying case to take out the infra-red mini-cam that could videotape in total blackness. Alison Gordon stepped forward with the Strobe gun in one hand and a large spray-can in the other.

With Tony Shephard leading the way—signaling when and where to move, they began to search the offices. There were alarms in every room, but no clues as to the real ownership and purpose of Blue Sky Promotions. Office by office, desk by desk, drawer by drawer, they searched and looked—and found nothing meaningful. They opened filing cabinets to examine the contents of dozens of folders, all with the same disappointing results. Latham videotaped the charts on the walls, the cards in the largest Rolodex and the canceled checks for the previous two months. Doc found a small safe in a closet, a mass-produced strongbox. He opened it up, studied the stamps and petty cash, and closed it.

Entering the command post was a lot more difficult. Doc faced the door marked "Audio-Visual," examined the lock and gestured to his wife. The lock was the most complex that he'd seen in these offices, so it was logical—probably inevitable—that

160

the door would also be rigged with electronic defenses. Tony leaned forward to study the door and pulled back immediately.

"Cute," she mouthed silently. The bastards had rigged the doorknob with a heat-sensitive device. Touching it would set off an alarm. She reached into her tool kit, found the cryogenic spray and blanketed the knob with freezing mist. She stepped aside to complete another sweep with the scanner before she gestured to her husband. He took out his kit of picks to attack the lock.

This one did not yield so easily. He began to sweat. He probed, tested, maneuvered—but the lock would not surrender. Something was defying his skills. It was infuriating, but he did not lose his temper. He tested the picks again, paused to breathe deeply and then extracted a small can of fine oil from his pocket. Two gentle squeezes were followed by a mental curse, and then a silent prayer. He inserted another pick. The lock surrendered.

He pushed the door open. Something inside glowed. There was a menacing growl. It was an attack dog, a big Doberman trained to kill. The dog snarled again and coiled to spring. Alison Gordon shoved Shephard aside, raised the Strobe gun and closed her own eyes as she triggered six blinding flashes in dazzling succession. Unable to see, the animal hesitated—just long enough for her to direct a blast of disabling spray at its face.

As the four retreated to safety, the Doberman tensed again to strike. Why wasn't the gas working? Alison Gordon triggered another barrage of stunning light and another jet of spray. The dog was disoriented, but it still bared inch-and-a-half fangs and looked ready to rip out their throats. Finally it staggered a few steps, whimpered and fell to the floor.

Inside the command post, Tony Shephard tapped her wrist-watch, and they all understood. They had used up twenty-six of their forty minutes. Now Alison Gordon pointed at the Doberman to remind them that there was no way to predict how long the animal would stay incapacitated. Latham began to sweep the walls with his mini-cam, moving in for closeups of the nine TV screens, then the unscrambling devices attached to each set.

There were six large clocks on the wall. Though they bore no markings to indicate what time zones they represented, her knowledge of geography told her that they spanned the area from Hawaii to the east coast of the United States. There were three high-backed swivel chairs behind a twenty-foot-wide desk, and at each position there was a phone with five buttons. At the end of the desk was a document shredder, a device infrequently found in legitimate business offices.

While the Shephards were working to open a metal door in the far wall, Alison Gordon prepared to open one of the drawers in the three-seat desk. She thought of all the alarms, crouched down to look underneath for additional security systems. The first thing she saw was three nine-millimeter Uzi submachine guns neatly held in quick release clamps—the weapons used by Secret Service men protecting the President, and by some of the Army's Special Forces "A" teams.

The wall clock set to Los Angeles time showed that they had eleven minutes left. She reached behind the gun nearest the drawer, touched a switch and pulled back her hand instantly. It could open the drawer, set off an alarm or blow up this entire room. She decided that the risk was too great. This was to be a covert reconnaissance, with the undetected acquisition of information the sole objective.

She stood up as Doc Shephard opened the door. Inside the closet were a Telex machine, two large state-of-the-art radio transmitters and several walkie-talkie sets that looked like military equipment. Latham videotaped it all, and the thieves relocked the door to go on to another one six yards away. It was

162

flanked by a large American flag on a floor-mounted stand.

A bit more than eight minutes remained. It took Doc and Tony almost three to make certain that this door was free of electronic traps, and finally to open it. Now this was really *interesting*, the master safecracker thought. He waved to them to come take a look at the massive special-steel vault. What the *hell* was such a complex and costly thing doing here? His wife had been right. Blue Sky Promotions was into something. Yeah, there could be twenty kilos of pure heroin in that box—a stash worth millions on the street . . .

He looked back at Alison Gordon. He owed her. She signaled five minutes. It was unlikely that he or anyone else—even Bernheimer or "Irish" O'Shea—could crack this box in less than twenty minutes, or even longer. It was a stony fact that the odds against them were shifting—moment by moment—growing inexorably in the night. Any second could bring disaster.

He would do his best for the next five minutes, but after that no more. Using stethoscope and a very sensitive electronic detector that picked up the faintest internal clicks, he did battle with the vault. At the end of four minutes he had determined one of the necessary dial settings. Some ninety seconds after that, he was reasonably sure about the second.

He was also a professional who survived by the lessons and rules a hundred other cracksmen had learned over the decades. He stood up, tapped his phosphorescent-faced watch and loaded his equipment to leave. None of the others resisted—they accepted his intuition and withdrew from the closet. He relocked the door and they left the way they had come—carefully and separately.

Doc and Tony were waiting in their van when Alison Gordon and Latham circled the building to join them in the shadows.

"Thanks—to both of you," she told the thieves.

"Did our best," Doc said.

"You did a fantastic job."

"Got it all but two lousy numbers. Sorry."

"Nobody could have done it better."

"Not in forty minutes," Tony Shephard said. "We had to split. You understand that."

"Of course," Latham agreed.

"The first two numbers are eleven and twenty-three. That's half, anyway. Remember them, eleven and twenty-three."

"I will, Doc. You were terrific."

"You were pretty good yourself with that Strobe and the gas, Al. You'd make a fine thief . . . Meant that as a compliment."

"That's how I took it." She watched their van roll off into the night. Latham drove her to the basement garage where her Porsche was parked, and then insisted on following her home in his car.

"Why would you want to do that?" she asked.

"You pay taxes?"

"Sure."

"Well, it's my duty to protect the taxpayers," he announced. She saw the look in his eye, and wondered whether he was going to be difficult when she reached her door. He was abrupt but polite.

"You like jazz?" he asked suddenly as she put her key in the lock.

"Most of it."

"Dizzy's in town. He's playing at Donte's in North Hollywood."

She waited for him to say more, but he simply stared at her with admiration and need.

"What is this—a *date?*" she asked, and immediately regretted her challenging tone. She had no wish to criticize or reject this man, no reason to set up barriers. As a matter of fact, he was —aside from the gun obsession—a rather attractive person. Listening to the Dizzy Gillespie quintet with Latham sounded very appealing.

"Sure. A date—the whole bit. I'll wear a tie and I'll bring you a corsage," he promised with a boyish smile. "What do you say?"

"You've got a date," she replied. She entered the house, turned on the radio and heard the piercing, dancing horn of John Birks Gillespie lighting up a recording of "Groovin' High." Maybe it was a sign of something.

# 24

In the District of Columbia, a different sort of music filled the White House ballroom. Diplomats and cabinet members, Supreme Court judges and top journalists, senior commanders in the U.S. armed forces, prominent political leaders and rich people who had helped elect them, film stars and a couple of tame poets enjoyed the contemporary country-rock offerings of Molly Sue Newbury and her Dixie Demons. With three number-one albums in the past sixteen months and a figure that made Dolly Parton look pre-pubescent, Ms. Newbury was an international favorite. Her admirers included this evening's guest of honor, President Njuguna of the uranium-rich African Republic of Kambo.

While Njuguna danced gracefully with the wife of U. S. Vice President Daniel Darnell, the latter made his way to one of the bars for another glass of champagne. Surveying the scene, he sipped and spoke with General Omar Reedy who was standing stiffly nearby. The anger in the face of the Chairman of the Joint Chiefs of Staff was almost tangible. After Ms. Newbury belted out the final poignant chorus of "Don't Never Love a Trucker," President Walker escaped from the boney clutches of the wife

166

of the British ambassador and started for the bar. He was nearly there when Reedy hurried away.

"What's burning Reedy, Dan?" Walker asked.

"He doesn't like big parties."

"No, it isn't the party. It's the host. You think it's me he hates, or just my guts?"

Darnell, whose good looks had led *Time* magazine to name him the handsomest U. S. senator of 1972, responded with an uneasy smile.

"He doesn't really hate you, Jack. That damn treaty makes him nervous."

Nodding affably toward Njuguna, as the guest of honor swept by, Walker drained half a glass of champagne before he answered.

"Makes me nervous too, Dan. It's obviously a calculated risk, but I think we've got to take it. Glad you do too."

"Politically it's dynamite," Darnell said. "And the Pentagon opposition scares the hell out of me. I never did trust the Russians anyway. Can we really trust them now?"

"We're going to find out," Walker said grimly. A very shrewd and wealthy widow who owned Washington's major news daily caught the President's attention as she came off the dance floor with his military aide.

"Please give this glamorous lady a Perrier," Walker told a bartender. "It *is* the Perrier that keeps you so slim, isn't it, Mrs. Richards?"

"You're such a charmer, Mr. President—the best since Kennedy," she said. "We don't have enough graceful charmers in Washington anymore."

"I'll try to appoint some more if I'm reelected," he joked. When she returned to the dance floor, he looked at Darnell again.

"I'll need your help in this treaty fight, Dan."

"Can't we stall for eight or ten months?"

The President finished his drink and shook his head.

"I don't think so. Be easier with the Senate if we had more Pentagon support. Brad Steele thinks they aren't all as bitter as Reedy. You were on the Armed Services Committee for twelve years. What do your military friends say?"

"Nothing that good," Darnell answered uncomfortably.

"Would you talk to them? Twist a few arms? Look, we've had some differences and I haven't forgotten the fight we had for the nomination. Ten votes the other way and you'd be President. But the issue here is larger than individuals. We both know that."

"I'll do my best," Darnell promised and excused himself to rejoin his wife on the dance floor. They were nimble and skilled, Walker thought as he watched them. Darnell was more than that. Though he represented the more conservative and hawkish wing of the party, he was loyal—as professional politicians must be. Unenthusiastic about the treaty, he would bite the goddamn bullet and do his duty. You could trust a man like Daniel Darnell when the chips were down.

It was late, and Walker felt tired. He was glad when Njuguna walked across to say goodnight. Five minutes after that the President of the United States and his wife left the noisy ball-room themselves. The party was over.

"No calls," Alison Gordon said into the squawk box, and then she led Latham, Hovde and Agajanian to the conference room to look at the videotapes of the Blue Sky offices. The mini-cam had done a fairly good job, providing pictures that were better than the usual surveillance films. They ran the tapes twice, stopping them to study specific frames or sequences. Latham took notes on a yellow legal pad while Alison Gordon spoke hers into a Pearlcorder S301. The second screening ended at 10:55 A.M., and Hovde turned off the videotape player.

"It's show-and-tell time," she announced. "We've shown Todd's tapes. What did they tell us?"

"That big room with the nine TV screens—that's a command post," Agajanian replied. "In my book, it's a poor man's version of the Strategic Air Command bunker—without the Plexiglas map of the world."

"They're not interested in the whole world, Andy," she said. "The clocks spell it out. From Hawaii to the Atlantic Coast—that's all."

"*Where* on the Atlantic Coast?" Hovde asked.

"We don't know," Latham said, "and we don't know why they need a command post or what they're commanding."

"Or who's in command." She lit a cigarette.

"We know they've got access to illegal first-class guns," Latham said. "Those Uzis are current military weapons, and that radio gear looked damn good."

"There isn't much better," Agajanian agreed.

"Is it just the guns that tell you they're bad guys, Todd?" she asked.

"That and the elaborate security. They're going to a great deal of trouble to hide something—something *big.*"

She nodded, and blew a smoke ring. "Anybody have a suggestion as to what it or they could be?"

"Counterfeiting? Dope? A Sov spy ring?" Hovde looked around the room at the others.

"A major weapons outfit," Latham said with authority. "Wholesale gun dealers. Maybe importers who smuggle large shipments ashore. That would explain the radios."

"Andy?"

169

"What the hell have gun dealers got to do with a tape-counterfeiting gang, Al? Why would a Red intelligence *apparat* want to waste you? Not for old time's sake. The KGB isn't that sentimental."

"There has to be a connection," Latham insisted.

"You didn't notice the calendar in the command post?" she said. "I did. April twenty-fourth was circled, just as it was on the calendar at Otto's flat. Something's going down on April twenty-fourth."

"That's *tomorrow.*"

"Doesn't give us much time, Don, does it? Cheer up, gentlemen. We're making progress. We've identified several of the mothers, located and penetrated their command post, video-taped their scrambler gear—"

"And gassed their dog," Agajanian added.

"She had to," Latham said protectively.

"Ignore the wise-ass remarks," she told them. "We taped their scramblers, and we've got the date they're going to do it. That's not all. Whatever *it* is, it's large and visual and I'll bet it involves that blimp. We'd better set up a video watch right away."

She explained to Hovde what was required, and he walked out to relay the message to the secretary/receptionist.

"*Nine* TV sets?" the woman asked incredulously.

"Nine."

"Why do we need *nine?*"

"*They've* got nine, so we need nine."

"Who's *they?*"

"Color sets—at least seventeen inches," he evaded, and returned to the conference room. Latham was rerunning the tapes of the Blue Sky Rolodex cards in closeup. Some of the names and phone numbers were those of advertising agencies or well-known stores, but there were others—in groups—that seemed odd. There were five different Greens, and the same number of Browns, Blacks and Whites. There were various Joneses with area codes that fixed their locations as San Diego, San Francisco, Chicago, Miami, Boston, New Orleans and New York. All these had to be discreetly checked—within the next eighteen hours.

By half past one, the array of TV sets was in place on the conference room table and the unscrambling device was operating by three o'clock. Using their federal status, two of Latham's most trusted A.T.F. agents were at the telephone company to review the long-distance calls made from the Blue Sky offices during the previous few months. The investigators did not quite understand why Latham had instructed them to lie and say that they were probing a criminal group smuggling untaxed cigarettes, but they obeyed the orders.

Another dedicated employee of the U. S. government was considerably less calm. He was worried, and his eyes—protected as usual by the dark glasses that inspired his CIA colleagues to speak of him as The Man With the Shades—hurt badly. They always did when he was under this kind of pressure. Downtown Washington was only eight miles away from the agency's two-hundred-and-nineteen-acre complex here in Virginia, but the deputy director's attention was focused on much more distant places as he strode through the main building's lobby of Georgia marble. Passing the romanticized bas-relief bust of former CIA Director Allen Dulles on the lobby's north wall, he thought of the latest bad news from Angola, the Philippines, Turkey and the budget makers of the U. S. Senate.

When he reached his third-floor office, he swallowed a pill and wondered what else would go wrong today. The answer came almost immediately. His plump secretary—*executive* secretary

171

—entered with a fistful of message slips.

"What's the bad news, Doris?"

Recognizing that he was in one of his moods, she simply thrust the cluster of papers at him. He riffled through them quickly. The Friday meeting of Working Group Six had been canceled, the director wanted a full report on the operation code-named "Skylark Tempo" by morning and Admiral Walford had called from San Diego with word that the air search had again found no trace of the vessel.

"Where the hell can it be?" he demanded.

"What?"

"An eight-thousand-ton freighter doesn't just disappear, damn it. What the *fuck* is going on?"

"Don't use that language to me," she answered indignantly. "Not on the day Shakespeare died."

Maybe she was losing her mind, he thought.

"It's April twenty-third. William Shakespeare died on April twenty-third, 1616—in England," she explained proudly. He guessed that this vital piece of intelligence had come to her in the evening course she was taking at George Washington U.

"Go away, Doris. Please just go away."

She did, but it didn't help at all. His eyes still hurt and the headache was growing worse by the second—and he had no idea what to do next. The Navy and Air Force had tracked the bloody ship four-fifths of the way across the Pacific, and it couldn't just vanish. It *had* to be there. The only question was *where*.

# 25

FOR REASONS that neither sociologists, food writers nor devout defenders of the Southern California dream have been able to explain, the Los Angeles area produces fine basketball teams but undistinguished Chinese restaurants. Todd Latham and Alison Gordon dined that night at one of the few good ones. Though Mr. Chow's modern decor was a bit much, they managed to concentrate on the food—and each other.

"No shop talk," she said as they were seated. She was tired of high-powered men who spoke of deals, properties, tax situations, lawsuits, office politics, contracts or corporate mergers.

Without touching on any of these dreary subjects, Latham proved he could be an interesting conversationalist. Shunning such standbys as inflation, the Arabs, tennis or the latest diet, Latham gently encouraged her to talk about herself. Even more unusual, he appeared to listen. She knew that some clever men did this as a pre-seduction tactic, but this one seemed to care.

By the time they had finished the dumplings and winter melon with ham soup, he had learned about her parents, high-school French teacher, college adventures in the drama club, Phi Beta Kappa key and reasons for joining the CIA in the mid

1960s—before the agency's name had been tarnished.

"Don't ask me about what I did for the agency. Even now, I've got this neurotic security hangup. They trained me well." She said it with a wry smile.

"And you performed very well. I wouldn't say that you were a household word, but people talked about Artemis and what she accomplished."

She stiffened.

"Sorry, Alison. If you'd rather not—"

"That name—it still bothers me."

"Alison, people respected you."

"I'm not ashamed of what I did for the agency, for the country. I didn't poison any wells or assassinate anybody," she said firmly. "I was the target . . . a lot of times. I shot the shooters, not innocent school kids. Jeezus, how did we get into this ancient history?"

"I was born in the Berkshires," Latham announced.

"You changing the subject?"

"It's a good place for children to grow up. My dad was a chemist for a paper company near Pittsfield, not far from Tanglewood where the Boston Symphony plays every summer."

"You're not bad at changing the subject."

"I wasn't good enough to play with the B.S.O., so I played baseball—high-school baseball. I was the pitcher."

"Pitch for Harvard?" she asked, and sipped more wine.

"How did you know I went to Harvard?"

"Somebody had to," she replied with a chuckle. "That was one of Mark's lines. He went to Yale."

"Somebody had to. Mark was a good man. I liked him."

"So did I. Listen, Todd. I don't have anything more to say about Mark. I'm not even sure that I'm a widow. If I was, it was a long time ago."

"I almost pitched a no-hitter once, but the other team got lucky. You're supposed to ask *how lucky*, Al."

"How lucky?"

"They pounded me for nine hits in one inning!" he recalled with a grin. "My big moment—and I blew it. Still, we took the Ivy League championship that year."

"Should we drink to that?"

"And to your fencing medal," Latham replied as the waiter set down scallops in brown bean sauce. "I've been reading about you, kid. Number-one female in the Pacific Conference three-weapons competition, right? You've got no secrets from this master detective, lady."

"The hell I don't. Eat your scallops."

"You sound like my mother."

"Stop hogging the rice."

"A *lot* like my mother." He asked about her next sculpture show. They finished dinner just in time for Gillespie's ten P.M. "set" at Donte's; the goateed jazz genius with the oddly angled horn performed brilliantly. Keeping his sometimes distracting but always colorful mugging and clowning to a minimum, he blew beautiful music—both fierce and delicate—and his excellent group added to the artistry.

Recognizing that tomorrow would be a critical day, Alison Gordon and Todd Latham left the crowded club at 11:30. They stopped en route to Beverly Hills for her to phone the video watcher.

"Nothing on any of the sets yet," Agajanian reported, "but I'm keeping busy. Got a book about L. A. that says Topanga and Malibu canyons used to be the haunts of bandits and smugglers."

"Wonder what ever happened to the smugglers," she replied and bade him stay alert. Two minutes before midnight, she led

Latham up the path to her door.

"All clear?" she asked suddenly.

"All clear," Hovde whispered from somewhere in the darkness. Though "they" were no longer following her, she was taking no chances. She told herself that she was not Artemis any more, but guarding the house around the clock was a routine and minimum precaution. When they reached the door, she turned to Latham. Perhaps it was the drink or the music, but he seemed very attractive.

"Go get your sleep," she said.

"Just like my mother. Funny, you don't look like her."

Now she wanted him.

"I don't feel like your mother," she answered.

They embraced and kissed, and she pressed against him as he stroked her back. His hands moved down her spine, and she began to move under his caress. Her heart was pounding; she heard herself making small guttural sounds. He pulled back, took her head in his hands and kissed her eyes and face gently.

"You're a better kisser than my mother," he said. "What are you doing tomorrow night?"

"Got a date with the Special Agent in Charge of the A.T.F. bureau."

"Lucky guy." Latham said.

They kissed again before he left her.

As he drove off, she tried to compute the unknown dangers that lay in the next twenty-three hours and fifty-six minutes. It was already April 24th. The battle would be joined soon.

# 26

SOME BUREAUCRATS might have played it safe, but Latham wasn't that sort of civil servant. The Los Angeles-area staff that he directed consisted of forty-seven agents, and this morning he was committing twenty-eight of them—more than half of his entire force—to an operation that he could not describe, being perpetrated by an enemy he could barely identify. He could not explain it at all.

As ordered, the agents assembled at A.T.F. headquarters in two groups. To avoid attracting attention, fourteen men arrived at 7:30 A.M. and the rest half an hour later. Each group was issued bulletproof vests, automatic weapons, radios and deliberately vague instructions. The 7:30 contingent was divided into four teams. Those designated Able, Baker and Charlie numbered four men each. Working with two agents per car, these teams were given stations near Century Electronics in Hollywood, the airport from which the blimp flew and Pacific Coast Security's building in Culver City. The "D" unit—a car with two agents—was to keep watch at the pilot's house where Mrs. Wilhite was hiding.

The men listened silently as Latham pinpointed each unit's location; they took notes as he specified the new radio frequencies and wondered why they were to report in only every two hours as a check of the communications gear. "And when you do," their boss said, "keep it under fifteen seconds on the air. No more. Any questions?"

"Did I miss something, Mr. Latham, or are you going to tell us now what this is all about?" a Chicano agent asked.

"Those are two good questions." The assembled men leaned forward for his answers, but they did not come. They looked at each other uneasily, and as they did Latham thought about the policewoman and the Riverside motorcycle cop and the strange situation at March Air Force Base. Could one of the men in this room also be involved? Whom could he trust?

"What kind of case is this, sir?" another agent asked.

"Big, and dangerous. We're up against some well-armed and violent people—a sophisticated outfit." He spelled out some additional rules. No man was to make any phone calls except in the presence of another agent, and at no time was any man to be alone. Latham did not have to spell it out. He was afraid that someone in this room might betray the bureau.

"One more thing. I might as well say it loud and clear so there won't be any misunderstanding. This is strictly our operation. No other law-enforcement agency—local or federal—knows about it. I don't want them to. I don't want the secretaries outside this office or anyone else in our own bureau to hear word-fucking-one about it. Not a word or a joke about it in the hall, in the elevators, in the john. Not a look or anything else that might indicate something heavy's going down."

A black agent named Frank Tolliver who had been with A.T.F. for some seven years shook his head. He had never experienced anything like this. It had to be really goddamn *baaad*, he thought.

"You'll get further instructions by radio—later," Latham told them. "Move out. Not in a gang. In twos, so you won't be noticed."

The agents exchanged glances again, and began to depart as Latham had ordered. They were troubled, but well-disciplined. Among the last to leave was Tolliver, who opened his mouth as he passed Latham but then closed it. One of the best men in the L. A. bureau, he was in charge of the "Baker" team.

"You're right, Frank," Latham told him. "It's *evil.*"

Tolliver smiled, for "evil" was one of his favorite words and Latham had borrowed it. The two men were comfortable with each other the way long-time comrades-in-arms become.

"Goes with the territory, man—evil, evil and more evil," Tolliver answered. "If I craved *good,* I'd have stayed in the Boy Scouts. I'd be the supreme world-wide chief in command of six zillion Scouts by now."

"No doubt about it." Latham watched him depart with the submachine gun. Tolliver had two sons in the Scouts—one a troop leader. Latham hoped that their father would be alive at nightfall.

When the other fourteen agents arrived at eight o'clock, he gave them the same instructions and minimal briefing. Then he told them that they were to serve as the mobile reserve, a strike force to go into combat later. He did not say that he didn't yet know where or when, or even why. What if the Blue Sky people didn't do anything today? What if he and Alison Gordon were wrong. What if whatever was to happen had no connection with the tens of millions of illegal handguns or their suppliers? The media and the government would crucify him, he thought.

He decided to risk it. His hatred of all those illegal and unnecessary guns told him he owed his unborn children at least that much.

The killing had to stop.

Across the city in the offices of A. B. Gordon Investigations, Agajanian slept on a couch while Ruth Tanaka O'Brien stared morosely at the television sets. Down the corridor in her own office, the head of the firm was staring too. She had not expected Hovde to bring an anti-tank weapon today.

"Indians jump the reservation, or is this World War Four?" she inquired.

"Did I miss Three?"

"Just testing to see whether you'd lost touch with reality. What's with the goddamn bazooka?"

"I was thinking . . . about Pacific Coast Security," Hovde said.

"Carew?"

"Him and the armored cars, Al. Lot of armored cars. I figured there was no harm in our having a bazooka, just in case."

She lit a cigarette, trying to understand.

"Why would we want to knock out an armored car, Don?"

He looked embarrassed, and a bit disappointed.

"Never can tell," he replied.

"What the hell! You're probably right," she said. "No harm in having a bazooka in your office these days. The way things are, you should have brought two."

"I did."

The phone rang. It was Latham.

"My people are all in position. What are yours doing?" he asked.

"Watching TV—a lot of TV—and playing with their toys.

We're all set for the Martians to land, if you know what I mean."

"I don't." He played along on the chance that the phone was tapped, "and I don't want to. Lord, I sure hope that we've figured this right."

"So do I." She took down his private number.

At half past eleven, he called to report that the "fat bird" was flying now—a message relayed from his team near the airfield. She wondered whether the fact that the blimp had lifted off an hour and a half later than usual meant something. Her recent experiences and the entire Blue Sky setup had convinced her that they were dealing with a covert operation, one that required strict communications security. All telephone conversations with Latham today would therefore be as ambiguous as possible.

The morning was gone, and nothing had happened. Maybe the nine video screens at Blue Sky had no role in what was to come. Bored and restless, Alison Gordon walked to the conference room to look at the line of sets. She found Ruth O'Brien seated comfortably, glancing up at the TVs every few seconds and knitting a sweater.

"Anything on the tubes?"

"Not even test patterns. I'd say that they aren't transmitting, Al. . . . What do you think?" Ruth held up a half-finished sleeve for approval.

"It's definitely *you.*"

"It's supposed to be for my *uncle* in Hawaii," she said gloomily.

Agajanian walked in and put down two large paper bags. Alison returned to her office, where the accountant found her a few minutes later. He thrust a waxed-paper package at her, and then added a container of coffee.

"What's this?" she asked.

"What do you care? You won't taste anything anyway." He opened a foil-lined bag containing half of a roasted chicken—his lunch.

He was right. Her focus was elsewhere as she began to eat her rare chiliburger with sprouts. She was nearly through with it before she spoke.

"Did I order this?"

"No. I was showing initiative. That's what they taught us at the infiltration and penetration school, remember?"

He was taking care of her. She felt both grateful and puzzled.

"What is this?"

"They didn't have shrimp salad," he announced. "You like shrimp salad. This is today's special—curried turkey on whole wheat with carrot strips. Good for night vision."

His clothes were rumpled and his face showed the effects of sleeping on the couch. She had no more appetite for an argument than for this sandwich. He was probably trying to cheer her up.

"Thanks . . . The blimp is up," she said.

"What does that mean?"

She did not know what to answer, so she finished the sandwich and drank some of the worst instant coffee that she had ever tasted. Even one and a half packets of chemical sweetener could not redeem it. Agajanian was talking about what he had discovered from studying Sidney Adams' credit-card slips. She was grateful that it was not important, for the nine TV screens were occupying her attention. Nine screens suggested nine cameras. Where?

"You're not listening," Agajanian complained.

"I'm sorry. Maybe you'd better put it in a memo, or we could talk about it tomorrow."

"By tomorrow, I might be shot to pieces, Al."

"You're right. The memo would be safer." She picked up the telephone to dial Latham's private number.

"Todd, it's me. What have you got?"

"Something, about the size of a grapefruit in my stomach, and a whole gang of very restless and unhappy people waiting for action. You see anything yet?"

She heard a shout.

"Just a second. Hang on, will you?"

She put down the instrument and hurried toward the conference room, Agajanian only a step behind her. She entered to find Ruth O'Brien pointing at the TV sets. The screens were filled with aerial views of traffic flowing in Los Angeles streets, a different location on each set.

"The blimp!"

"Got to be." Agajanian agreed. They watched the screens with her for another twenty seconds until they went blank. Then she ran back to the phone in her office.

"Saw a lot of things, all different. Just got a quick look. I figure it was a test, maybe a final check."

"Recognize any place or thing?" he asked.

"It was too brief. Even so, I take it for a good sign. I think they're warming up for the game, Todd."

"When does it start?"

"One hour and forty-one minutes," Roger Halleck announced in the Lexington headquarters, "and everything's right on schedule. Not a single one of those armored trucks is more than three minutes off."

"That's excellent, colonel," Zolner said loyally. Quietly pleased to have been chosen to help protect the command post, the former sergeant and another one of the men who had carried out the Century Electronics raid sat with machine guns at the ready.

"What do you say, George?" Halleck demanded.

The ex-squadron commander who now ran Blue Sky Promotions squirmed before he nodded. The fact that the goddamn Gordon woman had almost caught Jimmy Joyce at the hospital still bothered him. Perhaps it had been a mistake to stop watching her.

"So far, so good," Parks answered.

"Not good. *Great,*" Halleck exulted. "First time in history, George. Nobody else has ever taken eight armored cars full of cash at the same time—nobody. It's incredible."

"Be worth at least four million."

"And you helped plan it, George. Think of it. We're making history. They'll be naming streets after us. We'll be national heroes—all of us."

In the A.T.F. offices, the tension was becoming acute. It was after three o'clock now, and Latham had to consider other tactics. They had waited seven hours for the Blue Sky group to make its move, but nothing had happened. The units he had put in position early in the morning would be sullen and restless by now, stiff from sitting in cars and irritated from inaction. Maybe the Wilhite woman and those hiding her in the house at Largo Terrace knew the enemy's battle plan. He could reinforce Tolliver's team in half an hour, storm the house and seize them. He decided to discuss it with Alison Gordon at half past three. She called him first.

"They're on again—all the cameras," she announced. "Been on for six minutes. I think they're going to stay on. I think this is it."

"What do you see?"

"I'm in the conference room right now, and we're getting good pictures. The view is down. It's several parts of the city, but they're not paying any attention to buildings. It's trucks. Eight screens, eight trucks."

"What kind?"

"Can't quite tell. Seem to be medium-sized, gray. One is passing . . . yes . . . passing Cedars of Lebanon Hospital . . . Hey, another is rolling near the Civic Center where you are . . . Is that Hollywood Boulevard? The Chinese theater? . . . They're pushing in for a tight shot . . . Truck's stopping at a . . . I know that building. It's a bank . . . That's the Crocker National!"

Now Agajanian pointed at another screen.

"Wait a minute . . . That's the Bank of America on Figueroa," she said. "Men with bags . . . son of a bitch, those are armored cars."

"Pacific Coast Security?" Latham guessed.

"Got to be. Can't really see their markings, but I'd bet on it."

Hovde gestured toward the TV set at the far right.

"Another bank, Todd," she reported. "Don't know just where, but it's a . . . it's Barclay's . . . You recognize the area, Andy? Don?"

"Century City," Hovde said in his whisper.

"Sure . . . that's it . . . Okay, the truck at the Crocker National is leaving . . . Hey, that one on the left is rolling on Wilshire."

She put a cigarette in her mouth and the accountant lit it for her.

"Thanks . . . I'm trying to make some sense out of this, Todd . . . Got to be a pattern . . . No reason just to watch armored cars . . . Hey, one . . . two . . . three . . . four . . . *right,* five . . . are moving in traffic. I think they've finished their pickups . . . Sure, it's after three thirty. The banks are all closed."

"Heading back to Pacific Coast Security?" Latham asked.

"That's probably it . . . There's another . . . Now they're all rolling. Must be loaded with cash . . . Everything normal. Seven . . . eight . . . all moving at regular speed."

"What do you think?" Latham said.

"Don't know yet. . . . Maybe testing some security system. . . . What do you think, Andy?"

She glanced across at the accountant as he shook his head.

"Something lousy," he declared. He stood up, and began to strap on a bulletproof vest.

"What's that for?"

"Cold in here," Agajanian answered.

When she looked back at the screens, she saw one of the steel-sheathed trucks turn up an alley and move into a large courtyard almost completely surrounded by industrial buildings. It came to a stop.

"Something's happening," she reported and told Latham what she was watching. A second armored car neared that same alley. Just before it swung in, the driver in the first put on some kind of respirator and checked his watch. It was 3:40, time to turn on the gas that would disable the guards in the cash compartment behind him. He did so, then stepped from his vehicle as the other money car entered the courtyard. The driver in it turned off his engine, put on an identical mask and set off his gas. Within another ninety seconds, all eight armored cars were in the courtyard—visible only via the cameras in the blimp overhead. At 3:44, the drivers began to unlock the rear doors of their vehicles.

"Perfect . . . right on time," Halleck said.

"Couldn't be better," Parks agreed. The enthusiasm in the command post was contagious, irresistible. It was working exactly as they had planned, and the ex-USAF officer was feeling completely confident now. They were all grinning as they watched the masked drivers—each a loyal Lexington trooper—enter the money compartments. The group in the Blue Sky office could not see their allies step over the unconscious bodies of the gassed guards, but when the first bags of currency were tossed out, the men in the command post cheered.

"Look at that, will you?" Halleck shouted.

"Fantastic!" Carl Zelner said, watching raptly as the robbery continued.

While the money was being emptied from seven armored cars, the disabled guards in the eighth were carried to one of the other trucks and dumped beside their unconscious colleagues. The rear doors of the seven looted trucks were locked, and the drivers ripped off the uncomfortable masks and waved triumphantly to the cameras above.

"That's it. Damn it, that's the ball game!" Parks sang out and pointed at the screens. A green Dodge station wagon appeared on a screen, and stopped at the mouth of the alley. Meanwhile four of the drivers were taking off their caps and uniforms while the others threw the canvas sacks into the back of the empty armored car. Two of those still in uniform squeezed in beside the money; the other two took their places up front. As the motor of the money truck started, the "civilians" walked quickly to the street and slipped into the station wagon. They found sports coats and light zippered jackets on the seats, then reached down for the M-16s and handguns on the floor.

It was 3:46 when the armored car come out of the alley and turned left. The station wagon followed it for six blocks to Pico, where it slowed for the turn onto the busy thoroughfare. At that moment, the traffic light turned red and the driver of the armored car saw the black-and-white police car. He hit the brakes just in time to avoid violating the law. The policeman behind the wheel smiled, wagged his index finger in mild reproof and pointed to the light. The armored-car driver grinned back, saluted in apology—and hoped.

"Look straight ahead," he said to the man beside him, "and don't do anything dumb. Keep your hands away from your gun. Just talk to me as if everything's normal."

"*Jeezus*, Pete, you think it's—"

"I certainly do, and so do those cops. Hang loose. We're on our way."

"They're *looking* at us, Pete."

"That's fine. You talk away, chum. Look bored. Yawn. Fine. That's *good*. Couple of seconds more, and we're gone."

Now the light changed to green, and the traffic began to move. The policeman was not paying any attention to them now, he seemed to have found a busty blonde in a Mercedes convertible much more interesting. The armored car made its turn, and the threat was behind them.

"Let's go," Halleck said as he rose. "They'll be at the airport in twenty-one minutes, and we'd better be there. Guard the fort, sergeant," he told Zolner.

"Yes, sir. It was terrific, wasn't it?"

"It was highly professional," Halleck said as he started for the door. "A first-class military operation. In half an hour we'll be airborne with the money. We won this battle, and we're going to win the war. Nobody can stop us now."


"There she is," Halleck said, as he guided the jeep through the entrance of the Hawthorne Municipal Airport. He pointed beyond the twin-engine Cessna, lifting off three hundred yards down the runway, toward the blimp, tethered by a dozen ground lines but still swaying slightly in the late afternoon breeze. "And here comes the truck."

The armored car, crammed with currency, was less than two minutes behind schedule—no small achievement in the heavy traffic of the San Diego Freeway.

"You *really* did it, Rog," said Parks, seated beside him.

"Commander's only as good as his troops. Learned that at Benning more than thirty years ago," Halleck replied. They watched the truck and the station wagon pull to a halt beside the airship. Then Halleck descended from the jeep, looking around carefully.

"All clear, George. Let's help them load."

As they walked toward the blimp, the back doors of the armored car opened and two men in Pacific Coast Security uniforms emerged and scanned the area in a full 360-degree circle.

"Perimeter secure, sir," one reported.

"Right. Break out the sacks."

Peering down from the control tower ninety yards away, Frank Tolliver completed his count and shook his head. His Baker squad of four men would have a very hard time coping with eight or nine men. Latham's last radio message had warned him that the crew of the blimp was probably armed. If that wasn't enough, there was the problem of the armored car. Where the hell was Latham and the mobile reserve?

"Shit, shit, *shit,*" Tolliver whispered and raised the radio to try again. "Baker to SAC. Baker to SAC . . . We need you, man. Come in, SAC. Come in, SAC . . ."

There was no answer. This was the third time that he had tried to make radio contact in the past ten minutes. Now the armored car was empty, and they were beginning to carry the bags to the gondola. Time was running out before his eyes.

189

"What did you say this was about?" asked an uneasy air-traffic controller.

"Want to get arrested?"

"No, sir—"

"Then shut up. This is a federal deal, so do what I said. You wouldn't like Leavenworth."

Where the hell was the goddamn cavalry? Tolliver thought. It was never—well, hardly ever—this late in the movies. Latham's last radio message had been absolutely clear. Under no circumstances were those bags from the Pacific Security truck to leave the airport.

"I think you're making a mistake, sir," the controller ventured. "The blimp people are okay. I've spoken with Captain Budlett several times."

There was no more time.

"Look, you sure as hell aren't going to talk to him today—not a word," the black agent ordered. "I'm going down there in a second, and there's likely to be a lot of shooting. If you say one damn word on that radio I'll be back up to blow you away. Do you read me?"

The controller was so frightened that he could only nod his assent and stare at Tolliver's submachine gun. Tolliver waved the muzzle past him once more to reinforce the threat before he went down the stairs and joined the other three agents concealed behind a parked car.

"Where's Latham?" one of them asked.

"Don't need him. You've got Fearless Frank Tolliver, the new Clint Eastwood."

"You don't look like Eastwood."

"Watch your lip, honky," Tolliver joked as he checked the clip in his weapon.

"It's hero time, huh?"

190

Tolliver nodded to the man who'd spoken. "You got a way with words, Goldblatt. You should have finished law school."

Goldblatt's response was a grunt and an obscene one-finger salute.

Tolliver laid out his plan succinctly. He and Perilli would drive up to the men in one car to explain that they were surrounded and must surrender at once, while O'Leary circled around the control tower to cover the group in the station wagon. Goldblatt would wait with the radio in the other car.

"They're not going to surrender to three or four guys," Goldblatt said.

"This is no time for negative thinking."

"Frank, they'll shoot the crap out of you. They've got firepower."

"So do we."

Goldblatt looked at the others. Their faces showed no emotion. Only their eyes signaled their inward resistance to the unequal encounter.

"And what do I do after they've taken out you and O'Leary?"

"Wally, you just crash your car into that gondola at about seventy-five miles an hour."

Tolliver gestured to O'Leary. As soon as he was out of sight, the others climbed into their sedans. Tolliver waited twenty seconds to give O'Leary time to get into position before he started his motor. All but the last few bags were in the gondola. Tolliver thought about his wife, silently cursed Latham and stepped on the gas pedal.

He was forty yards from the armored car when one of the men standing beside the station wagon opened fire.

Then it happened. Several cars—Tolliver was too busy to count exactly how many—roared onto the runway.

They were moving at high speed, but that did not seriously

191

affect Latham's shooting. Leaning out of the lead vehicle, he shot the man who had fired at Tolliver.

There was a melée of bullets. O'Leary dropped one of the Pacific Coast Security guards and wounded another. The group from the station wagon returned the fire, and someone was shooting from the airship. Goldblatt raked the gondola with four bursts, and the glass in its windows shattered into hundreds of tiny javelins, blinding two of the Lexington men inside.

"In the truck! Get into the truck!" Halleck shouted. He dropped to the runway, crawled infantry-style to the front of the armored car and slipped in behind the wheel as Parks and a Pacific Coast Security guard jumped into the rear compartment. Another of the Lexington men tried to find safety within the steel walls, but staggered back under several bullets that hit him in the legs.

Now Halleck led a counterattack, using the armored car as its cutting edge. The federal agents, finding their bullets bouncing off the steel plates, were forced to fall back and take cover behind their cars.

Even that did not ensure safety. Halleck, seeing the effectiveness of Goldblatt's fire, turned the massive truck and drove it directly at him. Goldblatt barely managed to jump out before the armored car crashed into his own like a massive fist.

Encouraged by the success of the armored car, the Lexington gunmen maintained a heavy crossfire that kept the Treasury force pinned down. Two Pacific Coast Security guards zigzagged to the money bags and tossed the last few sacks into the gondola.

"We've got 'em!" Halleck shouted.

A Porsch convertible and another car had pulled up on the runway, and Alison Gordon was sprawled on the cement, firing short, accurate bursts from a very small submachine gun. Nine-millimeter slugs ended the life of one of the robbers and crippled another guard at the gondola. But two others were ripping at the ropes, clawing loose the nylon hold-downs to free the blimp.

"Don! Get that armored car!" she called to Hovde, already down on one knee with the bazooka. "Shoot!"

The rocket flew straight and true, blasting open the back of the armored car as if it were a plastic toy. The force of the explosion knocked the truck over on its side, and Hovde could see that George Parks and the guard with him in the money compartment were dead.

Groggy and bleeding from his mouth and ears, Roger Halleck managed to open a door and climb out. Eight of the dozen lines mooring the blimp were already loose. He was stumbling through the bullets and chaos, operating on desperation, not intelligence. He tore another line loose, and the blimp bobbed in response. One—perhaps two—more . . .

His hands were raw, but he was past feeling the pain. He was tugging at another line when Latham shot him twice.

The federal agents raked the disheartened and disorganized Lexington men with fierce fire from two sides, and within a few minutes it was over. Half of the men who had pulled off the greatest robbery in California's history were dead or seriously wounded. The three who were left saw that they would be slaughtered in the crossfire and laid down their weapons.

As a group of A.T.F. agents collected their guns, Alison Gordon and Todd Latham ran to the gondola. Stepping over the body of Roger Halleck, they climbed in just as the blimp pilot was about to sever another line with a broken piece of window glass.

"Drop it!" Latham commanded. Alison didn't say anything. She swung the Mac-10 into the side of the pilot's face, knocking him away from the key cord.

"It's over," Latham said.

Then they heard the explosion. They spun, looked out through the smashed windows and saw a car burning. It was her Porsche. A salvo of bullets had set off the fuel tank. Black smoke poured skyward from the wreck, enveloped by leaping yellow flames.

"You got insurance?" Latham asked.

"The hell with that," she said. "The government's going to pay."

"Don't hold your breath," he said as Agajanian entered the gondola.

"That car cost me nineteen thousand dollars, Todd."

"Nineteen thousand two hundred, to be exact," the accountant recalled. "I see you've met Mr. Budlett."

"Not formally. Get him out of here, Andy, and call me an ambulance."

"Garbage truck might be more appropriate," Agajanian said as he holstered his automatic. When they left the gondola, they saw seven corpses.

Four A.T.F. agents clustered around Hovde, who was pointing the bazooka at the airship.

"You can put that down now, Don," she said while Latham sent men to reattach all the ground lines to the blimp. Hovde lowered the rocket launcher and trudged off to his car to stow the anti-tank weapon in the trunk.

"My name is Goldblatt. That's some iron. What agency are you people with?"

"Mighty nice to meet you, Mr. Goldblatt," Agajanian answered briskly. Then he walked over to Alison Gordon and to Latham, who was speaking earnestly to Tolliver.

"I need an hour, Frank, and I'm counting on you to buy it for me. Cops will be ten deep here in a couple of minutes. Do whatever you have to do—threaten, lie, talk about national security, I don't care. We've got to keep this off the radio—even the police radio—until we pick up the rest of these people."

"I'll do a medley of my biggest hits," Tolliver promised. He recognized Alison from the photos in the newspapers. "Thanks for dropping in with the bazooka, Miss Gordon."

"I didn't see any bazooka," Latham said. Alison knew she would hear from him about the illegal rocket launcher later. Even though it had saved their lives, he could not ignore such a powerful military weapon in private hands. But now Blue Sky Promotions came first. Latham had four agents follow him and escorted Alison Gordon to his car. They heard distant sounds of police sirens as they drove out of the airport. She wondered how much currency was in those bags. Latham wouldn't even care, she realized suddenly—and for some reason that pleased her.

"What are you smiling about?" he asked.

"None of your business." She turned on the radio. Lauri Adams was singing "You Are the Sunshine of My Life." Stevie Wonder had done it better.

# 27

At 5:25 P.M., Latham decided that he couldn't wait any longer for Dilchik to arrive with the search warrant.

"Chop 'em," he said into the walkie-talkie. With that an A.T.F. electronics specialist in the office building basement severed the telephone lines that served Blue Sky Promotions, then walked to the freight elevator where Goldblatt stood silently with a fibreboard instrument case. A janitor getting ready to go home noticed it.

"That a trumpet?" he asked.

"It's a machine gun."

The janitor laughed and the two agents took the elevator up to the ninth floor. They changed over to the stairwell, where Goldblatt took out the automatic weapon and sat down to rest his tired feet.

On the tenth floor, the receptionist at Blue Sky Promotions looked at her watch again. Parks should call in at any moment with word that the blimp was airborne. A minute after that she'd walk out of here for the last time. By morning, Blue Sky would have promoted itself out of existence, and Lexington would be operating from the new command post in San Diego before the police could connect it with the armored-car robbery. She was enjoying this prospect when a well-dressed woman carrying a dispatch case walked in.

"I'm the Avon lady," Alison Gordon announced brightly.

"Sorry. We're closed."

"You haven't tried our *gorgeous* new fragrance, have you? Just a whiff? It's marvelous . . ."

The receptionist controlled her annoyance. Colonel Halleck had repeatedly emphasized the importance of discipline and normalcy for Lexington today, and for the whole new nation tomorrow.

"No, thanks. Try the people next door," she suggested. The pushy vendor went right ahead opening her case, rattling on how this fresh scent was *delighting* women *everywhere*. She extracted a spray can and beamed.

"It's called *Irresistible*."

A single squirt of the same disabling gas that knocked out the dog had the receptionist dazed and choking. The room blurred, then began to spin. With her strength fading, the woman fought to reach the buzzer under her desk. She was vaguely aware of someone vaulting over the low barrier, striking her arm a numbing blow and shoving her against the wall. Then there was more gas and, finally, blackness.

Latham and three other Treasury men came through the door. Alison Gordon stood up and pointed at the limp body.

"Works on people too," she said. Latham drew his .38, and shot out the "eye" of the closed-circuit TV camera concealed in the wall. She watched as he led his agents down the corridor on a dead run, one pair sweeping through the offices on the left and other bursting into those on the right. He had told her that this was a federal raid, and the government didn't want to pay for her funeral. She understood that, and his unspoken caring for her.

Someone was testing the doorknob. Doc Shephard entered, stiffened at the sight of the .357 she was pointing at him and noticed the unconscious receptionist sprawled in the swivel chair.

"Nobody you know," Alison assured him, as she led him down the passageway to the command-post entrance, where the A.T.F. team was handcuffing three grim-faced men in shirt-sleeves.

"What's the charge?" one of them demanded.

"Loitering with intent to commit a felony," Latham replied.

"What felony? We've got rights. This isn't Russia, you know. You've got to read us our rights."

"You have the right to remain silent," Latham said, "and if you don't I'm going to break your face. You also have the right to cremation at public expense if this gun goes off *by accident.* If you're just crippled, your mother has the right to see you every visiting day. Did I leave anything out, Perilli?"

"That about covers it, sir. Should I dump them in a closet?"

Latham nodded, and Doc Shephard went to work on the door. This time it only took him two and a half minutes to solve the locks, but the heavy portal would not budge. He considered the situation for a long time.

"We've got a problem. Some bastard has bolted it from the inside."

"We got a solution?" Alison Gordon asked. Shephard unbuttoned his shirt, reached in and pulled out what seemed to be a bulging money belt. He sliced it open with a switchblade, took out a yellow putty and began to mold it into mounds that covered the door's hinges. Latham recognized the odor.

198

"C-three, huh?"

"Yeah. Hate to use it unless I have to. It's so crude." Doc Shephard inserted fuses into the plastic explosive, and when they all stepped back twenty feet he blew the door off its hinges. Zolner opened fire at once. The other Lexington man guarding the headquarters, partially stunned by the blast, fell forward onto the door.

Zolner went on shooting until a ricocheting Treasury bullet pierced his throat. The government agents found him—barely alive—in the command post, his eyes still shining with hate. The expression on Doc Shephard's face was a combination of shock and revulsion. To a skilled burglar whose professional craft made violence unnecessary, this was primitive horror.

"The first two numbers are eleven and twenty-three," Alison reminded him.

Doc Shephard didn't seem to hear her. He surveyed the bullet-ravaged command post, the linoleum floor splattered with blood, the broken glass from several of the TV screens and the body of Carl Zolner.

"I suppose you people get used to it," he said.

"Not really," Latham answered.

"*Never,*" Alison Gordon said.

"Eleven and twenty-three," the burglar repeated. While Latham radioed below for the backup team and a medical unit, Shephard resumed his efforts to unlock the massive door of the vault. Twice he called out for silence. It was only after Zolner had been carried away in a litter and the talky federal agents were out of the command post that he could focus all his experience, cunning and intensity.

"Seventeen," he said softly.

Alison wanted to sit down and light a cigarette, but did neither. Until technicians had gone over each inch of the chamber searching for fingerprints or fragments, hair, dust particles or any other evidence, she must touch or disturb nothing. Shephard had the third number of the combination, so the wait would not be long. Suddenly he stopped, looked across at her and sighed.

"Last one's a bitch, Al."

"You'll get it."

"Maybe my hands are sweating because I'm not used to working with cops around. It feels . . . unreal."

"It is, but it'll be finished soon. You'll get that fourth number and then you can take off—with my thanks. Come on, get back to work."

He dried his hands on his trouser legs and closed his eyes to reestablish his concentration. He forced himself to focus utterly . . . there was nothing in the world but this vault. The perspiration was running down his back, but he didn't feel it. He rotated the dial very slowly, listening to each click. Then he turned it again even more tenderly, like a surgeon probing an exposed brain. Was that *it?* He repeated the process. Yes, that had to be be the fourth goddamn number.

"Here goes, Al."

Eleven . . . twenty-three . . . seventeen . . . four.

It worked. He pulled, felt the heavy door move and stepped aside immediately—there could easily be some kind of booby trap inside. He drew the door wider inch by inch, his heart thumping, and then warily opened it all the way. He waited behind it for forty-five seconds in case there was a delayed-action bomb. Finally he leaned past the door and peeked in.

"This is crazy, Al. Take a look."

There was nothing in the vault but a chair, an end table—and a phone. It had neither dial nor push-buttons—just a plain black telephone sitting on a small wooden table. The steel walls were naked and seamless, unmarked by any panels, openings or compartments. Doc Shephard had broken into more than forty large vaults and they had all been lined with safety deposit boxes. This one was not. He started to feel let down.

"A box like this to protect a *telephone*, Al?"

"It must be a very special telephone."

She saw no documents, no plastic bags of dope, no heaps of currency, no gold bars, diamonds or guns. Latham would be disappointed too, she thought. She looked up to see Doc glancing at his wristwatch.

"There should have been bugles, Doc. You did a great job. Tony's right. There's *nobody* better."

He dried his palms on the pants again, and they shook hands.

"You ought to get a medal," she told him, "but all I can give you is my thanks."

"That's enough. I was glad to do it for you, Al."

He took a last look at the strange contents of the vault and walked out. "It's open," he told Latham as they passed in the corridor. The sudden sound of the telephone bell shocked Alison, and she hesitated. It rang again; there was only one thing to do. As Latham reached the entrance to the vault, she picked up the phone and listened.

"This is Caesar. Report on the operation."

It was a strong, masculine voice, full of authority. Caesar was probably a code name. What should she say? The man who called himself Caesar was expecting to speak to a specific person, almost surely the head of Blue Sky Promotions. The vault made it obvious that no more than one or two people were to have access to this telephone. That was it. This was a "hot line"— a direct link from Blue Sky to some higher authority. Who? Where?

"How did it go?" the voice demanded.

Could the call be traced? Maybe she could stall him, get him to say something more that might be valuable; even one additional fact would help.

"The operation was a complete success," she answered in as deep and muffled a speech as she could. The line went dead immediately. Caesar, whoever he was, was smart, quick and decisive.

"Who was it?" Latham asked.

"Called himself Caesar. He said, 'This is Caesar. Report on the operation.' I guess he meant the armored-car heist."

"Caesar?"

"Right. He said, 'How did it go?' When I tried to string him along he hung up."

Latham scanned the almost empty vault, shook his head and reached out to caress her face.

"You gave it a good shot."

"I think it's a direct line, Todd. Maybe you can trace it to Caesar. He's the one with the answers."

"I'm still working on the questions," Latham admitted. "Where was that blimp going? Why such an elaborate setup for a robbery, even one this large? What sort of a mob is this? Who put this caper together?"

"Caesar's the boss. I could hear command in his voice—flat power," she explained as they left the vault. "Take a look around. You ever hear of any armed robbery outfit with this kind of gear? This is something big."

"Christ, I was hoping it was over."

"Not yet. Not until we find out what *it* is—the whole thing. Not until we take Caesar," she predicted.

They heard A.T.F. reinforcements entering the Blue Sky suite and started down the hall to meet them. Penetrating that vault was supposed to clear up all the loose ends, she reflected wearily. Well, it hadn't. Now Latham saw Dilchik.

"Glad you could make it," he said sarcastically.

"Don't blame me. The judge was on the phone with his broker for twenty minutes, and the traffic was rotten," Dilchik replied. "Everything okay?"

"Just fine. We raided this place without any legal authority, arrested some guys, took a door out with a plastic blast people must have heard in Glendale, and then shot a couple of fellows—"

"Holy shit!" Dilchik erupted.

"—then we illegally opened a vault. You should have been here, Eli."

"It's all legal now," the agent said, handing him the two search warrants. Latham examined them and shoved the papers in his breast pocket.

"So you got the warrants, everything's okay," Dilchik said, puzzled to see Alison shake her head. "What's wrong?"

"Plenty," Latham answered.

When they got to the lobby, he saw a crowd outside the front of the building that looked like an opening night. "Give the people what they want, and they'll all come."

Alison Gordon pointed to the back door. They left by that exit, followed by four other agents. When they reached their cars, Latham gave them final instructions.

"We want to take these people alive. Fact is, we *have* to. Let's roll."

They got into their cars and set off for 286 Largo Terrace in Hawthorne. There wasn't a cloud in the sky or a trace of smog, and the temperature was a pleasant 79 degrees. The orange solar ball was just beginning to touch the horizon—another of the sunsets that made Southern California such a desirable place to live.

# 28

THE CENTRAL American night was hot and thick with humidity, but the El Panama Hotel on the fashionable Via Espana was air-conditioned. Visitors from a dozen countries who had flown to this duty-free paradise were shielded from the heat by their gracious Hilton hosts, whose compassion included lining the lobby with a flower shop, expensive gift shops and the newsstand where the two intelligence agents were meeting.

Ignoring the heaps of today's *La Republica* and *Star & Herald*, they were pretending to browse among the guidebooks, paperback mysteries, two-day-old editions of the *Miami Herald* and a variety of magazines that ranged from the Japanese edition of *Reader's Digest* to the Spanish versions of *Cosmopolitan* and *Billboard*. Unable to find this month's *Playboy*, Major Orloff studied the bare-breasted Cuna Indian maidens in a pictorial souvenir book.

"This better be good," Orloff said tersely.

"I'm afraid it's bad," the black photographer replied. "Our man checking out that mental ward at Amador has missed three meetings. That's not like him."

"You called an emergency rendezvous for *that*, Bob? Have you lost your mind?"

"They say *he* did. They've got him in the nuthouse."

"Maybe he is crazy."

"Like a fox. He's a damn good field man, major, and he's in trouble."

Orloff raised his eyes from photos of the colorful *molas* woven on the San Blas isles and looked around to see if anyone was watching.

"Can we slip somebody into that ward?"

"They won't let anyone near him, major. *They* say he's homicidal. *I* say we have to get him out—fast."

"This is tough, Bob. If we . . . well, we could very easily blow his cover . . . and ours." He saw immediate anger in the photographer's face reflected in the display-case glass.

"We don't abandon our people, do we, major?"

It was more than a naked challenge. It was close to an insult to Orloff, to the entire Criminal Investigation Division and the U. S. Army itself.

"I'll need authority to move. Have to cable Washington. Jeezus, they won't like this. I'm not sure they'll *believe* it."

"A.S.A.P.?" asked the black man.

"Tonight. You know—if you're wrong, we'll look like total imbeciles."

"I'm right."

Orloff shrugged unhappily, trudged across the lobby through the tourists heading for the gambling casino and stepped out into the steamy night. He wondered how he could really expect those comfortable staff officers and Pentagon desk jockeys to act on this unlikely report. They might decide that he was crazy too.

It was six degrees cooler in Hawthorne and the humidity was less than half of that in Panama, but the two men who unloaded the nineteen-inch color set from the Sony TV Services truck were perspiring. It wasn't because of the weight of the video machine or the bulletproof vests under their coveralls. They were sweating out the timing of the assault on 286 Largo Terrace only fifteen yards away.

Perfect coordination was essential in order to avoid bloodshed. No one inside knew about the violent confrontations at the airport and the Blue Sky offices, according to the A.T.F. team watching the house. As far as the federal agents could tell, there were four people in the house—Gloria Budlett, the blimp pilot's wife; Mrs. Wilhite—who had not actually been seen since she arrived; some unidentified, stocky Caucasian, photographed when he went out twice to buy groceries; and Sergeant Elizabeth Wade who had returned at three P.M.

"Wade is armed," Latham had said, "and the others could be too. Mrs. Budlett has a pistol permit. Maybe they've got a couple of M-16s in the freezer. Be careful."

The agents were in position. It was time to start the assault. Seated in Latham's car thirty yards away across the street, Alison Gordon and Todd Latham watched Tolliver and Dilchik carry the TV set up the flagstone path to the front door. They set it down and rang the bell.

"Everybody stand by," Latham said softly into the walkie-talkie. "Okay, get set . . . door's opening . . . a couple of inches. Go, Smitty."

A block away in a phone booth, A.T.F. Special Agent Oscar Smith finished dialing Budlett's house. If the plan worked, the phone should distract at least one of those inside.

"Yes?" Mrs. Budlett said.

Tolliver could only see a thin sliver of her, for the door was barely open. There was a goddamn chain on it. He could hear the phone ringing.

"Set's all fixed, lady," Tolliver announced. "That's one thirty-one even. We can't take checks."

"What?"

"Don't blame me. It's company policy," he apologized as Dilchik reached to pick up the TV. The ringing stopped. Someone had picked up the phone.

"You've got the wrong house," Gloria Budlett said as she jerked the door shut. It did not close; Dilchik had rammed a three-inch piece of pipe into the opening. Mrs. Budlett began to scream, and Tolliver tossed the concussion grenade that knocked her into a coat tree.

"Mrs. Budlett? This is Mr. Livermore at Sears," Smith said into the telephone. "There's a little problem with that check you sent us."

Elizabeth Wade did not reply. At the sound of the blast she dropped the phone and ran into the front room. She barely heard the agents smashing the windows in and breaking through the panel on the back door.

Tolliver stepped back a yard, hurled himself against the weakened front door and burst the chain. He charged in, but spun under the impact of three rounds. The bulletproof vest saved his life. The man at the top of the stairs who had shot him was not wearing one, and Dilchik's bullets brought him tumbling down in a pinwheel of arms and legs.

"Hold it!"

Elizabeth Wade turned to face a man with a submachine gun.

"You're under arrest," Goldblatt ordered. "Drop that piece."

She did not. Instead she stood there calculating her chances.

"I'm a federal agent. Put it down."

"Sure." But she suddenly raised the .38, forcing Goldblatt to shoot at her right arm. The handgun flew from her fist and left the woman bleeding and cursing.

"You okay, Wally?" Latham called from the front door.

"Terrific. Get a meat wagon."

As Alison Gordon entered the house, she nearly collided with Dilchik who was bending over Mrs. Budlett and handcuffing her. The concussion grenade had half shredded her blouse, injured her eardrum and somehow blown off one shoe.

"You have the right to remain silent," Dilchik informed her.

"She can't hear you," Alison said. "Eardrum's gone."

"I know. Hell, she's unconscious too, but rules are rules."

While Dilchik finished the litany, Latham, Alison Gordon and Tolliver went upstairs.

There were four closed doors on the second floor. Any one of them could be booby-trapped or sheltering more people with guns. Latham gestured the others to step back. He turned the knob of the first slowly. When there was no explosion, he swung the door wide.

"I shall not speak unto the idolaters," Juanita Mae Wilhite declaimed loudly, "or unto the atheistic traitors who shall all be struck down. Vengeance is mine, sayeth the Lord." She pointed an index finger at them accusingly and began to sing a psalm.

"What do you think?" Latham asked.

"She's out to lunch," Tolliver replied. They searched the room, found no weapons and summoned another agent to take the woman downstairs.

The next door Latham opened exposed a closet filled with sheets, towels, pillowcases and a carton of incendiary grenades. Alison Gordon tried the third door. It was a windowless room crammed with shortwave radio equipment—gear that could reach halfway around the world. Why would armored car robbers need it?

"My turn," Tolliver announced as they reached the last door. He twisted the knob just enough to disengage the metal tongue, then kicked it open. There was no blast of explosives, no burst of bullets, no sound at all. The room was empty. The closet, however, was not.

"Meet Mr. Carew," she invited.

"Thank God, you're here," he said loudly. "I was praying that you'd find me. I've been a prisoner of these devils for days."

He was obviously lying.

"It was a *nightmare*, Miss Gordon. Kidnapped by thugs, threatened and beaten—a total horror."

He was smooth-shaven, neatly dressed in clean clothes and smelled of some costly cologne. There was not a bruise or mark of any sort on him.

"Mr. Carew, I'd like to introduce your rescuers—the U. S. Treasury."

"Treasury?"

"This is Mr. Latham, who's the Special Agent in Charge of law enforcement operations for the L. A. office of the Alchohol, Tobacco and Firearms Bureau. And that's Mr. Tolliver of his staff."

A fake smile wreathed Carew's face as he held out his hand. Latham didn't take it.

"Where are the guns?" he demanded instead.

A realist and a coward, the president of Pacific Coast Security realized that he had to choose—right now. If *they* were here, *they* must have killed or captured everyone else in the house. *They* could not have found this "safe house" by accident. Others in Lexington must have been taken and broken too. Maybe all the leaders—perhaps even Colonel Halleck and the admiral— were in their hands. He had to convince Latham that he'd had no part in it—prove that he really was a prisoner and an upstanding citizen. The Treasury agents must know a lot already. Christ, Lexington was falling apart—maybe already demolished.

He'd buy his own ticket out of here by telling them about the guns. Why not? The weapons were outside U. S. territorial waters, so whatever Carew said could have no effect. If Lexington prevailed, that's what he could say to Halleck later. Meanwhile, it shouldn't be that hard to string along these lower-class civil servants and the pushy Beverly Hills woman.

"Where are they?" Latham insisted.

"On a freighter—about two hundred miles off Ensenada. I heard them talking about it. They didn't know I was listening."

"How many?"

"Thousands and thousands. Machine guns, mortars, anti-tank weapons. It's simply awful."

Latham's eyes shone bright and bitter in triumph. He had finally found his guns, his ghosts . . . his mortal enemies.

# 29

THE NUMBER on the door was 508 and the gold-leaf letters beneath it spelled out KRAWITZ & SEYMOUR, CERTIFIED PUBLIC ACCOUNTANTS. Two of the eight men who worked here actually did audits, but not for sportswear manufacturers or liquor wholesalers. They worked for the U.S. Government. This was a clandestine sub-branch of the Los Angeles "station" of the CIA.

"You look tired," Alison Gordon said to Todd Latham. That was hardly surprising; the booking of the various prisoners and the interrogation of Carew had lasted until close to midnight. It was all work. Then they had been on the phone to Washington for another two hours.

"You look beautiful," he replied.

"Are you sure you want to do this? Your people won't like it."

"I'd like to get those guns."

They entered the suite and found themselves facing a receptionist through a glass panel open just an inch.

"Mr. Jennings?" Latham asked.

"Out. Can anyone else help you?"

"How about Mr. Nelson?"

The receptionist nodded. The passwords—names of country music stars—would continue until the end of the month, when they would be replaced by baseball players of the 1960's. She pressed the buzzer that released the inner door's lock. As soon as they entered, the door clicked shut and they saw a heavyset man coming toward them.

"Yes?"

"My name's Latham. This is A.B. Gordon."

"Uh huh."

"We're looking for Mr. Acuff."

"Uh huh."

"We'd like to use the phone."

"Been expecting you. You're right on time." Then he led them into a windowless office, unlocked a desk drawer and took out a brown push-button telephone.

"Secure line," he said.

When he left, Latham locked the door from the inside and pointed at the phone.

She was talking to the deputy director (Ops) in Virginia, a brilliant and dedicated cloak-and-dagger veteran with thirty-two years of experience. They had known each other for more than a dozen years. Somehow, even though there was mutual respect, they were not comfortable with each other.

"How are you?" he asked. He really wanted to know. He was still concerned.

"All right. And you?"

She could visualize him behind the big, old-fashioned wooden desk that he'd had so long. He had been gray-haired for years, and he'd be wearing the sunglasses that he'd needed since The Other Side did something terrible to his eyes in Germany in the 1950's, when the Cold War burned at its hottest. Among professionals in the trade, he was known as The Man With the Shades.

"No complaints. Well, there are some new faces. Alison, your message said you needed a secure line. How can I help you?"

"I'm helping you." She told him the entire story.

"Two hundred miles or so off the coast of Ensenada," she repeated, "and they were supposed to deliver the money by blimp. Latham's team counted over five million one in those bags. He's right here. He can tell you about it."

The brief silence that followed told her a lot. He was mentally drafting a scenario for evasion, half-truth or deception. There was no malice involved, of course. He did it routinely, effortlessly.

"Perhaps Mr. Latham ought to tell his superiors at Treasury."

"He did that. They said they'd look into it, but he has the impression that they don't place their full trust and confidence in his assessment."

Two hundred miles off Ensenada. Almost exactly what the informer in Hong Kong had reported.

"This sounds like navy business," he said, testing her.

"That could be risky because I've got another one for you."

"Yes?"

"There's a naval officer in on this. Code name is Popeye." She heard the man in Virginia suck in his breath.

"So you don't trust the Navy either?" he asked slowly.

"Can't. If we tell the Navy, Popeye could tip the freighter or Caesar—"

"Also unidentified."

"Completely, but maybe not for long. Latham's men are checking out that hot-line setup."

More silence.

"It's all very complex," he said with his usual cautious understatement. "You've done quite a . . . a fine job."

"Didn't phone for compliments. That shipload of weapons

has to be stopped. Those aren't the standard Saturday-night specials. That's combat infantry hardware, and a lot of it."

"In international waters. The U. S. Navy couldn't touch it anyway," he reminded her.

"This sounds like Navy business. There's just one government agency that could handle this, and it isn't the goddamn Department of Agriculture. You know it, and I know it—and so does Todd Latham."

He coughed and cleared his throat before he replied. "Things have changed, Alison. It's all different now. There are substantial limitations on our activities, legal restrictions. The intervention in international waters that you seem to suggest—"

"Say it straight out."

"We don't do that sort of thing anymore."

"Bullshit."

"We don't do it because we can't. Why don't you try the French or the Israelis?"

"Why don't you cut the crap and spare me the sanctimonious jokes. Somebody's moving enough hardware to start a small war, and you're singing me The Ten Commandments. Here . . . you talk to him." She thrust the phone at Latham.

The conversation ran for only a minute. The Man With the Shades did almost all the talking.

"But what about those guns?" Latham asked, having been told why it was "utterly impossible" for the CIA to "meddle." He listened to the brief answer, and shook his head.

"I understand," Latham announced in a New England accent that was suddenly stronger. She wondered whether it happened when he was frustrated or angry, some odd throwback . . .

"Yes, I'll tell her. Goodbye." He hung up the telephone.

"What?" she asked.

214

"He doesn't think he can do anything, but he'll ask some people to look into it."

She lit a cigarette.

"Anything else, Todd?"

"He thanked us for bringing this to his attention. He was very polite—which is more than my director in D.C. will be when he finds out we phoned the CIA on this."

"You *care?*"

"Only about the guns—and you."

He obviously meant it.

"You're quite a romantic," she said, "and I'm a sucker for it. I wonder why."

"Because the lady's a romantic too."

She smiled. Then she put a finger to her lips, and pointed at the ceiling to remind him that the room was probably wired.

"It's too late, Al. *They* must have known for years."

He suddenly kissed her, and then they left the offices. He did not speak again until they reached the street.

"This thing isn't finished, Al."

"Us or the freighter?" she asked.

"Either. Both. There has to be something more that we can do—and soon." He seemed completely determined. It was unrealistic, and very appealing.

"You're right," she agreed, "there is something. I have one question though."

"Sure."

"My place or yours?"

At naval headquarters in San Diego, Admiral Walford continued his report.

"The ship captain has agreed to hold his position until the

twenty-ninth in exchange for an extra million—as you proposed."

"And you're wondering where we'll get that money now, right, Popeye?"

"I'm sure you have a contingency plan, sir."

"Damn right. We'll go on April twenty-seventh without those weapons. We'll have to. We've got dedicated people, and I'll make sure—personally—that the Panama operation succeeds. When we strike in Los Angeles, we'll take two banks immediately and use *that* cash. Since the blimp is gone, you'll supply a chopper to deliver the money."

Walford nodded in admiration. Caesar was a born field commander with that essential ability to improvise in crisis. He would make a great leader for the new America.

"We'll do it," the admiral promised.

"The other senior commanders all feel the same way, Popeye. Now it's a question of timing. Our people have guts, and none of those taken alive yesterday know enough of the plan to hurt Lexington."

"I've reached them through a cop assigned to the prison ward, sir. They've given their solemn oath to hang in until we rescue them on the twenty-eighth," Walford said.

"Damn good troops—every one of them. Now get your units ready and wait for the signal that we've succeeded in Panama."

"We're ready now."

"Good. Taking out that gullible weakling is crucial, even though we have plenty of support. They should seize him easily, but there's a backup plan for that too."

"Yes?"

"If they can't take him alive, I'll kill him myself."

Suddenly the line was dead. In fifty-one hours, the President of the United States might well be too.

216

# 30

ALISON GORDON awakened with the morning sun on her face, looked at the man sleeping beside her and smiled. He seemed so relaxed, and boyish somehow. She could not resist the impulse to lean over and kiss him. Her lips brushed his, then she sat bolt upright.

"Todd, Todd, wake up!"

He opened one eye, still groggy.

"Wake up, Todd," she insisted. "We've got to talk."

"It'll keep," he answered and closed his eyes.

"No, it won't. We've got to move right away. Todd, this is business."

"No business at this crazy hour in the morning. You're a *romantic,* remember?" he sighed.

"It's about the guns."

He opened his eyes as he sat up.

"I thought that would do it. Listen, Todd. Last night was wonderful. I'm looking forward to tonight and a lot more. But today we have something to do."

"What about the guns, Al?"

"There's only one way to get anyone in Washington to believe us. If we want them to hit that freighter, we've got to give them something *more*—something that will establish our credibility. One man's unconfirmed word about a ship out there isn't enough."

He saw that the bedside clock showed 6:55, and shook his head. "Okay, *more* might do it. Where do we get it?"

"From Carew. Think about him, Todd. That conniving sleaze couldn't possibly give us *all* of it at one time. He's got to be holding back something in case he needs to trade it later."

Naked and intent, she looked very beautiful.

"Maybe. Yes, he'd do that. How do we get it out of him now instead of next month?"

"I have an idea that could work."

*"Could?"*

"If you do it my way." She began to explain her plan. They were still arguing about it—refining it—when they finished their coffee forty minutes later.

At five minutes after ten, the control-tower operator at the Hawthorne Municipal Airport heard a radioed request for landing instructions from an executive jet approaching from Sacramento. A gray Gulfstream bearing the markings of Cascade Air, Inc., touched down a dozen minutes later. When it had taxied to a halt, the pilot and copilot/navigator remained in the plane while four men in tan coveralls got out and stretched. Then they began to unload wooden crates, each about four or five feet long, half as wide. They seemed to be heavy.

The two deputies from the Sheriff's Office guarding the blimp watched from a hundred and fifty yards away. They were glad to have even this small distraction, for it had become quite boring ever since all the journalists left at ten the previous night. Now a black Ford sedan parked near the control tower, and an

218

accountant named Acuff approached them with an envelope in his hand.

"Name's Twitty," he announced. "Looking for some fellows from Cascade Air."

One of the sheriff's men pointed at the group unloading the jet.

"Right. This here's a court order signed by Judge Rudin of the Supreme Court. Officially impounds that plane and seizes it, and authorizes those boys to fly it up to the capital for . . . lessee what it says . . . for complete examination and investigation as evidence in a criminal proceeding under Section 903 of the State Code."

He handed the envelope to the officer. The policeman read it carefully.

"Looks okay. Yessir, Section 903," he said.

Twitty gestured to the quartet who were unloading the last crate. They waved back—a rather ordinary-looking group in their thirties wearing dark aviator glasses. All of medium build, all wearing mustaches.

"Give you an official receipt, of course," Twitty said.

"Bet your ass, you will. No way we'd release this hunk of property without it, mister."

While one of the men from the plane took a wheeled dolly from the rear door, Twitty returned to his car for his briefcase. The men in coveralls got one of the crates on the dolly and rolled it slowly to the gondola.

"Just a second, fella, till we get this signed all proper and official. You're not loading anything . . . you're not touching that machine . . . till Mr. Twitty puts his John Hancock on this . . . thanks."

He studied the signature, grunted in approval when he saw that Twitty was a marshal.

"She's all yours," he said.

"Thanks. Could you give these guys a hand?"

The sheriff's officer grinned.

"Loading crates doesn't fit my job description, marshal."

Then his partner laughed, and so did Twitty. The "boys" would get the boxes in themselves, explained the marshal, but they might need a couple of extra hands to help the pilots release the ground lines properly. No lifting would be required.

"Why not? I've never seen one of these creatures take off," the policeman confessed, "and I don't mind helping a fellow lawman. What do you say, Preston?"

The other officer agreed. They were both eager for a change of pace. It took a while to get the boxes stowed properly and the blimp checked out, but it was ready to launch at ten minutes to noon. They let loose the lines, then watched the airship rise slowly into the midday sky.

"I'd say that's *majestic*, Preston," one policeman declared to his partner.

"Definitely *majestic*."

The pilots thanked them, returned to the Gulfstream and radioed to the tower that they were filing a flight plan to Sacramento.

Once out of sight they turned east. Their orders had been specific. They were to be out of the state by one o'clock. They were to land at an Air Force emergency strip in the Nevada desert where a fuel truck and a painting crew would be waiting. By 3:30, this plane would be dark green and identified as the property of A.B.C. Flight Services of Miami.

When it was beyond the radar at Hawthorne, the blimp went down to 2,000 feet and headed out over the blue-green Pacific. Two men flew it, while the others used hammers and chisels to open the crates. When the airship was a hundred and thirty miles off the coast, it circled south toward the Mexican border.

To conserve fuel but maintain minimum mobility, the freighter steamed at five knots in a lazy loop around the rendezvous point. The crew basked on the deck, wondering when something would happen. There had not been a plane overhead in days. Of course, the sailors were not complaining and they certainly were not asking questions. They knew better than that. They were patient Asians, glad to have jobs at a time when so many seamen were unemployed. They thought about the bonuses and the women who were waiting for them.

At three P.M., a lookout spotted the blimp through his binoculars. The captain had insisted on lookouts but had never said why. He was in command; he owed them no explanation.

The airship was cruising toward the freighter at about eighty miles an hour, flying some 3,000 feet above the waves. The captain lifted his own binoculars. It was good, he thought. They would not have to wait until the 29th, after all.

The blimp was descending for the man to climb down the rope ladder to the deck. These Americans were not children. They would inspect the merchandise—probably open a dozen boxes—before they lowered the cash. The blimp was no more than two miles away, perhaps 1,900 feet high.

"Open the main cargo hatches," the captain ordered. Americans were always impatient. Waiting around while the hatches were removed irritated them. One should not be angry with them, the captain thought, for they had no sense of perspective and lived hurried existences devoid of the wisdom or philosophy of Lord Buddha or the comforting faiths of India.

The airship was down to 1,000 feet, a mile away. The nose

was still pointed down as it continued to lose altitude. By the time it reached the freighter, it would be no higher than four or five hundred feet. Crew and captain alike stared skyward as it slowly and ponderously slid by, blotting out the afternoon sun. The gondola was not that large, nor were the engines nearly as noisy as those on airplanes. The blimp swung in a broad circle. The Americans had been prudent to inspect his ship, the captain thought, but then anyone carrying such large sums should be wary of traps.

The blimp was moving more slowly, maybe fifty-five or sixty miles per hour. The men in it were opening windows and a door in the side of the gondola. The captain looked up and waved. Someone in the gondola returned the greeting, and then something fell. Now another, and then two more. It took the captain several seconds to recognize what they were.

Bombs. He opened his mouth to shout a command as two cylinders plummeted into the open forward hold. Sailors were screaming now, pointing up and running toward the stern. More bombs were dropping. A moment before the first pair exploded below, three more rained down on the fantail of the ship—fire bombs. One detonated behind the bridge, spraying chunks of white-hot phosphorus across the deck. Some bits struck panicky crewmen, searing through their light garments and burning into their flesh.

Others went off in the after hold starting fires in seconds. The blimp turned in a tight loop. It was coming back to attack again. The captain saw three sailors diving over the rail, but he had no time to deal with cowards. He yelled to the second mate to man the 20-millimeter cannon concealed under a tarpaulin near the prow, and as the young officer began to run, the captain sprinted to open the gun locker. There was a score of automatic weapons inside—neither heavy-caliber nor ideal to counter air attack, but they would have to do.

More bombs dropped—flat disks, Claymore antipersonnel mines, each of which hurled hundreds of murderous steel balls across the deck. A score of men fell as more incendiaries dropped from the gondola. Three lifeboats were burning and smoke was pouring out of both hatches from the fires roaring below.

The second mate heard them and felt them. The deck plates beneath his feet were getting warm. He ripped the tarpaulin loose, took the firing position behind the cannon and released the safety. Then he tilted the 20-millimeter weapon up. The blimp was almost overhead, but it was too late. An incendiary bomb dropped less than a yard behind him, and he was ablaze.

The fires below reached some ammunition crates and mortar shells began to explode. Suddenly a larger blast made the whole ship lurch. Flames engulfed an entire cargo department, and there was another explosion—even bigger. A jagged hole opened and tongues of yellow fire leaped out. Parts of the deck began to glow dull orange, and more sailors leaped into the sea.

The blimp cruised on a thousand yards past the burning ship, and circled in a broad arc. The men in the gondola saw two more blasts rip out sections of the stern. The rear of the hull was taking water, enough to lift the bow out of the water. Fire was everywhere, spouting from the hatches and dancing across the decks and superstructure in flickering yellow streams. Rigging, hoists, railings and men were all ablaze.

It could not last. A massive blast broke the keel, tearing the crippled ship into two parts. The stern slid beneath the surface first, sucking down with it three frantically swimming crewmen. The men in the blimp refilled their Styrofoam cups with coffee, looked down and waited for the rest of the ship to go under.

"Survivors," one of the bombardiers said. He pointed at several dots on the surface.

"Five . . . six . . . seven," the blimp's navigator counted as he peered through his binoculars.

"I make it eight."

To the leader of the strike team, the only number that mattered was zero.

"Do it," he ordered.

The blimp headed back to where the freighter had died, a patch of cold sea marked by a large oil slick and those heads. When the airship was two hundred feet directly above them, the commander spoke again.

*"Now."*

Two incendiary bombs fell. In moments, the surface was a solid sheet of fire. Nothing could live in that inferno. When the blimp flew back over a few minutes later, they saw two charred corpses floating face down in the ocean—no survivors, no witnesses.

The airship flew north again until it was just above the U. S. border, then headed toward the California coast. It was down to a mere hundred feet above the water to avoid radar detection or notice by distant aircraft. The sun set when they were seventy miles off the coast. The night was black with clouds masking the moon. Only a few pale rays filtered through.

"Bombers' moon," the navigator said, recalling Royal Air Force terminology.

"How far?"

"Maybe twenty-two or twenty-three miles."

"Black out the gondola," the commander ordered.

With only the instrument panels illuminated, the blimp sailed on like a silver ghost for a quarter of an hour. The navigator looked at the chart again, glanced at the phosphorescent face of the clock and turned on the radio location device.

"Bingo!" The transmitter on the shore was sending the prearranged pulse on the selected frequency. For a moment he wondered who and what was on that freighter, and why total destruction had been ordered. "Six miles," he announced.

"Suit up," the commander instructed. The attack team reached into an open box, took out rubber wet suits and struggled into them.

"Two miles."

"Say hello."

The navigator turned on the transmitter, spoke.

"Hello, Dolly. Hello, Dolly. Hello, Dolly. Where are you, Dolly?"

Twin beams of light flashed on and off—four times—from a point directly ahead.

"Right on the bleeding button. How about *that?*" the navigator said.

"Not bad," the team leader acknowledged. He turned the lights on and off, looked at the fuel gauge and reached down to set the timer for thirty minutes. The blimp would be forty-five miles out when it exploded.

"One mile. Stand by. We're going down."

It was flying at less than thirty feet—perhaps two hundred and fifty yards offshore and cruising at low speed—when the first man jumped into the sea. Two more followed seconds later. The commander set the controls that would send the blimp out over the Pacific, then leapt. The ocean was rougher than he had expected, and visibility was irritatingly poor through the spray-splashed face mask. He swam steadily, helped some by the tide. Still, it was an effort—even for men as fit as this hand-picked assault unit—and they were gasping when they reached the shore.

225

They removed their flippers and walked toward the van dimly visible fifty yards away. Bringing up the rear was the commander, who used his flippers to brush and smooth away the footprints in the sand.

"I want a clean operation," The Man With the Shades had said.

They reached the van, took off the wet suits and found their clothes on hangers inside, complete outfits with underwear, socks and shoes stacked neatly below. They dressed, piled their frogman outfits in the van and watched it roll off into the night. Then they entered the station wagon parked a dozen yards away.

"How did it go?"

"How did *what* go?" the commander said, exhausted.

The driver did not say another word all the way to the airstrip in the Nevada desert where the green Gulfstream jet was waiting.

# 31

WITH HALF a glass of Chivas Regal in hand, Carew rose from the red leather armchair and walked past the French windows again. This was the seventh time in the past three hours that he had scanned the small portion of street visible from his living room. He had been quite uneasy when he first got home, but his confidence began to return when he realized that he had outwitted the stupid civil servants. He had fooled them with his account of kidnapping and with his useless information about the freighter. Then he spotted the men in the car—just across the road—shortly before five o'clock.

*They were still there.*

The Federal agents didn't have a shred of evidence to connect him with the armored-car robbery. There was no scrap of paper —not a word in writing—to tie him to it or to Blue Sky. Lexington's security procedures had been first-class. The only ones who knew about his role were dead. The government could not touch him.

*What if they weren't Feds?*

He sipped the whiskey, cursed the money grubbers and social climbers who had made a mess of America and thought about the major attack that Caesar would launch in less than forty-eight hours. Carew had never been told who Caesar was. He was definitely tough and resourceful, a born aristocrat who would put the Chicanos, Spades and Heebs in their places and cleanse the media of bleeding-heart liberals. Caesar might pull it off yet, Carew thought as he walked to the kitchen for more ice.

*There was another carload of men at the rear.*

It was sixty yards from the back door to the avenue behind the house, but the residence was on a low hill that allowed him to see over the tops of the shrubs that masked the garden. He decided they were local police there to protect him. After all, he had been told that he would be a material witness. If Lexington succeeded that trial would never happen.

Could they be Caesar's men? He must have other units besides the ones chewed up in yesterday's triple debacle, plenty of them. Maybe Caesar had sent these men to protect him from harassment. After all, he had contributed a great deal to one of Lexington's key operations. He was hardly a nobody.

*Had Caesar sent them to kill him?*

He threw three ice cubes into the glass and started back to the living room. He was halfway there when the front doorbell rang, and he twitched in startled reaction. He looked around for his maid, recalled that she'd gone out on an errand and wondered whether to open the door himself.

His hand began to shake. It wasn't that he was afraid, he analyzed, but merely fatigued. He had hardly slept at all in that dirty dreadful place where the A.T.F. had questioned him all night, badgering him as if he was some common criminal. He heard the ice cubes rattling against the side of the glass, forced his hand to steady and swallowed the last drops.

*Was it an assassin at the door?*

Gathering his self-confidence, he opened the door to face Latham.

"I've got to talk to you."

"Can't it wait until tomorrow? First the kidnapping, then all that endless questioning. I'm exhausted."

"It won't wait."

With a sigh of resignation, Carew told himself that the sooner he let this bureaucrat speak his mind, the quicker he would be gone. It might not be a bad idea to go away for a few days himself, he thought, as he led the way into the living room.

"It was *disturbing,* and quite unwarranted," he complained as he settled down in the red armchair. He poured more whiskey. "It was as if I wasn't the victim but one of the . . . uh . . . what's that word . . . oh, yes. The *perpetrators.* The criminals."

"That's what I'm here to talk about."

"So you've come to apologize? Well, you damn well ought to."

Latham shook his head.

"I'm afraid that's not it, sir."

Carew drank more Scotch. "Then stop wasting my time and get to the point."

"Time is what's involved. Maybe five to ten years. It could be more. One of my agents is on the critical list, and another is dead. The district attorney of Los Angeles is going in to ask for indictments tomorrow or the next day."

"Thank you for keeping me informed. I seem to be getting an awful headache—"

"You're one of the people who'll be indicted."

The ice cubes rattled again.

"*Me?* That's preposterous. That's insane!"

Terror made his voice shrill. It often did that to people. Now was the moment to throw the second bomb.

"That's what I told him," Latham said. "I explained how cooperative you'd been, how you were a respected man . . . an important member of the business community. I told him how helpful you'd been with that ship. They'd never have found it without you, sir."

*Christ, they had the goddamn ship.*

"He's a stubborn man. Ambitious, too," Latham continued. This much was true. This D. A. was honest enough, but ruthless. His eyes were on the governorship, and he'd trample anyone or anything in the way.

"But I'm innocent—"

"I believe you, sir, and so does Miss Gordon. She tried to speak to him on your behalf too. We both pointed out that you came from a fine family. You wouldn't have anything to do with anyone like Caesar."

"Caesar?"

"The FBI arrested him an hour ago. Quite a shootout, I heard."

*If they had Caesar, it was all over.*

Carew blinked as he battled to hold down the panic. His mouth was dry. He could barely swallow. His eyes darted to the French windows.

"Those are D.A.'s men, sir," Latham said gravely. "They've got the back covered as well. Orders are to keep you here till the indictments come down. There's no way out."

"But I didn't do anything."

"Mrs. Wilhite swears you did. She'll testify you were one of the leaders."

*The psalm-singing bitch was making a deal.*

"It's a goddamn lie! She's just trying to save herself."

Carew was coming around.

"Help me, please. Please!"

230

"I can't—unless you help yourself. Is there any more information that you can give them—something like the ship?"

"What?"

Latham saw his eyes narrow. The devious bastard was already calculating how to buy his way out.

"Anything to prove that you're not with this gang. Think. You're not the sort who could survive years in prison. Abuse, loneliness, degradation—maybe even rape."

*"Rape?"*

"Those convicts are animals. A good-looking man like you wouldn't be safe for a day. Think, Mr. Carew."

*Rape? No, it was every man for himself.* "I don't know. I only heard snatches of . . . wait a minute. There's *one* thing that I forgot."

Latham managed not to smile.

"It sounded crazy, so I didn't take it seriously. They said a lot of crazy things, Latham. They were strange. I heard somebody talking about the twenty-seventh. They were laughing about it —the vermin. Lord, they were loathsome."

"What about the twenty-seventh?"

"They were going to try to do something to the President. Maybe kidnap him. Insane, isn't it? *Kidnap* the President of the United States? Common criminals?"

"This was a desperate group, sir. They might try anything. I'd better report this immediately."

There might be still more, Latham realized. One real jolt could crack it loose. He rose to his feet.

"Can you remember anything else? Even the smallest phrase? You're going to need protection for a long time, Mr. Carew."

"I don't understand."

"We may not catch all of them. Some may . . . well, to put it bluntly . . . try to waste you."

"*Waste* me?"

"The more you give this ambitious D.A., the more he'll owe you—and the longer and stronger the protection."

*Nothing for nothing. Even the cops and the D.A. were making deals for their own benefit.*

"It's ugly, but those are the facts of life," Latham apologized. Carew finished his Scotch.

"Panama. They may try in Panama. Would have remembered sooner but this headache is terrible."

"Need a doctor?" Latham asked.

"Sleep and rest. You tell them I did my best to help the government. Tell them the whole thing, and don't let them take those guards away. Make them *promise.*"

He was practically whining. Latham gravely assured him that he would be protected indefinitely and left to join Alison Gordon in his car half a block away.

"You were right. The yarn about the ship shook him but it was the rape that did it," he reported. "This is wild, Al. They mean to kidnap the President—of the United States—in Panama on the twenty-seventh."

"You believe him, Todd?"

"He's too scared to lie. God, the *President.*"

"We'd better call right away."

"That accounting firm may be closed, Al."

"No time for rituals anyway. Find a phone booth."

Three minutes later, she recited her telephone credit-card number to a long-distance operator and then she was speaking to someone at the CIA switchboard at Langley.

"351-1100," the operator said.

"Night-duty controller, fast."

She heard the buzzer sounding.

"N. D. C.," answered a man with midwestern speech.

"Now get this straight because I'm only going to say it once," she announced. "This is a Priority Blue call, and I'm on a non-secure line. I must talk to the deputy director for OPS immediately."

"Who's that?" the controller tested.

She gave his name.

"Who is this?"

"Tell him it's Artemis."

She was talking to The Man With the Shades in ninety seconds.

"We've got something else—bigger and more urgent. *Most* urgent. Those folks we spoke about yesterday—the ones in the shipping business—have a large deal going down in Panama on the twenty-seventh."

"I'm listening."

"They're going to grab someone. I don't know what code name you're using this year. It used to be Sunbeam."

"*Sunbeam?* Are you certain?"

"Reasonably. I wouldn't call if I wasn't."

"I wasn't doubting your word," he assured. "This is definitely *most urgent*—as you said. We'll look into it right away."

"Like you looked into that freighter?"

"Forget that ship. It doesn't exist." There was something absolute and final in his voice.

"That's definite?"

"Excuse me. I've got some people to call," he told her and hung up.

"He never even said thanks," she said as she stepped from the phone booth.

They were still analyzing the conversation an hour later at her house when the telephone rang.

233

"This is Mr. Acuff at American Airlines," a voice announced. It was the man who had guided them to the secure line at the dummy accounting firm.

"Yes?"

"We can confirm your first-class seat on Flight Thirty-Six departing at ten forty-five this evening."

It was the red eye to Washington.

"By the way," he added, "I'm advised that your travel agent is taking care of ground transportation from Dulles. There'll be a car waiting. . . ."

And there was, driven by two men in civilian clothes. One she recognized immediately.

"This is General Reedy," The Man With the Shades said. "I've briefed him fully, and he has some ideas that may be helpful. General, this is Alison Gordon."

The chairman of the Joint Chiefs of Staff thrust out his hand. He looked disturbed and angry as hell.

# 32

"TALL TURKEY to Albrook . . . Tall Turkey to Albrook."

"Here we go," the controller at the U.S. air base near Panama City told his aides. Tall Turkey was the code name for *Air Force One*, the President's jet.

"Albrook to Tall Turkey. An honor to have you with us, sir. You're on our screen nice and clear. Visibility ten miles. Winds from two-seven-zero at five . . . repeat, five . . . knots. Ground temperature eighty-two degrees Fahrenheit, humidity forty-nine percent."

"Kind of sticky, Albrook?"

"Just a bit, Tall Turkey, but General Backlund has eight air-conditioned cars waiting, and a bus for the press." No harm in letting the commander-in-chief know that Albrook was on the ball, not just a drowsy sun-baked outpost in the tropics.

"God bless the press," the pilot of *Air Force One* joked. Only a handful of top journalists were aboard. Another group of them was following in the "zoo" plane two minutes behind.

"Tall Turkey, you are now passing Beacon Charlie. Turn left sixty degrees and descend to fourteen thousand."

"Left sixty and down to fourteen thousand."

When he had started his descending turn, the pilot announced the ground weather over the speaker system and noted that they'd be on the ground in eight minutes. The President went on reading the speech he would deliver upon landing. He glanced up a few moments later as a shapely Secret Service woman walked by with a glass in her hand.

"Drinking on the job?" he said.

"Club soda, Mr. President," A. B. Gordon assured him. "Got to stay one-hundred-percent fit."

"You look one-hundred-and-ten-percent fit to me," he said and returned to his chore.

At Albrook, the air controller made an announcement alerting the soldiers, airmen, U.S. and foreign diplomats and Panamanian dignitaries lined up in the midafternoon sun.

"Estimated time of arrival is under eight minutes," he said over the outdoor speakers.

The man who had tortured José Garcia nodded to the waiting honor guard. Captain McKee had confidence in these handpicked fighters, all Lexington volunteers who had been concealed in the mental ward at Fort Amador for weeks. It had not been easy to assemble them, but Major Dunlap's deft manipulation of the Pentagon personnel computer had made it possible.

Within ten minutes, *Air Force One* would taxi to a halt about fifty yards from where they waited. Three minutes later, they would shoot all of the Secret Service agents and seize the President. They'd drag him to the helicopters waiting behind Hangar Two for the trip to a secret jungle. base. McKee scanned the assembled VIPs again. They would scatter like chickens when the bullets flew.

"What the *hell* is that?" the senior controller asked, pointing at the radar screen. There was a large blip marking an approaching plane less than fifteen miles away.

"Unidentified aircraft . . . altitude sixteen hundred . . . air speed three eighty," said the controller on the scope.

". . . Albrook, this is Med Evac Flight Nine with an inflight emergency, requesting landing instructions."

"It's a hospital plane, sir," the junior controller said.

"How did he get this close without being assigned, damn it? What the hell is he *doing* here?"

Before the senior controller could radio the questions, the approaching pilot spoke once more.

"One engine out and another failing. This is an emergency, Albrook. Request immediate permission to land."

The senior controller watched the scope. He could not turn away a crippled U.S. Air Force hospital plane . . .

"Put him on Runway Three and park him as far as you can from where Tall Turkey will unload. Better have a firetruck and a crash wagon ready too."

The U.S. Air Force jet that touched down a few minutes later was one of the biggest planes in the world, a huge C-5A some 245 feet long. Lockheed had built the C-5s to move heavy loads of up to 125,000 pounds—even M-60 tanks—as far as 8,000 miles. They were rarely used for medical flights. All four engines seemed to be operating, as far as the men in the tower could see.

"What's that C-5 doing?" demanded the senior controller. "Why didn't he turn left onto Runway Three?"

"Maybe he's on the wrong frequency, sir . . ."

Ignoring repeated instructions, the pilot of the C-5A was taxiing directly toward the VIP area. The chief controller picked up the microphone himself to order him away, but there was no reply as the plane rolled on. The big machine finally stopped less than eighty yards from the canopy shielding the waiting dignitaries.

"Tall Turkey's on final approach sir. About six miles out . . . altitude seventeen hundred . . . right on schedule."

The senior controller looked from the radarscope to the field.

"Tall Turkey, you are cleared to land on Runway One," the controller radioed. He informed the dignitaries, band and troops waiting below that the President would touch down in ninety seconds, then asked the head of the honor guard to hurry to the C-5A and order the pilot to move it out of the area at once.

Eager to have the President disembark exactly where planned, McKee dogtrotted toward the huge Lockheed as its front and rear doors began to open.

"Get that bird out of here!" he shouted up to the pilot. "This is where the President's plane will park. Move it—*fast.*"

As if in answer, armored personnel carriers rolled out, two emerging from each end of the plane. They were M113A1 diesels with welded aluminum alloy armor that varied from one and a half to five inches in thickness. When combat-loaded with a dozen infantry and a driver, each weighed twelve tons. And they were combat-loaded—with elite assault troops, men of Green Light, the top-secret unit that handled the most difficult missions. Crack commandos, the boldest and the best. The officer who led them this afternoon was someone special too.

He jogged out of the plane after the armored vehicles, sturdy but visibly older than the dozen infantry in full battle gear right behind him. There was no sign of a stretcher, a medic or a nurse.

McKee looked past the C-5A to see the President's jet down to four hundred feet—a mile from the start of the runway.

The disembarking troops were fanning out quickly now, and there was a soldier manning the .50-caliber machine gun atop each armored carrier. One round from this weapon could take off a head. The rate of fire topped four hundred a minute. At this range, the M85 heavy-machine gun was a meat grinder—a weapon of slaughter. As the uneasy Lexington men eyed the unscheduled new arrivals, McKee stared at the commander's face.

*Air Force One* was only about one hundred feet above the runway. It would land in twenty seconds unless the tower took over and waved it off.

"General Reedy? What are you doing here?" McKee asked.

"I'm with Caesar."

"We're *all* with Caesar," McKee said proudly and nodded toward the honor guard. Then he pointed at the President's plane. "In two minutes, he'll be ours, general."

Reedy shook his head. "You just blew it, captain. Tell your men to lay down their arms."

McKee reacted instantly, first with shock, then fury at the deceit. He felt a visceral surge of determination. No tricky old bastard would put Ned McKee into Leavenworth for twenty years. Lexington wasn't done yet. *Air Force One* was already on the runway. He'd rally his men, and they'd storm the plane at any cost. He began to back away.

Reedy called out for McKee to halt. The captain kept backing slowly, wondering who had betrayed Caesar and the plan. He was surprised when Reedy yelled out a command and a soldier at one of the .50s blew off most of McKee's head.

Two of the Lexington men fired back, and in seconds the battle began. The dignitaries dove for safety as Green Light commandos charged from the armored carriers. The .50s swept the rebels with a hurricane of bullets before they could throw their grenades.

In the tower, the senior controller reacted swiftly.

"Tall Turkey, Tall Turkey. Abort. Get out. Security alert! It's an ambush!"

He tried to recall the emergency code phrase.

"Flash Gun . . . Flash Gun . . . get the *fuck* out of here!"

The pilot of *Air Force One* hesitated for a second but played it right from the book. He followed the procedures he never expected to use—step by step.

"Flash Gun," he repeated to the copilot. "Let's go."

The man in the right-hand seat shifted immediately into his checklist for a "hot" takeoff. The jet was already slowed to seventy miles per hour and they had used up most of the runway and three quarters of the jet's fuel was gone, but none of that deterred either of them. It was their duty to get the President out of the frying pan. They'd fight the fire later.

Brakes off . . . retro thrust off . . . more power . . . goddamn it, *more* power. Pratt & Whitney had built 43,500 pounds of thrust into each of the four J-T9D engines, and now it was time for these mothers to deliver.

"Ninety," the copilot announced as the speed indicator turned up.

"Go, baby, go," the pilot said.

"Two hundred."

The whole goddamn thing was impossible. The pilot had been flying *Air Force One* for more than three years with no incident more serious than a burst tire. Flash Gun? *Here?* In peacetime at a U.S. field in a friendly nation? It was crazy.

"I don't believe this," the navigator said. Then he saw the fighting and the gunners on the APCs swiveling the heavy machine guns, and he changed his mind.

"One twenty. Think we'll make it, Duke?"

They could feel the surging power. So could the President and the others in the passenger compartment.

240

"What's going on?" the press secretary asked.

"Don't know," replied the military aide seated beside her. A CBS-TV newswoman pointed out her window at the mini-war.

*"Hey,"* she said, then fell silent as she felt the plane speeding up. The ABC correspondent in the seat behind her adjusted his toupee, looked at the shooting and tried to size up the situation.

"Something's happened," was all he could manage as he reached for his tape recorder.

"One forty, and we're running out of concrete, Duke."

"Full thrust."

The plane lunged forward under the impact. It shuddered, then there was a groaning sound and only a hundred yards of runway left—a life-and-death strip the Jet could hurtle in the blink of an eye. In that final second, the pilot accepted the twin facts that he'd never be promoted to full colonel or get buried in Arlington. It was not a place for losers who killed the commander-in-chief. His body tensed for the impact of the crash.

The front wheels of the 747 were five feet from the end of the main runway when they lifted from the concrete. The copilot swallowed the lump in his throat as the nose of the large Boeing rose. The rear wheels came off the end of the runway. In seconds, *Air Force One* was up to 200 . . . 300 . . . 500 . . . climbing steadily. Miracle time.

"Not bad, Duke," the copilot finally said, "but what do we do for an encore?"

"No encore," the pilot answered grimly and patted the instrument panel.

In the passenger areas, excited and disturbed people were talking, reacting to the shock. Among those most troubled by the unexplained incident was Major General Steele, the President's military aide. He managed to get to his feet, even though the plane was still climbing sharply, and to force himself down the aisle to where the President sat.

"Are you all right, sir?" Steele asked.

"Think so, Brad. What's going on?"

The two-star general leaned over to answer, holding onto the President's seat with one hand and fumbling with his half-buttoned jacket with the other. Even in crisis, the West Pointer in him had to be neat.

"There's shooting at the airfield, sir," he told President Walker. "I don't know anything more, but I'll ask the pilot to radio the tower and I'll report back to you."

That was when Alison Gordon put the cold muzzle of the .357 magnum in Steele's left ear.

"Don't move, general. And keep your hand away from the piece under your arm."

"What is this?" the President demanded.

"*This* son of a bitch is Caesar, Mr. President. I recognized his voice. It was the way he said *report;* that nailed it."

"You're crazy—" Steele protested.

"Crazy enough to pull this trigger if you so much as sneeze, general." She jammed the barrel into his ear. "This officer was planning to kidnap you, Mr. President. Maybe kill you."

"This is ridiculous," Steele said. "May I straighten up?"

He looked to the President for sympathy, began to stand up —and reached for his shoulder holster. She hit him on the side of the head with the .357, cracked his collarbone with the barrel and then crashed it against the back of his skull in three quick movements. Steele staggered, half turned and slumped to his knees with his mouth open. She held the muzzle under his chin.

"That was a *very* dumb move," she said.

The President looked at her warily, then studied the military aide he had trusted for so long. Which one was telling the truth? Where the hell were the rest of the Secret Service people?

242

It took her a while to convince Walker that Major General Bradley Steele was a traitor who led a large but shadowy conspiracy. Senior naval and Air Force officers were probably involved too.

"Reedy's friends," President Walker said.

"General Reedy's down there, Mr. President. He's leading the Green Light commando team that's mopping up Caesar's people at Albrook right now. He planned that whole operation, saved your neck. I'd say you owe him one."

John Walker nodded in assent as he considered how badly he had misjudged both Reedy and Steele. He reminded himself that no one was perfect, but that did not help much. If it had not been for the intervention of the chairman of the Joint Chiefs, the Green Light commandos and this attractive stranger who was pressing a gun against Steele's head, he might well be dead. It was a disturbing thought. What other mistakes was he making? Who was this woman anyway?

"How long have you been with the Secret Service?" he asked.

"I'm not with them, but they're fine people. If you'd buzz for them, they could take charge of General Steele and I could tell you the whole story, starting with Sidney Adams."

Steele blinked in groggy confusion.

"Who's Sidney Adams?" he asked uncertainly.

He had never heard of him. Walker summoned the Secret Service, and three agents took Steele's gun and handcuffed him before they led him away.

# 33

THE HEAVY street fighting, attempted assassinations and sabotage efforts that erupted in five U.S. cities during the next thirty-six hours proved that "Caesar" was right about one thing. Cutting off the head of an organization terminates its ability to resist.

With its commander in federal custody, Lexington failed in all its assaults. There were hundreds of casualties on both sides, but by the morning of April 30th its fighting force was beaten. At Walker's request, Alison Gordon was present in the Oval Office when Reedy reported on the rebels' collapse.

"We've got Marine patrols in L. A.—two full battalions, and there's a company of the Eighty-second Airborne still at March Field where we found that motorcycle cop Miss Gordon mentioned. The base security officer was hiding him and a load of weapons."

"New York?" the President asked.

"Still a few snipers, but they'll be gone by tonight. The tanks did a real fine job in Chicago, and it looks like Miami's been deloused."

Walker half turned in the leather swivel chair and pointed out the window.

"How long will they have to be there, general?"

"A week, maybe longer. Those light tanks and troops are here to protect the commander-in-chief, and they'll stay for as long as we think it's necessary."

"Anything else?" he asked as Alison Gordon put a fresh Sobranie in her black onyx holder and crossed her legs.

"I'd better tell you the rest about Panama," Reedy answered. "After you bugged out, we mopped up at Albrook. Biggest fire fight I've seen since the Pusan perimeter. Green Light did a terrific job. Then we hooked up with a C.I.D. guy who'd been checking out the nuthouse at the Fort Amador hospital."

"Explain that."

"A computer security spot check tipped us that someone was diddling the Army's personnel computer to ship certain people to Panama, so C.I.D. slipped in two guys to find out why. The *outside* agent was a black photographer. *Inside* man was a private—name of José Garcia. They caught him and tortured the hell out of him, but the kid never cracked. He's been a lieutenant since last night."

"Hero, huh?"

"Hero and a half, Mr. President. I took the Green Light team to hit the Amador mental ward where the Lexington hoods had been hiding. It was their base. We had some shooting before we found the private in a straightjacket—battered, blood-caked, half dead."

"The men who did that will be punished," Walker said earnestly.

"The ones still alive will be. We shot our way in to rescue this man and blew the lock off the door of a padded cell. Garcia's inside with maybe three fingernails left, one eye open and trussed up like a goose. The photographer says to him, 'You're safe now, José. This is General Reedy, chairman of the Joint Chiefs.' I began to untie the poor kid, and just as he's loose he looked me in the eye and said it."

Reedy paused and smiled.

" 'Took your own sweet time, didn't you?' That's what he said to a four-star general. Lord, I didn't know whether to hit somebody or cry. I still don't."

"And the shipload of arms?" asked Alison.

Reedy hesitated a second.

"I'm told it doesn't exist. There's no trace of it."

These were almost the same words used by The Man With the Shades. Was it a coincidence?

"What about Lexington's naval friend in San Diego?" she asked.

"An admiral and a commander are being interrogated now—*vigorously.*"

"I didn't hear that," Walker said.

Alison puffed on the cigarette and recrossed her legs.

"Do you think that's all of them, general?"

"Probably not, miss. Must be a lot we haven't found. FBI is looking, but maybe they've infiltrated the FBI too. Perhaps the CIA as well. I wouldn't know. My job is to protect the country from *external* threat."

He stared directly at Walker as he spoke. Reedy was reiterating his opposition to the treaty.

"We've got to talk about that some more tomorrow," Walker said.

"The Sinbad pictures?" Reedy asked.

The President nodded, and the general seemed less hostile as he left.

"The general and I have had our differences on . . . a certain policy question," Walker said uncomfortably, "but they may be narrowing. It seems that . . . well . . . I may have been premature."

The latest photographs and electronic readings taken from the Sinbad satellite strongly suggested that the Soviets were already breaching the missile limitations agreement. How the hell could you sign a nuclear disarmament treaty with them now?

"You believe in disarmament, Miss Gordon?"

"Sure, with complete access for full inspection. Lots of people would disagree with me. I'm no expert."

"Lots of people," the troubled chief executive agreed. For a moment he reflected on the irony of the situation. A major reason for the whole Lexington conspiracy had been to wreck Walker's foreign policy and prevent signing of the treaty. Now the man Lexington wanted to destroy was uncertain about how to proceed, and it would be some time—maybe years—before any such pact was signed. The scheme and slaughter had been more than wrong—it had been unnecessary.

"The general's quite a soldier," Walker said suddenly in an effort to change the subject. "Wonder why he took the risk of going down to Panama himself."

"For the same reason he didn't tell you what little we knew about Lexington," she answered. "He wasn't really sure that it was true, or that U. S. military people were involved. He wouldn't let anyone else make that bitter decision to send American troops against other Americans."

"Looks like Reedy's a hero too. Guess I ought to give him a medal . . ." Walker saw something in her eyes.

"What is it, Miss Gordon?"

"I don't know if you can do this, or if you'd want to . . ." she began cautiously. She described the invaluable contributions Doc Shephard had made in breaking the conspiracy. "If he hadn't opened that vault, I'd never have heard that voice on the phone and Steele probably would have killed you."

"You want me to give a medal to a *burglar?*"

"You've appointed worse men ambassadors—I'm sorry I said that, Mr. President."

"You sound like *The Washington Post,*" he answered wryly. "I have an idea. Let the CIA give Shephard *their* medal. They hand them out secretly, so why not this one?"

"If you think they would."

"I'll suggest it—*vigorously.* You ought to get one too, Miss Gordon."

He could see that she was trying to phrase a reply.

"You've already got one?" he guessed.

She almost blushed as she nodded in silent confession.

"Isn't there something that a grateful President—and nation —can do for you?"

She thought about the gun control. No, there was little more that he could do in the face of the opposition of the self-serving politicians. Only the will of millions of people—organized and implacable—could do that.

"My car," she announced. "They blew it up when we were stopping the blimp. It was totalled."

"Yes?"

"The book value on that Porsche was $19,000, Mr. President."

"I see."

"Mr. President, that car would be intact if I hadn't risked my —for Chrissakes, they'd have delivered the money to the freighter. *Don't* tell me it doesn't exist. I've had a bellyful of that."

Walker saw no reason to argue with her.

"You want nineteen thousand dollars from the federal government?"

"Exactly. Todd Latham of the A.T.F. in Los Angeles said that I had a valid claim, but I wouldn't get paid for two or three years because of red tape."

Walker rose, smiled paternally and advanced around his desk toward her.

"Don't you worry about it, Miss Gordon. The drawbacks of bureaucracy are grossly exaggerated. I've instructed my press secretary to arrange for your air ticket back to California, and I want you to know that I'll get your claim moving."

She stood up, feeling much encouraged as they walked to the door.

"No three years?"

"You've got the President of the United States with you, Miss Gordon. Not a day over eighteen months," he showed her his grand presidential grin.

Eighteen months? He wasn't a perfect human being, she thought as they reached the door, but General-for-Life Steele would have been a hell of a lot worse.

# 34

When Alison Gordon descended from the DC-10 at Los Angeles International Airport, there were five men—and a tank —waiting for her. She stared for several seconds at the armored vehicle and the nearby platoon of Marines in full battle gear. Could it still be happening *here?*

"*We're* your private welcoming party," Latham said. "The tank and troops are here for everybody."

He reached out and took her hand. She sensed that he wanted to embrace and kiss her but was holding back in the presence of Hovde and Agajanian. Ever the proper Easterner, he did not want to embarrass her in front of her friends and staff.

"You all right, Al?" Agajanian asked.

"Sure. And you?"

"We finished the report on Sidney Adams," Hovde whispered.

"That's good." She tried to recall the names of the other two A.T.F. agents with Latham. The black man was Tolliver, but who was the other? *Goldblatt.* Sure, Wally Goldblatt.

"Nice of all you fellows to show up," she told them. Why *had* they come?

"Firepower," Goldblatt said.

"My friend is telling you that we're here to protect you, Al," Latham translated. "It could be that some of the unsung members of the Lexington group hold grudges. You've got a way with words, Wally. Make one charming lawyer."

"I thought I'd concentrate on tax problems and charisma," Goldblatt answered. "If a lawyer is good at those things, the rest doesn't matter."

"You've got charisma, Wally." She decided not to be embarrassed. She turned her face up to Latham, and they kissed for several seconds.

"You've got charisma too, Al," Latham said—and now she felt better.

The unsettling effect of the military presence at the airport did not leave her immediately. It was still down there in her consciousness as Latham drove her to Beverly Hills. He wanted to take her home for reasons that were both implicit and appealing, but she insisted on going directly to her office.

"There's something I have to do first," she said.

"You sound angry."

"Not at you, Todd. You're right, though. I'm angry, and I'm annoyed that I'm angry, and I won't feel okay until I clean this up."

Then she told him what had happened since they had parted five days earlier, and when she described the President's solemn commitment on the eighteen months he laughed. She wanted to kiss him again, but it seemed unwise at fifty-five miles an hour. After she had finished what she had to do, they could do what they wanted to for as long as their love, bodies and telephone answering services would permit. Maybe she'd break both their beepers, an act that was practically an engagement announcement in greater Los Angeles.

When she reached her office, she read the entire report carefully. Only her bitterness kept her from weeping. Hovde and Agajanian had not found every detail of the final three months of Sidney Adams' life, but there was more than enough to paint a clear and pain-filled picture.

"You did a good job—as usual," she told her aides.

"Too good?" Agajanian asked, seeing the effect that his report had on her.

"Who's to say?"

"We'll send the file over to Maxie tomorrow," Hovde said.

"No. I'll deliver it to her today. Find her."

The accountant could not recall such hardness and hurt in her voice in a very long time. He telephoned the mansion in Bel Air, and reported that Lauri Adams was "too busy to see Miss Gordon" because it was 5:05 P.M. and she was due at a champagne reception at the Motion Picture Academy in twenty-five minutes. That would make her a fashionable half-hour late, Alison Gordon calculated.

"Ready when you are, A. B.," Latham announced as he rose from the armchair.

"I don't need a bodyguard for this, Todd."

"It's purely social. Look, it's after five. I'm off duty—and you don't have a car."

When they left her office with the fat envelope, they found Hovde and Agajanian waiting at the elevator.

"Where are you going?" she asked suspiciously.

"Party," Hovde answered.

"At the Motion Picture Academy?"

Agajanian nodded as he adjusted the knot on his forty-dollar brocade tie.

"This isn't necessary," she told them.

"We get invited to a *lot* of parties," Agajanian said.

They got into the elevator.

"Who invited you to this one?"

"Marilyn Monroe," Hovde offered.

"She still lives in his heart," Agajanian said, and Alison Gordon sighed in surrender. They drove out of the basement garage a few minutes later, trailed by Hovde and Agajanian in one car and Tolliver and Goldblatt in another.

"How long will this go on, Todd?"

"They'll be with us for a month."

"Us?"

Latham took his right hand from the wheel to pat her knee.

"Orders are orders. My boss phoned from Washington three hours ago. I'm assigned to your personal security until further notice."

"Who thought up that one?"

"John Walker, your loving President. Don't fight it, Al. He's too big for us."

She did not speak again until they were almost at the Academy.

"Do you think it really could happen, Todd? I mean Lexington."

"Maybe."

"In *this* country?"

"Why not, Al? Democracy's not the norm on this planet yet. Look around. Three quarters of the people on earth live under regimes that nobody could call democratic. Some tyrannies are Left, others Right. It could happen. There's enough fear and hate around for it, Al."

She thought of the legend chiseled into the stone of so many courthouses and public buildings across the nation.

"So we're stuck with *eternal vigilance?*" she asked.

"Only game in town. I know it sounds like a cheap slogan, but from my experience it could be damned expensive if we ignore it. Hey, do I sound like a high-school orator?"

"No, lover."

He beamed when she said that. He pointed ahead to the Academy building on the other side of Wilshire Boulevard. He had to circle the block to park near the entrance, where a stream of limousines and the usual Mercedes and Rollses were unloading expensively dressed men and women.

Alison Gordon waited on the sidewalk, wondering whether these people really believed what they had read and heard and seen on their six-foot Advent TV screens about the Lexington conspiracy in the past few days. Did they take it seriously, or was it just another pilot film that bombed?

There she was. As Lauri Adams emerged from her Rolls Silver Cloud, Alison hurried to hand her the file—almost as if it were an award or diploma.

"Miss Gordon, I'm really much too busy for *this.*"

"Take it. I don't suppose that you know what you started." Alison Gordon thrust the envelope into the hands of the bejeweled and startled superstar. Quickly she told Lauri Adams about everything that happened, right up through the hundreds slain in the street fighting.

"I thought that you were hired to find out about my brother." Apparently the account of the carnage had not moved her at all.

"Your brother's in there," Alison said, pointing to the file. "He was a sad person, and he had a lousy life. He was a masochist, a gay slave and a drug addict. Maybe *some*body could have helped him. Maybe he didn't have to get slaughtered in that record factory."

Lauri Adams stared through her.

"Is there anything else you have to tell me, Miss Gordon?"

"Yeah, your mother was right. You should have married a

254

dentist and settled down in Scarsdale."

Lauri Adams' face showed shock for a moment, then suddenly a smile as the photographers charged toward her. Alison Gordon got back in Latham's car as the cameras began to click.

"Feeling better?" he asked.

"Just a little. That woman is an animal."

"Me too," he said.

When they reached her house, she did not break the beepers, but she put them in a bedroom drawer filled with her lingerie. She was three quarters naked and only half listening as Latham explained why she should not smash his beeper . . . Destruction of federal property was a serious offense . . . Even the President could not "fix" that, he told her . . .

Then he stopped talking. She didn't mind a bit.